Praise for the
NOVELS
OF
SYDNEY CROFT

Tempting the Fire

"A spicy and fabulously entertaining tale. Even the subplot has richly drawn characters and a smartly developed plot."
—*RT Book Reviews*

"*Tempting the Fire* is a thrilling addition to the ACRO series, and will keep readers riveted from beginning to end."
—Romance Reviews Today

Taming the Fire

"Sydney Croft creates a thrilling paranormal read with action and scorching romance at every turn."   —Darque Reviews

"Totally outstanding . . . [a] sizzling hot series that has never failed to keep my undivided attention. The collaboration of Sydney Croft is nothing short of brilliant."   —Fresh Fiction

Seduced by the Storm

"If you like intrigue, espionage, danger and sexy secret agents with psychic abilities, you will love this book—especially when one agent has to disperse a hurricane with sexual energy! Croft's realistic characters have real, flawed motives that keep the action suspenseful and the sex extra hot."

—*Romantic Times*

"Ms. Croft pens a tale where she manages to combine action along with sizzling hot passion. You will not be disappointed in this book, it is a keeper." —Night Owl Romance Reviews

Unleashing the Storm

"Red-hot romance and paranormal thrills from the first page to the last! Sydney Croft writes the kind of books I love to read!"

—LARA ADRIAN, *New York Times* bestselling author

"The tension, both romantic and plot-driven, was well created and upheld. . . . This is an author to watch."

—All About Romance

"This second book in the ACRO series is fabulously sexy and intriguingly hot. I have become addicted to the collaboration of the two authors known as Sydney Croft, and I'm ready to find out what happens next. Definitely a must-read."

—Fresh Fiction

"*Unleashing the Storm* is one of those rare reads where the characters linger long after the story ends. Intense intrigue, action, eroticism, and a fascinating world combine to create an enthralling winner. Sydney Croft is a fabulous new talent."

—CHEYENNE MCCRAY, *USA Today* bestselling author

Riding the Storm

"In this action-packed, inventive tale, each character's strengths and weaknesses are more fantastic than the next. The various plots and characters ebb and flow together seamlessly. . . . Croft redefines sizzle and spark with weather-driven passion."
— *Romantic Times*

"Absolutely fabulous!! *Riding the Storm* has the perfect balance of action/adventure and hot, steamy sex." — Fresh Fiction

"*Riding the Storm* will ride your every fantasy. . . . A power punch of erotic heat, emotion, and adventure. Remy takes you on an adventure you won't soon forget."
— Lora Leigh, *USA Today* bestselling author

Taken
by
Fire

Taken

by

Fire

SYDNEY CROFT

Bantam Books Trade Paperbacks

New York

A Bantam Books Trade Paperback Original

Published in the United States by Bantam Books,
an imprint of The Random House Publishing Group,
a division of Random House, Inc., New York.

BANTAM BOOKS and the rooster colophon are registered trademarks of
Random House, Inc.

Croft, Sydney.
Taken by fire / Sydney Croft.
p.   cm.
ISBN 978-0-385-34229-2
eBook ISBN 978-0-440-42336-2
1. Twin sisters—Fiction.   2. Psychic ability—Ficiton.   I. Title.
PS3603.R6356T35 2011
813'6—dc22   2010053284

Printed in the United States of America

www.bantamdell.com

2 4 6 8 9 7 5 3 1

With huge thanks to all our readers who have
supported us through the ACRO adventures.
We appreciate every one of you.

And special thanks to Gina Scalera.
Your enthusiasm from the very beginning
means more than we can say.

Taken
by
Fire

Prologue

The acrid stench of burning flesh filled the air, tangling with the sound of screams and the sight of a man engulfed in flames. Gunfire rang out, clean, crisp pops that seemed distant and unimportant.

The man on fire was too distracting. He flailed, running blindly into trees until he hit the ground and rolled, but even as the flames began to snuff out, his movements flagged, until he was nothing but a charred, quivering lump on the jungle floor. Gray wisps of smoke rose from his body, reaching out to her, telling her the fire had done its evil work . . .

Melanie Milan jackknifed upright in bed, her lungs seizing in terror, a cold sweat coating every inch of her body. Panic wrapped around her as she slapped a trembling hand down on the mattress, groping blindly for something familiar. Anything.

Please, please, let me be alone.

Sweet relief washed through her at the feel of her own satin comforter. Now that her vision had cleared of the dream-smoke, she could see the position of the alarm clock, the mirror near the foot of the bed, the window that was cracked to allow a cool breeze inside.

She was at the Rome apartment. Thank God. She never knew where she was going to wake up.

Usually, waking up in the body she shared with her sister was the nightmare, but sometimes, like tonight, her dreams were far worse than waking up in some strange bed, possibly with some strange man. Or woman. Or both.

The burning man's screams still echoed in her ears, and the foul odors clogged her nose. It didn't matter that she hadn't actually seen or heard the man burning alive. She knew it had happened, and she knew her sister was responsible.

Seeing Phoebe's memories as nightmares was one of the worst things about sharing a body and brain. Melanie wasn't consciously aware of anything that happened while Phoebe had control of their body, but sometimes, like now, Phoebe's actions played out on the movie screen of Melanie's mind.

This particular event had happened eight months ago—Melanie knew, because she'd suddenly come awake to take over the body after Phoebe retreated during a rare moment of terror. The first thing Mel had seen was the face of an extremely pissed-off man who was trying to kill her. The second thing was the dead, burned man on the ground, and she'd instantly known Phoebe was responsible.

And now, thanks to her nightmares, she was bone-chillingly aware of exactly how it had all gone down.

Melanie flopped back down on the pillow, afraid to sleep . . . but what sucked was that she was even more afraid to be awake.

CHAPTER
One

Rome wasn't a place where Stryker Wills was comfortable. Sure, the women were gorgeous, the food amazing, and fucking and eating were two of his favorite pleasures in life. But man, there was a lot of history here he could potentially destroy. The cathedrals and the Colosseum, not to mention the Vatican, had all survived hundreds, or even thousands, of years and he could take them out in one fell swoop with a flash of temper.

Knowing that made him more wary than usual. He'd been tense all morning, despite the beautiful women who'd been propositioning him as he ate at an outdoor café—he didn't like mixing business with pleasure. And this trip was business, pure and simple, as he tried to get a bead on the fire-and-ice woman, a split-personalitied agent who'd killed his friend and nearly taken Stryker out—twice—eight months earlier in the Amazon jungle.

Stryker had been out for blood ever since—his easygoing personality fading into the background as his hunger to avenge his fellow murdered ACRO agent grew with each passing day.

Now the woman responsible for the murder was close. His hands fisted and he realized that he was no longer the same man who'd left ACRO for this assignment all those months ago.

Itor operative Phoebe Milan had killed his supervisor and friend, Akbar Shatar, setting him on fire while Stryker watched, helpless to do anything. And when Stryker returned to ACRO after Phoebe escaped, he'd gotten his new instructions from Devlin O'Malley, head of the ACRO agency.

Kill her, Dev told him. No further discussion needed.

It was an instruction ACRO agents heard often. As an operative with rare abilities, Stryker had actually lived on ACRO's massive compound since birth, as his parents were also both longtime agents with the Agency for Covert Rare Operatives.

His parents had assumed he'd have abilities, but man, had they been surprised at both the type and the extent. Mating a telekinetic with an excedosapien with superstrength hadn't seemed like a crazy idea at the time—and most agents tended to marry other agents anyway. But the first time two-year-old Stryker's temper tantrum ripped a fault through the middle of his house, everyone at ACRO had taken quite an interest in him.

So yeah, he'd grown up within the organization and, thanks to that, he was one of the few agents with special abilities who didn't have major adjustment issues, but that didn't mean that sometimes he didn't feel intimidated by his own might.

He could cause earthquakes and volcanoes. Tsunamis too, of course. Mudslides. Avalanches. Thing was, once he started them, he couldn't stop them, so he had to make sure to put just the right spin on his power. Typically, if he was forced to use it, he'd start small. Really, really small, because hey, there was always room to advance to life-threatening.

But there was a downside to his gift—there always was, for all the agents.

Stryker didn't have to watch the news to find out about natural disasters that occurred globally. Most were underreported anyway, but he was conscious of every single one, no matter their size.

Mainly, because they pulled at his libido, an unfortunate and common side effect for any elementalist. Mother Nature had a way of getting back at humans who could manipulate her world, and her nasty punishment for Stryker was a hard-on whenever someone used elemental powers around him—or when the planet rocked out an earthquake.

It was a constant—ranging from mild to highly uncomfortable—reminder that he had no control over Mother Nature at all, because even though he got advance notice, it came only mere seconds before the destruction, leaving no time to actually help any victims in the path of the oncoming natural disaster.

Most of the time, his sense of guilt was immense. More than once he'd gone to the ACRO scientists and psychics to seek a way to refine his abilities into an earlier warning system, but to no avail.

You can't beat yourself up over this, Dev would tell him, but Stryker would anyway.

Over the years, Stryker had watched men and women filter into ACRO—most dragged in, kicking and screaming until they could get their powers under control. He'd been there, done that with the control thing, and by the time he'd hit the all-too-volatile teen years, complete with raging hormones and plenty of testosterone, he'd gotten it. He knew, for the most part, how to keep his temper in check and, more important, the reasoning behind the why.

The next years found him learning to temper his . . . temper, so he could use his power to help, not hurt. Because that's what ACRO agents did—they helped to save the world, thanks to their blend of extraordinary gifts.

Some could control the weather. Others could communicate with animals, some with ghosts, and there was a small army of men—excedosapiens—who had superstrength or -speed.

ACRO was a pretty cool organization that assisted the government in saving the world from evil—and from Itor Corp, its most dangerous enemy to date.

Dangerous not just because of its self-serving, take-over-the-world goals, but because of the operatives it employed. Operatives like Stryker's current target. Phoebe was the fiery bitch and her alter identity was the icy one; from what little information ACRO had been able to gather, it seemed that the icy personality was the more vulnerable of the two.

Stryker had seen that firsthand, would wake nightly from the same recurrent nightmare that played out as it had in real life in the jungle, with the icy personality pleading with him for her life—but he refused to let his resolve down.

He would kill her as soon as he got the chance, because his nightmares about the smell of burning flesh, and Akbar's screams of pain, were just as vivid.

"Can I get you another espresso?" The young waitress, dark and curvy, was asking, before peering into his eyes. "I'm sorry, signor, I don't mean to stare, but your eyes—they look like . . . a kaleidoscope."

He nodded, had heard that before. His eyes were different, just like he was, crystal clear with a hint of blue and green, but the rest of him was classic all-American—blond, lean, and tall. "I'm all set here."

He stood to leave, ignoring the woman's continuing gaze, and that's when he felt it. A chill passed through the air, as if someone had poured ice down his back. But when he raised his head, he noted he wasn't the only one feeling the effects.

Spring had just hit and Rome was brimming with tourists. Although March in Italy was always iffy weather-wise, Stryker knew this sudden chill had nothing at all to do with Mother Nature.

And still, his body responded as if a major earthquake was about to happen. A pull that got him up and moving fast, hands jammed in his pockets to hide his sudden arousal.

He did not want to get closer to that bitch—not like this, had not thought through the fact that her powers could be a major turn-on to him. Mainly because he hadn't been affected at all the first time they'd met. He didn't know if it was because of the horror of watching Akbar die, but this was an unfortunate development neither he nor his trainers had considered.

Shit.

He hated her—did not want to need sex because of her. He cursed her as he walked against the icy wind, taking in the icicles hanging off storefronts and the hoarfrost coating windows. He knew he was close.

His gaze strayed upward, and he caught sight of a woman on a balcony, a blond woman who waved her arms wildly and was apparently having a rather animated conversation with . . . herself.

It was the ice lady, and although he much preferred her to the one who shot fire, he had to stop both of them. ASAP.

Quickly but covertly, he stashed all but one of his weapons and let himself into the secured building—illegally, of course—and headed up the stairs to the third floor.

Her icy door knocker gave her apartment away, if the film of frost on her door hadn't.

He drank the potion ACRO scientists had given him, the one that would render him immune to both of Phoebe's powers, albeit for only a few minutes, but it did nothing to stop his arousal. If anything, the salty liquid seemed to heighten his sexual needs.

He cracked his fingers. He could control himself for a few minutes. That would be more than enough time.

Melanie Milan knew she'd just done something incredibly stupid, but at the moment, she was far too pissed off to care. She was so pissed, in fact, that if her apartment—or, more accurately, Phoebe's apartment—were any higher than the third floor, she'd take a swan dive from the balcony just to teach her sister a lesson. A nice, long hospital stay would go a long way toward making Phoebe miserable.

All around her, the air had gone still. The mild March weather had taken a temporary vacation thanks to her temper tantrum, and on the streets below, in probably a three-block radius, it was winter again, complete with frost and ice. Shivering, but from fury, not the cold, Melanie went back inside the apartment, which had also gone chilly, because her fit of anger had started in the kitchen, where she'd found her pet goldfish impaled on the tines of a fork.

The fish was Phoebe's handiwork, a punishment for something Melanie wasn't even aware of yet. And now, because she'd just drained the battery on their special powers, Phoebe would devise another way to torture her.

She was so tired of this.

Cursing up a storm, she trudged to the bathroom where, sure enough, there was a note taped to the mirror—one of three methods of communication she used with Phoebe.

You stupid, lazy cow. You know I hate to find dishes in the sink. How many times do I have to tell you to make sure the kitchen is clean? And do the fucking laundry today. I want my favorite jeans to be clean and pressed.

Melanie's hands shook as she ripped the note in half and tossed it into the garbage. She was sick of being Phoebe's slave, sick of being abused, and sick of the face that stared back at her in the mirror. It wasn't hers. The long, blond hair was Phoebe's—Mel would prefer a chin-length cut. The ice blue, bloodshot eyes that spoke of late nights and drugs that left Melanie exhausted and hungover were Phoebe's doing. Worst of all, the swollen lips that had probably done some wicked things to God only knew how many men and women were all Phoebe's.

Phoebe liked sex, drugs, and violence, often all at the same time, and it was always Melanie who paid the price when she woke up in the body Phoebe had used hard.

At least this morning Melanie had awakened in their own bed instead of some stranger's. That was always a plus.

Melanie tightened the sash on her robe, though even that wasn't hers, was it? Almost everything in the apartment, from the furniture to the clothes to the food, was Phoebe's. Every time Melanie bought something for herself, Phoebe destroyed it. Melanie's only possessions consisted of a few paperbacks and college textbooks in the nightstand drawer, and her mother's gold ring in the wall safe that Phoebe had promised not to break into.

Mel also had a few files on the computer—her college courses. It was stupid, she knew, but she wanted desperately to do something for herself, even if that something was an art degree she'd never use. Obviously, when she had possession of the body she and Phoebe shared for only around ten hours a day, the degree was going to take forever to earn, and at some point would require Phoebe's cooperation.

How Melanie was going to manage that was the question of the century. Especially when all they did now was fight and see who could hurt who the most. Mel had no idea how she was going to pay Phoebe back for killing her fish . . . though as she eyed a pair of scissors on the counter, she wondered how her sister would like *really* short hair . . .

The buzzing of a cellphone reminded her that she needed to get her butt in gear. The ringtone belonged to Itor's big boss, Alek.

Who was also their father. Not that he behaved like one. And why should he? He was nothing but a sperm donor who had jerked off into a cup so his semen could be used to fertilize an egg in a petri dish. Melanie had no idea how he treated Phoebe, but she knew very well how he treated her. The son of a bitch despised her, acted like she was a traitor, even though she had nothing to do with Itor, didn't know anyone inside the operation, and, really, didn't even know what the agency's entire purpose was. Phoebe had kept everything a mystery, and only by piecing together tiny chunks of information over the years had Melanie learned what little she did know.

Such as the fact that Phoebe was some sort of superagent, and Itor employed a lot of people like her.

Like Melanie, whose gift of ice was the opposite of Phoebe's fiery touch. But since Mel had refused to use her ability to hurt people—even after being tortured—Itor considered her useless.

Assholes.

Melanie might be useless, but she wasn't helpless. Eight months ago, she'd encountered Itor's enemies—and what was that saying, the enemy of my enemy is my friend?

Since then, Mel had spent every spare moment trying to find the people she'd seen in the jungle, had questioned Phoebe about them, had scoured her memories raw in an effort to glean any information about the group of individuals who might be able to help lift her out of this hellish existence. So far, she had very little to go on, but she wasn't giving up.

The cellphone rang again, and Mel hurried to the bedroom. The text message was in code, as usual, so she had no freaking clue what it said. If it had been important, there would have been nothing on the screen but an exclamation point—which meant that Melanie had best retreat into the darkness of her mind and force Phoebe out.

Thank God that wasn't the case this time. She'd just drained their abilities, and she needed to charge. Quickly. Before Phoebe took over and discovered that she couldn't use her gift.

The problem was that charging up meant finding a man, and not only was Melanie not practiced in that particular skill, but she wasn't allowed to leave the building. Phoebe had made some very dangerous enemies a couple of weeks ago when an arms deal went bad, and apparently the small but deadly organization was hunting her.

A knock at the door made her jump, which was silly. The building was owned by Itor, was supersecure, and when she glanced at the clock, she realized it was time for the mail, and she was expecting a new textbook.

Smiling, she opened the door . . . and froze. The person on the other side wasn't an Itor guard delivering packages.

It was the very man she'd been looking for. The man who, eight months ago, had watched his buddy go up in flames, thanks to Phoebe. The man who had promised to kill her the next time they met.

She might have wanted to find him, but not like this, and a scream welled in her throat even as she tried to slam the door shut. But he was fast, and he moved inside with the speed of a striking snake, pinning her to the wall with his big body while fisting her hair in one hand and pressing the tip of a knife into the soft spot beneath her chin with the other. He kicked the door closed, and now she was completely, utterly helpless.

"So, Phoebe," he said in a smooth, calm voice that was far more frightening than if he'd yelled. "Wish I could say it was nice seeing you again. You should know that if you try to use your fire or ice, you'll end up with a blade in your brain. Got it?"

Oh, God. Wanting to find this man or the people he worked for was a huge mistake. Now she wanted to retreat, to let Phoebe out to handle this. Even without her gift, Phoebe was lethal— Mel had seen videos of her sister fighting like some sort of martial arts master. This was the kind of thing Phoebe lived for.

But she would be beyond pissed that Mel had drained the battery, and the last time that had happened . . . Mel shuddered.

No, somehow, she had to handle this herself.

"Well?" He pressed the knife, which had to be of a nonmetal construction to pass through the building's metal detectors, into her skin a little harder. "Are we clear on this?"

"Yes," she rasped. "Please . . . I'm not . . . I'm not Phoebe."

His eyes, hypnotic, swirling with sparks of anger, narrowed. "Who are you?"

"M-Melanie. Phoebe is—" She swallowed drily, hoping he'd

buy what was sort of a lie. "Phoebe is my twin sister. She's not here. She's at the market. She'll be home soon."

He smiled, his full lips peeling back from straight, white teeth, and wow, if he wasn't the scariest man she'd ever seen—outside of her father anyway—she'd have been seriously attracted to him. "See, the thing is, I know she's not at the market. I know she's you."

"We're identical twins—"

"You're the same person. Split personality." He tugged on her hair as he moved in even closer, so the entire hard length of his body was pressed against hers. He was bigger, stronger, and if that was the point he was trying to make, he'd succeeded. "So if you aren't Phoebe, why don't you tell me who you are at the moment."

Oh, crap. Very few people knew what she was, even inside Itor. Granted, this guy was wrong, but he was on the right track. This wasn't a case of multiple personality syndrome. Broken down into the most simple of concepts, this was a case of one egg splitting into two and then being shoved together again in a lab. Melanie and Phoebe really were two very different people fighting for control of the same body.

And unfortunately, Phoebe was a lot stronger, and had been for years.

"I told you, I'm Melanie," she insisted. "Who are you?"

"You don't remember?"

"I remember some." She jerked her head to the side in a futile attempt to break his hold. "But I'd remember a lot better if you took away the knife."

"Nice try," he said.

"You can't expect me to chat while I'm worried about bleeding out."

One corner of his mouth tipped up in amusement, which pissed her off, because bleeding out wasn't on her list of funny topics. "And you can't expect me to hand over the advantage so you can freeze me to death."

He shifted, and . . . good God, did he actually have an erection? She squirmed, and yes, there was a definite hard bulge in the front of his pants that was pressing into her belly. How nice that the thought of killing her turned him on.

"I can't freeze you to death." She glared at him. "I'm out of power. Used it all up a little while ago, and it takes several hours to recharge." Took sex to recharge too, but he didn't need to know that.

One blond eyebrow cocked up. "Now, why don't I believe you?"

She exhaled slowly and tried to keep her temper in check. "Dunno. Maybe because you're an asshole?" So much for the temper.

He snorted. "Like I haven't heard that before."

"No doubt you have." She swallowed, winced at the bite of the blade in her skin. "Look, if I could turn you into an ice cube, I'd have done it by now, knife or no knife. So tell me who you are, and let me go."

There was a long, tense silence, and then he backed off, but he stood a few feet away, coiled like a spring, and she had the feeling he was ready to put her down if she so much as flinched.

"Name's Stryker. And I'm guessing you remember me."

"You tried to kill me in some godforsaken jungle. You think I'd forget that?" She raised her chin and met his unnerving gaze head-on. "Are you here to finish the job?"

He considered her question for a long time, which did nothing for her nerves. Finally, he moved toward her. Stalking her.

A fresh jolt of fear spiked through her as she retreated. His prowling gait backed her all the way into the kitchen, where she bumped up against the counter.

"Am I here to kill you?" he asked softly, in a voice that filled her with dread. "Honestly? Yes."

A ball of terror dropped into the pit of her stomach. She couldn't speak, couldn't even move as he inched closer. He could have been a little less honest.

"But I'd really rather kill fire-bitch, so get her for me."

Okay. Yes, she needed to get Phoebe. This was so beyond Melanie's ability to handle. Concentrating, she called out to Phoebe in her mind. No response, as expected. For the first couple of hours after Melanie woke up, Phoebe was often next to impossible to summon.

Please, Phoebe, wake up! Still nothing. Dammit!

"Well?" Stryker's voice was gravelly with impatience, and Melanie began to sweat.

"I can't reach her."

"Too bad for you, then." The hand holding the wicked-looking knife came up, level with her heart, only a foot away. "Did you enjoy it?" he growled. "Did you like seeing my friend burn?"

Hurt and murder swirled in Stryker's eyes, and she knew her life could very well end in about five seconds.

"I'm sorry . . . I didn't do it . . . it was horrible." Stinging tears welled up, but they didn't drown out the visions of that man dying the way he had.

"You're sorry." He bared his teeth and stepped closer, pressing the tip of the knife into her breastbone. "Well, your *sorry* means jack shit."

She couldn't help it. She trembled so hard that the blade vibrated, punctured the fabric of her robe, and bit into her skin. His raw curse blistered the air, and he jerked the knife away.

"I'm not doing this with you," he snapped. "Until Phoebe grows a pair and decides to show her psychotic face, you're coming with me."

Panic wrapped around Mel, squeezing until her breath was coming in shallow pants. She wasn't stupid; she might not be safe right this minute, but at least she was in an apartment she knew, in a building owned by Itor. If she left with him, her chances for survival plummeted. "I can't. I can't leave. Phoebe will be mad. I have laundry to do, and I have to eat, and . . ." God, she was babbling, but at this point, she didn't care.

Stryker looked at her like she was nuts. "Phoebe will be fine." He reached for her, but she wheeled away, knocking dishes off the counter.

He cornered her near the pantry, and terror ripped through her. "Please don't. Please don't make me go. I can help you—"

"This isn't up for debate, and begging has no effect on me."

Her gaze darted around the kitchen. A weapon. She needed a weapon. Anything. But there was nothing. He was going to take her, and she was going to die. Abruptly, defeat closed in on her like a shroud. Years of living only half a life collided with the knowledge that the only glimmer of hope she'd had—finding Itor's enemies—turned out to be a letdown. Itor's enemies wanted her dead, and now she could do nothing but pray for mercy, something that had never, ever worked before.

"The thing with the knife," she rasped. "In my brain. Would it hurt?"

"What?" He blinked, clearly thrown by the question. "I guess I could make it hurt. Why?"

"Would you do it so it won't?"

"Look, if you cooperate—"

"I'm not going to cooperate," she said. "So just do it. But . . . I don't want it to hurt." She couldn't believe she was asking her murderer for a favor. She really had lost it.

Stryker looked completely dumbfounded, but at least he'd lost that homicidal glaze in his eyes. He stared. Scrubbed his hand over his face. Took a step back, even. As if maybe her crazy was contagious. After a long moment, he made the knife disappear into his leather jacket.

"What's your game?" he said gruffly. "Phoebe isn't going to hurt you. I did a little research into your condition, and from what I learned, alters are formed to protect. Not hurt. At least, not hurt each other."

Laughing bitterly, she gestured to the fork-impaled fish near the coffeemaker. "That was punishment for leaving her with no coffee. You don't want to know what she did to my parakeet."

"Well, there don't appear to be any other pets she can kill, so what else can she do to you?"

"You can't even begin to imagine." She wrapped her arms around her body, mainly to hold herself up. "I mean, I give as good as I get, but she has her creepy colleagues on her side." Mel didn't have anyone, and hadn't since her mother died.

His gaze sharpened. "Her colleagues? You work for Itor too, don't you?"

"Only Phoebe works for them," she said tiredly. "I don't really know what they do."

There was skepticism in his voice when he said, "So you're saying you have no idea what was going on in the Amazon when you were there?"

She shook her head. "The last thing I remember before coming to in the jungle was being on a plane with Itor people who wouldn't say a word to me. And then I was in the jungle and there was that man . . . and you were trying to kill me."

"Yeah, well, your buddy Phoebe and her Itor henchmen were planning to murder three dozen people, all to gain a powerful weapon." He paused as though expecting her to deny his accusation, but she knew her sister and father well enough to know that what Stryker was saying was no doubt true. When she said nothing, he continued. "Her team managed to slaughter some innocent people as well as kill my friend, and I'm here to make sure Phoebe answers for what she did." He gestured at her robe. "So get dressed, and come with me." When she stood there, paralyzed by indecision, he cocked his head, asked her softly, "Why did you ask me for help?"

Her heart nearly stopped. She'd forgotten how, in her confusion over what had happened in the jungle, her shock at the death and destruction, she'd whispered a terrified "Help me" to Stryker, even though he'd clearly rather have killed her.

"Because I was afraid." She'd been desperate, terrified, and grasping at the first glimmer of hope she'd seen in years. Itor's enemy could help her, right?

But then reality had set in at the murder in his eyes, and she'd cut her losses and run.

"Are you afraid now?" His voice was so deceptively quiet. "Yes."

"Good," he said, as he shoved her toward the bedroom. "At least you're smart. Get dressed."

That she was out of options was now obvious. She'd have to go with him and either convince him to help her, or leave their fate to Phoebe. She brushed past him. "Don't want to kill me while I'm in my pajamas, huh?" Her gallows humor came out in a thin voice that only emphasized the danger of her situation.

"Behave, and maybe I won't need to kill you at all. At least, not right away."

She stumbled to a halt at the bedroom doorway. "What do you mean?"

"I might have other uses for you," he said, sounding almost disappointed, as though he really wanted to kill her, but a smarter though less appealing option had come to mind. "Now stop talking and start dressing."

His tone said there was no room to argue, and really, when it came right down to it, Stryker couldn't do anything to her that hadn't been done before. And if he wanted to kill her, she'd die. If he was some sort of good guy, she'd probably end up in a mental ward somewhere, and Phoebe wouldn't have the freedom to torment her.

So . . . a mental ward or death.

Yep, things were looking up.

CHAPTER *Two*

Melanie was maybe the worst would-be hostage ever—or the smartest. Begging for death was a brilliant move to throw him off track, except Stryker didn't think she was kidding. At all.

She appeared genuinely afraid of her alter personality and, having met that Phoebe bitch personally, he could understand.

The forked fish on the counter confirmed that if what Mel told him about how her alter ego tortured her proved true, she was truly living a horror show existence. Having enemies was one thing, but sharing a body with one . . . well, he could read the fear wafting off Melanie in waves.

If she wasn't totally shitting him. And while he'd listened in on the ACRO scientists discussing multiple personality disorder—though they'd also called it dissociative identity disorder—he still firmly believed that Phoebe and Melanie were both the same person—and they should be punished.

But he'd get a lot more satisfaction taking it out on that fire-bitch. And the only way to ensure he could take his time and maybe even torture some Itor intel out of terrified Mel before he met Phoebe again was to get her the hell out of here and into the ACRO safe house.

Melanie moved into the bedroom and attempted to shut the door between them.

He slammed a flat palm out, making contact with the door and pushing it wide open. "I'm not letting you out of my sight."

She started at that, pulled the robe more tightly around her. He conceded her some privacy by angling away from her slightly, so he could still see her in his peripheral vision. She let the robe hang open as she turned to the side and slid on a pair of purple, lacy underwear. He couldn't miss the curve of her breast, the hint of a nipple, and he wanted to see her with that robe off completely.

Which was odd, considering she'd killed his friend and tried to do the same to him. Usually, he didn't find that such a turn-on.

Except Melanie . . . she was different.

In the case of multiple personality disorder within special-ability types, the more timid personality is usually the dominant, the ACRO psychologists had explained to him. *If she's stressed, the stronger personalities will come out to protect her.*

Stryker was walking a fine line with that, but so far, the only woman in front of him was Melanie. And he sure planned on stressing her more, and soon.

Finally, she shook the robe off, keeping her gaze averted from his the entire time.

He shifted, his erection nearly to the point of painful, and fuck it all, he would need relief soon. Just because the woman's ice tantrum was over didn't mean that the atmospheric shift didn't fuck with his cock.

And he knew she'd noticed, both earlier and again now when she slid a furtive glance his way and quickly went back to pulling on a pair of tight, dark jeans and a black sweater cut low, with a pair of leather boots that he hoped like hell she could run in, if need be.

"I'm ready," she said finally.

He looked her over. "Good. Let's go."

He motioned for her to walk ahead of him. She hesitated, and then grabbed a jacket hanging off a rack by the front door.

"You're going to act like you know me," he instructed, his hand on the knob. "Slip your arm through mine. Smile. Pretend you're Phoebe."

They walked down the flights of stairs and out the front door of the building with no problems. The safe house was about half a mile away on foot, a nice stroll through some heavily populated areas, which would be great.

They just had to pass through two residential neighborhoods, the first of which was where he'd stored the gun and Taser, since he knew he'd never get them through Itor's security at the apartment. And they were there, right behind a Dumpster parked in a narrow alley, and so he tucked the Taser into the side pocket of his cargo pants and the gun in his front pocket.

Stryker felt a tingle of warning and he began to walk faster, even as the passages between the buildings became more narrow, closing in on them as quickly as the footfalls behind them did. Melanie kept up, and for a second he thought maybe they'd be okay, until . . .

"Hey, Phoebe!" an angry male voice called out, and Stryker and Melanie both turned to see two men stalking toward them.

Too fast.

"Any idea who they are?" he asked.

Melanie looked between them and him. "Maybe . . . and they don't look happy."

They didn't, were too close for a quick escape—and Stryker knew a fight was in his future.

"Phoebe, we're here to collect on the money you owe us."

"I don't owe you anything," Melanie told them.

"You lose at poker, you pay a price," one of them said, his voice level despite clenched fists.

Stryker growled, "Why don't you just back off?"

Instead of doing that, the taller of the two men heaved a small metal Dumpster into the air with one hand and slammed it back down to the ground with the ease Stryker had come to associate with an excedosapien—humans who possessed either super-strength or superspeed, but never both.

"They're not Itor," Melanie said quietly, and yes, Stryker knew that too, had seen the flash of a tattooed palm as the man began his Dumpster toss.

Things never really ever did go as planned, but this time, he knew he could be fucked royally.

These men weren't Itor, but they could be just as bad. This was a gang of men and women with superpowers who had formed some kind of rogue upstart agency. Or, more accurately, a terrorist organization. He'd been warned about them thanks to The Aquarius Group, ACRO's sister agency based in London, whose operatives were on standby to help him with situations like this.

Except he really didn't have time for a phone call right now.

These men and women didn't have any loyalty among them. Bonded by anger and the glyphlike ink on their palms, they fought dirty, had no desire to learn to control their strength or channel their powers appropriately.

And it looked like they pretty much wanted Phoebe dead. Unfortunately, Melanie would take the brunt of the action, although by the weary look on her face, she was used to this happening.

"Phoebe, you need to come with us," Dumpster Guy said, his Italian accent thick with anger, and yeah, Phoebe wasn't exactly the make-friends-easily type.

"You want me, come get me, assholes," Melanie called back fiercely, and while Stryker appreciated the sentiment, the invitation she'd tossed out would only make them angrier.

"Now's not the time to grow a spine," he muttered. He wanted to tell her to run, but if the guys had backup, they'd catch her. No,

she was safer waiting for him, trying to stay out of the way and behind him. "If you want her, you'll need to go through me."

Widening his stance, he sank into a defensive position that
gave them an eyeful of his pistol. He didn't want to have to use
it, not out in the open like this, but letting these assholes know he
had it couldn't hurt.

Dumpster Guy just grinned. It was the short guy who
charged Stryker, slamming him easily to the ground, jarring
the pistol loose and sending it clattering across the cobblestone
paving. A railroad spike of pain shot up his spine and rattled his
skull.

Strength. Definitely strength for both excedos, he thought
groggily as he rolled away and shoved to his feet. Shortshit, his
eyes glittering with blood thirst, threw a punch. Stryker ducked,
felt the whisper of air caress his cheek as the blur of a fist flew by.
Hungry for his own shot, he spun, driving his heel into the guy's
sternum, and then he used the momentum of landing to make another sweep with his leg. Shortshit yelped in surprise and pain as
Stryker's foot made contact with his ribs.

A satisfying crunch echoed off the surrounding walls, audible
even over the sound of traffic at the ends of the alley, and yeah,
it was worth getting the crap kicked out of him every couple of
weeks during training with Ender and Trance in order to learn
the excedos' weaknesses.

He wheeled around to avoid an incoming strike from Dumpster and thanked his lucky stars these guys were strong, but not
fast. The trick would be avoiding a killing blow while taking
them to the ground.

Out of the corner of his eye he saw Mel, backed against a
wall. She held his pistol in shaking hands, and even from here
and while ripping kicks at these two guys, he could see that the
safety was still engaged.

A glancing blow to the shoulder spun him into Shortshit.
Stryker stepped off, but not fast enough to avoid a fist in the gut.
With a grunt, he doubled over, used his position to conceal his

hand as he palmed the Taser. In a smooth motion, he slammed into Dumpster with a linebacker hit while nailing Shortshit with the Taser. The short guy went down, eyes bulging, body twitching.

"*Merda!*" Dumpster spat, and jammed the heel of his palm into Stryker's nose.

Cartilage crunched and pain screamed through his face, and shit was right, because motherfuck that hurt, and he'd be popping his own nose back into place when this was done.

Breathe. Stay calm.

Kind of hard to do when he was getting thrown against a wall by Dumpster Guy.

"Mel—" He broke off as Dumpster's forearm came down on his throat, and where the hell was she anyway? Gasping for breath, he cranked his head to the side, just barely, but enough to catch sight of her as she turned the corner up the alleyway and he wondered why the hell this asshole wasn't following her.

A heartbeat later, he had his answer. As suspected, another asshole had been waiting in the wings to grab her. Somehow— with sheer dumb luck, probably—she evaded him by bumping into two restaurant workers hauling garbage bags.

But fuck . . . where there was one bad guy there were more.

And this shit was about way more than Phoebe owing money from a lost poker game.

Summoning the last of his strength and calling on all his training, he simultaneously jammed his knee into Dumpster's junk while angling the Taser at his neck. Too late the guy realized what was happening, and he hit the ground with a thud.

Unable to spare the time to kill the guys, Stryker sprinted after Melanie and the guy chasing her. He ran as hard as he could, his body screaming with an aching pain that promised to get worse as he pushed himself to the limit.

A crowd loomed ahead, and he shouldered his way through it, ignoring the angry curses. He scanned the bobbing heads . . . there. Melanie had crossed the street, was trying to blend in with the herd of pedestrians, but someone had to fucking teach her that a bright pink jacket did shit to help that.

To his left, a dark-haired man had zeroed in on Melanie as well, his gaze sharp with predatory intent. Adrenaline surging, Stryker jogged across the street, dodging cars and wildly swerving bicyclists. Suddenly, angry shouts rose up over the sounds of honking vehicles, and he turned to see two men, one of them Dumpster Guy, charging at Melanie.

Shit! He darted down the walk, nearly colliding with a woman stepping out of a boutique, arms laden with shopping bags. Cursing, he targeted Melanie once more, as she wove her way between some café tables ahead. Stryker gave chase. A toddler waddled into his path, and he lunged to the side, leaping over an empty four-top and sending chairs tumbling. The startled screams of the patrons had Mel looking over her shoulder as she ran, her eyes wide when she saw both him and the pissed-off excedo barreling through the tables with as much grace as a bull in a china shop.

"Mel!" He caught her by the wrist and tugged her toward the thickest of the throng in an attempt to lose both the massive man hot on their tail and the two smaller men who had come from freaking nowhere.

Not good. Still running, he took in the area, every window, doorway . . . hell, if he could steal a car he would. He spotted a shop that backed up to an alley, which meant a rear exit.

"This way!" He dragged Mel through the front door of what turned out to be a curio shop. Halfway in he stripped the damned jacket off her and threw it to the floor before leading her back outside and along the cobblestone streets.

They were attracting attention—far too much for his liking, because the last thing he wanted was the local authorities involved. That would take hours of questioning and God knew what Mel would tell them about him.

No, he had to do this on his own.

They traversed the streets and alleys, taking shortcuts

through shops and then slowing to walk casually through a crowded piazza. They paused next to a fountain to catch their breath and gain their bearings, and so far, so good. No sign of the enemy, but he didn't want to assume they'd lost them.

Still holding her hand, he maneuvered her down another busy street, in the opposite direction of the safe house.

The safe house was out for now. Too far away, and he didn't want to risk leading the enemy to it. A hotel would have to do, and almost as though she'd read his mind, Mel pointed to the west and said, "That way."

They cut through the kitchen of a restaurant, earning scowls from patrons and scoldings from the chef, but they saved time.

"There's a block of hotels over here." She tugged at his arm. "I've woken up in them a few times."

They bypassed the first one—too exposed, with large windows and not enough people. The second, sandwiched between a corner grocer and a shoe shop, was perfect. It was your basic shithole tourist trap, but for now, it would work.

He stopped before they went through the street entrance. "Try to catch your breath. Keep looking at me, head down, like we're lovers who can't wait to get back to our room."

Thankfully, the lobby was crowded, and they managed to walk through and grab the elevator up to the second floor. Better than the first, and still they could escape easily out the window if they needed to.

He stopped next to a door, knocked, and when no one answered, he used his breaking-and-entering skills to open the door. Suitcases lined the floor. Occupied. Dammit.

Keeping her close, he tried the next three rooms until he found an empty one.

Undetected. So far, so good. As soon as they were inside, door closed, he rounded on Melanie. "Now, let's talk about you running while I was saving your ass."

She shrugged. "Looked like you were going to lose. Had to save myself."

He grabbed her arm, pulled her close, his voice a low growl. "You're fucking with me, Melanie. And I don't like it. Running was a really stupid move."

"Yeah? I thought it was pretty damned smart," she spat as she struggled uselessly against his grip.

He noted red marks on her cheek that were beginning to bruise. She had blood on a pouty lower lip and he found himself wanting to reach out and wipe her face. She was pretty. Really delicate features that softened the ice blue eyes and blond hair.

He yanked his thoughts away from her injuries and his sudden need to wrap her up and keep her safe and thought about the plan. It would have to include backup, but Mel didn't need to know that. Yet. He released her, grabbed a tissue to wipe his bloody nose as he stalked to the window.

"Those guys aren't going to stay away for long. They'll find us and they'll bring backup. We've got to be ready. Have a plan of action. Another escape route. You said earlier that you couldn't use your powers if you wanted to."

"Right."

"Why?"

"I drained them on my balcony."

"And is there a way besides time that will restore them?"

"Yes." She licked her bottom lip nervously. "But it's complicated."

He peered out the window and then looked back at her. "Break it down and bottom-line it—we may not have a lot of time."

"You'd have to have sex with me."

He stared at her. She blushed, and hey, well, he'd asked for it in the simplest terms.

And at least now he knew exactly how to keep both fire and ice at bay.

* * *

God, Melanie couldn't believe she'd just blurted it out like that. Then again, she was sorely lacking in social skills.

Stryker was still looking at her with a distinct, are-you-fucking-kidding-me expression on his face, and she just wanted to throw up.

Phoebe was going to freak out, would no doubt blame Mel for this crazy situation they were in, even though Stryker was here for Phoebe, and the insane men who'd attacked them were too.

"Forget I said anything," she said, sinking down onto the too soft bed that spoke of age, worn springs, and way too many couplings. The ancient comforter was a tacky blend of reds and golds, like nearly everything else in the room, from the oil painting on the wall to the vase full of fake flowers on the tiny sitting table, and she fought the urge to shudder. Phoebe had landed them in some horrible places over the years, but this was the first time Mel had.

"Forget you just said that if I fuck you, you get your powers back? You told me at your apartment that it takes time. How much time?"

She scrubbed a hand over her face, wincing at the twinge of pain as her palm brushed the swelling flesh around her right eye. For a moment she considered lying, but she was too tired and too rattled to think right now. So the truth it was. "Sex gets it back immediately. Otherwise it takes between twenty-four and forty-eight hours for a full charge."

"If you're telling the truth, that's pretty damned inconvenient."

"You have no idea," she sighed.

He tugged back the age- and cigarette-smoke-yellowed curtain and peeked outside again. Sunlight streaked across his face, bathing his handsome profile in a golden glow. The harsh line of his jaw tightened as his gaze scanned the narrow side street, but after a moment he turned back to her. "I'm not fucking you, so I guess we wait."

Thank God. The man wanted to kill her; she doubted he'd be all that considerate with her body during sex. "Well, we can't just sit here. I need to eat."

He gave her another one of those looks of utter disbelief. "Yeah, let's just waltz down to the corner café and see if we get grabbed."

"We've got to do something." She came to her feet. "If Phoebe comes out with an empty stomach, she'll be pissed." Well, that was true enough, but the *real* truth about why she wanted to eat wasn't something she was prepared to share.

"She'll deal."

Fear knotted in her empty stomach. He wasn't going to budge, was he? "Please . . . you have to promise me one thing."

He folded his arms across his broad chest. "You haven't figured out by now that I don't have to promise you shit?"

She raised her chin and tried hard not to let desperation bleed into her voice. "This is easy enough. When Phoebe comes out, tell her I fought you. Tell her it was you who injured me instead of those thugs."

"I already said I'd make it clear that you didn't cooperate with me." His eyes narrowed, as though he suspected a trick. He watched her with that intense, intelligent gaze for a long time before saying, "Something here isn't making sense. If you want anything from me, I want the truth."

"That works both ways, you know."

"Not when you're the one who's not in charge. Keep in mind that killing you would be a lot easier than keeping you alive."

Good point. "Can you at least tell me who you are? Who you work for?"

"You don't know?" When she shook her head, he said, "Ever heard of ACRO?"

Several times, actually. People who worked for Itor seemed to constantly be at odds with whatever this ACRO was. "I have, but I don't know what it is, exactly. I know Itor doesn't think well of them."

"That's because my agency opposes everything Itor stands for. We're the good guys."

"That's funny," she said quietly, "because I didn't think good guys kill innocent people."

"You aren't innocent."

"I wasn't responsible for what happened to your friend."

Instantly, she regretted bringing up the dead man, because everything about Stryker went cold, from his gaze to his voice. "Fuck you," he snarled. "I'm not buying your multiple personality bullshit. You might have a bunch of alters, but deep down, it's all the same person. So here's the thing. I want to know why Phoebe would do things to hurt you, because that doesn't make sense. Which personality is dominant?"

She didn't want to tell him anything, but really, what would it hurt? She held no loyalty to Itor or Phoebe. Besides, if he knew the truth, maybe he would be a little more hesitant about killing her. "I used to be dominant, when we were kids. But now Phoebe is," she admitted, eyeing him warily, because he still looked ready to throttle her for killing his friend. "But she's not a personality. I'm not an alter."

He snorted. "Is that what some quack psychiatrist told you?"

She started pacing, doing her best to contain her nervous energy. "I'm not suffering from multiple personality disorder, and don't give me that look. I'm telling you the truth, and no, I'm not delusional." Reaching deep for some elusive sense of calm, she continued. "Phoebe and I are the result of laboratory experimentation. One egg was fertilized, and it split. We should have been born identical twins, but scientists forced the eggs back together. Sort of how sometimes you hear some freaky story about how one twin absorbs the other in the womb. Except this was more of a joining than an absorption."

Stryker's expression was contemplative now. "So you're saying that you really are two different people. Each with your own soul."

"Yes. Doctors determined that while we share the body, we

each have our own separate area of the brain. She controls a portion of the logical left and I control a region in the creative right."

"Okay, let's say I believe you," he said in a tone that made it clear he didn't. "Who performed this experiment, and why?"

"It was Itor. I don't know exactly what their goal was. No one tells me anything. I asked my mom once, and my dad, and Phoebe—"

"Wait. How did you ask Phoebe?"

"We communicate in a few ways. Notes taped to the bathroom mirror, text messages left for each other on the phone, and sometimes a handheld voice recorder or video camera on the computer." She shrugged. "So anyway, she said they were hoping to create the perfect spy. Someone who could be anything in any situation because they were two different people. The problem is that they wanted both of us to be aware of what was going on when the other was in control. Turns out that when Phoebe is in control, I know nothing about what happens during the time she has the body, and vice versa."

What she'd just told Stryker wasn't entirely true, but he didn't need to know about the nightmares that often turned out to be true slices of Phoebe's life.

"So the experiment was a failure." He spoke while peering out the window once more, his sharp gaze taking in everything outside. He might scare the crap out of her, but she couldn't help but appreciate how alert he was, how confident he was in his abilities.

"No. *I* was the failure according to Itor."

He frowned. "Why do you say that?"

"I'm the weak one," she said. "The one who couldn't learn all the spy stuff. I can't fight very well, and I suck at lying."

The light in the room dimmed as he let the curtains fall back into place. His frown deepened, putting lines in the corners of his lush mouth. An insane question popped into her head, one that asked if he could kiss as well as she suspected. "So Itor created you," he mused, "but how were you raised? And where?"

Tired of the pacing, she sank back down on the bed and drew her knees up to her chest. "All over, really. Our mother was a powerful elemental telekinetic. She could manipulate both fire and air, which she said was really rare."

Stryker whistled, long and low. "No shit. I've never even heard of anyone with a double element talent. Not until you."

"Well, not me. Not technically. I can't manipulate fire, and Phoebe can't manipulate temperature and water vapor. But still, my mom figured she was the source of our differing gifts. She lost hers during pregnancy and never got them back, so she was useless to Itor after that, except as a mother to us." A mother who had been protective and kind, if distant, as though something inside her had broken when she lost her powers. Mel didn't remember a lot about her, except that she'd always seemed nervous when their father paid an unexpected visit, hovering, as though she was worried he'd take Mel and Phoebe with him.

Stryker drifted toward her, and she wondered if he even realized he was doing it. "So where did you grow up?"

"For the first five years, Australia. Itor poked and prodded, tested and made us come out and retreat. Then my mom's brother got sick, and she took us to live with him in Japan for a couple of years." Melanie still didn't know why her father allowed it, but then, he didn't seem to care all that much about her or Phoebe on a personal level. As long as their mother kept up their education and training, he seemed content to let them live with her. "While we were there, an earthquake struck. Phoebe was in control at the time, and she was trapped beneath some rubble when a building came down. Mom was killed."

Realization dawned in Stryker's remarkable eyes, and for the first time, she saw a true softening in his expression. He sat down next to her, not touching, but close enough that she could feel his heat. "And that's why Phoebe retreated in the jungle, isn't it? The earthquake."

Mel nodded. "She's terrified of them. It's the only thing she's afraid of, and she's practically phobic."

"What happened after that?"

"My father came for us." She took a deep, calming breath, because it was at that point in her life when everything went to hell. She'd awakened after the earthquake to find herself in the hospital, recovering from a broken leg and several broken ribs. Her father had arrived shortly after that, cold as a robot and just as efficient as he had her whisked from the hospital to a waiting plane staffed with a medical team. He'd barely spoken to her, had been more concerned for her special abilities than her health or emotional well-being.

"He took you back to Australia?"

"Yes. He figured we were old enough to do without a mom, so we were raised on the Itor compound. We had tutors and trainers, and our existence was all about becoming effective tools for Itor." She rubbed her eyes again, too late remembering the blow she'd taken from one of the attackers, and she hissed in a breath at the throbbing pain that exploded in her face when her palm struck the bruise over her right cheekbone.

Stryker's fingers closed on her hand and pulled it away. "We need to get ice on that," he said, his voice soft—soothing, even. Lightly, he feathered his fingers over her cheek, and a strange tingling sensation replaced the pain. She couldn't remember the last time anyone had touched her out of . . . concern?

No, that couldn't be it. The man wanted to kill her. She jerked away from him, but he caught her chin, holding her immobile. "Hey," he murmured. "I'm not going to hurt you. I just want to see how bad your injuries are."

"O-okay." Okay? She could hardly breathe as his gaze roamed her face and his fingers probed the edges of her injury.

He leaned in, so his massive chest brushed her arm, and a lightning strike of awareness shot through her.

Dear God, was she getting . . . turned on . . . by this?

He seemed to know she had frozen like a deer facing an oncoming vehicle, and he drew back, but it didn't matter. She still felt the shadow of his touch on her skin. "So who is your father anyway?"

She swallowed to bring moisture back to her mouth. "Alek Kharkov. He's—"

"The head of Itor." Stryker's voice had gone deadly flat, like his expression, and she got the feeling she'd just given him the wrong answer. "Jesus fucking Christ."

"Closer to Antichrist," she muttered, and suddenly, she found herself pinned to the mattress, Stryker's big body holding her down. "What did I do now?" The words came out in a breathless rush.

His face was a mask of fury. "You're the fucking daughter of Itor, and you expect me to believe that anything you just told me was the truth?"

"Y-yes. It's the truth. All of it. I swear."

"Why?" he snapped. "Why help your father's enemy?"

"I'm not helping anyone." She struggled beneath him, but he only pressed down harder, his legs locked down on hers, his chest a dead weight. Panting with exertion, she finally gave up, figuring she should conserve her strength in case she needed to surprise him later. Besides, the struggle seemed to have aroused him, and as his erection ground against the juncture between her legs, something inside her stirred.

"Then what are you doing?"

"I'm trying to keep myself safe," she snapped back at him, not bothering to hide her irritation at being held down against her will, and her greater irritation at the fact that she was just a little turned on by the physicality of it. Maybe Phoebe had conditioned their body to respond this way. Or maybe she was more like Phoebe than she'd thought. "And right now, you look better than the alternative."

"So you're saying that if conditions change and you think someone else can keep you safe, you'll switch sides?"

Say no, say no . . . "Yes." She couldn't lie for shit. Phoebe seemed to have gotten all of that particular talent.

Stryker stiffened, seeming perplexed, as if he couldn't believe she'd told the truth, so therefore it must be a lie. But if it was a lie, then it meant she wouldn't change sides, which meant he could trust her. Yep, she'd just trapped him in a web of his own skepticism.

"Fuck." He rolled off her and lay beside her, staring up at the ceiling. "This would have been so much easier if Phoebe had been in the apartment instead of you."

"So sorry I ruined your homicide party." She sat up and shook out her arm, which had fallen asleep when it had been pinned awkwardly between her hip and the mattress.

With a snarl, he shoved away from the bed and stalked to the window. "When will Phoebe make her appearance?"

"Around two in the afternoon."

"Can you stop her?"

She narrowed her eyes at him. "I thought you wanted to see her."

"Oh, I'm dying to see her," he said in a dark, ominous voice. "But not until I'm ready."

Okay, so she needed to stay in control as long as possible. "If we go back to my place, there's a way. A drug Itor developed to help Phoebe stay in control at critical times on missions. If I take it, it will keep her suppressed for a few extra hours."

"Fine. We head back to your place."

"But won't that be dangerous? With those guys after us? Maybe we should . . . you know . . ."

"I already told you, it's not going to happen."

"I swear, I won't use my powers on you."

"That's not my issue."

"Then what is?"

"My issue is that I'd rather face a battle than fuck the woman who killed my best friend." His gaze raked her from head to toe, and then, with a sneer, he said, "Besides, if I'd wanted you, I'd have had my chance a minute ago."

How crazy was it that what he'd just said actually stung? She should be happy he didn't want her. "Guess the fact that you're a good guy saved me, huh?" She shoved to her feet. "It's a really good thing you told me you were ACRO instead of Itor, because right now I'm having a hard time telling them apart."

With that, she slammed into the bathroom.

CHAPTER
three

Stryker stared at the closed bathroom door.

He couldn't believe he'd let himself have a hard-on for her, how easily he'd let his guard down, and he cursed himself for the same instinct he would've trusted before Akbar's death.

Kindness had always been one of Stryker's best qualities, and Akbar had encouraged him not to lose that, not to get so much of an edge that he lost his instincts about people.

Akbar had been too fucking kind himself—if he hadn't stepped out in front of Stryker . . .

Fuck, he couldn't go there now. There was too damned much to do—for Akbar and for ACRO.

Fire-and-ice woman might as well be the spawn of the devil, because seriously, being Alek's daughter wasn't any better.

Dev was going to flip. And, of course, tell Stryker not to kill her. Melanie was more valuable than any of them even knew.

Stryker needed to call Dev with the news ASAP and he also needed the backup from TAG—and Devlin would be the one to call in the cavalry for him. Because come two P.M., fire-bitch would emerge and Stryker knew he'd have a hard time not killing her.

Of course, he'd like to spend some time in a nice, quiet location scaring the shit out of her with a few earthquakes. Torture had never been his speed, but these months of searching for Phoebe—and for revenge—had left a metallic, bitter taste in his mouth and his normally even personality in shreds.

Yeah, not good. He checked his watch. It would be close to six in the morning back in New York. That wouldn't matter— Dev could often be found in his office as early as five A.M. and, no matter what, would pick up the phone. Which he did now, on the first ring.

"Is she dead?"

"Not exactly." *Not that I wouldn't like her to be, despite the fact that I got a raging hard-on from lying on top of her . . . not that icewoman's playing me like a fiddle. Christ.* "I managed to get some intel from her that I thought would make her valuable. If she's not lying, one of Itor's bases might be in Australia."

"She just handed us a huge advantage if that's true."

"Which is why I'm skeptical, but it can't hurt to check into the possibility." He glanced at the bathroom door. Still closed. "There's more. I hit pay dirt—fire-and-ice woman is Alek's daughter."

He heard a sharp inhale from across the line. It took a hell of a lot to surprise Dev, but it seemed like forever before his boss spoke again. "Don't kill her."

"Yeah, I figured you'd say that. We ran into some trouble with a rogue group—I'm going to need TAG's help getting us to the safe house."

"Consider it done. What else have you found out?"

"I'm dealing with Melanie here. She's scared as shit and she doesn't know much else, or so she claims. We're heading back to her apartment and then to the safe house. She says Phoebe will emerge soon if we don't get some Itor special medicine, and I know that bitch will be far less compliant than Melanie."

"Agreed. TAG will contact you. Call me when you get to the safe house." Dev's tones were clipped and left no room for discussion. As if to ensure that, his boss disconnected the line, and Stryker slowly closed his own phone and listened to the running water on the other side of the bathroom door.

Now all he had to do was wait for TAG to take care of the rogues. But if TAG didn't hurry, Stryker would find himself face-to-face with Phoebe, and he sure as shit didn't need the suntan.

The bathroom door opened slowly and Mel emerged. It was obvious she'd been crying—no amount of cold water could mask that.

Right now he didn't want to deal with feeling bad for her. She was enemy personified. "Help is on the way—we'll get to your place with protection."

"Good, that's good." She wrung her hands together. "I know it kills you, to have to spend time with me."

"This isn't personal—this is a job."

"How can you say it's not personal—my sister killed your friend."

"Your sister killed an agent, that's why I was ordered to find her," he said through clenched teeth. "This isn't about personal revenge."

"Bullshit."

He didn't answer, didn't want to admit to himself that she might be right on the money—that this was way more than a job from ACRO. That he would've gone out without Devlin's approval to hunt down fire-bitch.

"Look, I get it," she said. "I'm either feared or hated—usually both—for who my father and sister are." She shrugged but her eyes were red-rimmed.

And no, he couldn't begin to imagine the childhood—hell, the lifetime—of pain she'd endured. Still, the nagging thought that Mel could've been complicit in what happened to Akbar . . .

She was staring, but not at his face. No, her gaze had dropped to his now clenched fists, which shook, as if he was trying his best not to reach out and punch someone.

She looked as though she was waiting to be hit and that alone was enough to make him open his hands. He didn't hit women. He fought operatives, and Melanie did not fit that profile.

When she finally let her eyes meet his, she looked weary—and resigned. "If it makes you feel any better, I'm already punished. Every single day of my life."

"It doesn't."

She nodded and then suddenly she tensed, her face pale. "No, not now—it's too soon," she rasped, more to herself than to him.

"What's wrong?"

"Phoebe's stirring—we'll have to go now."

He hadn't gotten the call from TAG that things were in place, and leaving now to get the Itor meds would be too risky. So the only thing to do was take advantage of this new development. "Good. Bring her on, Mel."

"Trust me, you don't want this."

"Don't you dare tell me what I want—what I want is for that bitch to die." Dev might want this woman back at ACRO, but if Phoebe came out now, Stryker could have some fun with her and *maybe* bring her back alive.

But the way he felt at the moment, with the anger bubbling to the surface, he didn't think the alive thing was an option at all. "Come on out, Phoebe." Melanie backed up, managed to get a few steps out of his reach before he was on her, slamming her against the wall. "Phoebe, you little bitch—I know you can hear me. Come on out and we'll have some fun. Correction—I'll have some fun ripping your fucking throat out."

An image of Akbar flashed in his mind—he heard Akbar's screams from that final day ringing in his ears as he cupped Melanie's throat in his hand and squeezed. "Bring the bitch out. Because I can kill you both right now, but it won't be nearly as satisfying."

With that, the floor beneath them shook—and slammed him out of his tirade. He realized that he desperately needed to get himself back in control and wondered if it was too late this time.

But the earthquake his anger had created was only one of his problems. The other was the rock-hard erection and the feeling of uncontrollable arousal that passed over him and made everything hazy.

His hand had slipped from Melanie's throat to her breast and she drew in a sharp gasp as through her shirt he worked a nipple between his thumb and forefinger.

The fury and the arousal would combine to create a hell of a show, both outside and here . . . against the wall . . . on the table . . . on the floor . . .

Whether or not he'd allow himself to go there was suddenly, sickeningly, out of his control as the haze enveloped him in its grasp.

Hand still on the phone, Devlin O'Malley almost called Gabriel or Marlena. Normally, either one of them could bring him instant comfort with their mere presence.

This morning, nothing would help the feeling of impending doom spreading through his body.

Fire-and-ice woman is Alek's daughter.

The words echoed in his head, a terrible cacophony, until his eyes watered and he was sure he'd throw up. Unable to sit still, he paced the office floor until he could control his breathing.

Stryker was still angry—wanted nothing more than to kill the woman he now held hostage. He'd delivered the news of who she was to Dev carefully, but his operative had no idea of the impact of the information.

Stryker would have no way of knowing that Melanie/Phoebe was also Dev's sister, likely half sister.

He had a sibling. One who had murdered one of his agents. She'd probably murdered more—ACRO had an entire file of operatives who had been either killed at the hands of an unknown assailant or gone MIA and were presumed dead.

He sat down heavily in his chair and stared out the window into the gray dawn.

Very few things threw him these days. The death of Oz, his former lover, best friend, and ACRO agent, had done so, but with Gabriel's help, he'd slowly come out of mourning. And he'd spent the last year meticulously planning Itor's demise and falling in love all over again.

Things had been good. The best they had been for him since taking over ACRO after the deaths of his parents ten years earlier. He'd spent those years besting Itor Corp more often than not, as well as helping the U.S. government nail terrorists who threatened the country. Although the government officially denied ACRO's existence, something Dev insisted on, they would pass on information to ACRO when they suspected that a member of the military or another organization had special or rare powers. It was a win-win all around, and Dev's time at ACRO's wheel had gone well.

Until two years earlier, when Itor's leader, Alek Kharkov, had used his genetic link to Dev in a way that had left ACRO vulnerable and had nearly broken Dev completely. Learning that Dev's greatest enemy was a biological part of himself was the only thing that had put him back together. That, and the need to avenge not only the psychic violation that had taken place but the danger Dev had inadvertently put his own agents in.

He turned back to his desk now and, in a habitual move leftover from years of blindness, ran his fingers over the mission report Ryan Malmstrom had dropped off the night before. Ryan, who had been one of the very agents Dev had put at risk. The man had been deep undercover in Itor at the time, having infiltrated the organization after months of careful planning. Ryan's cover had been blown, and he'd been tortured, his mind scrubbed, and it had been only by the grace of God that the agent had been returned to ACRO last year.

Ryan had forgiven him, but Devlin couldn't forgive himself. He'd promised his operative that he would take Itor to the ground or die trying.

This year, things had begun to fall into place. Thanks to Ryan's infiltration, they'd gotten some important inside information that included a possible highly dangerous weapon.

And now . . . now they had Alek's daughter.

Alek had killed Dev's birth mother—Dev had learned that only a few years earlier. His parents had never let on that he wasn't their biological son, that they'd rescued him from Itor's evil leader when he was a mere newborn.

Dev wondered if Melanie/Phoebe's mother had suffered the same fate.

He could trust Stryker not to kill her, no matter the man's personal grudge. He needed to spend the day planning how best to use the information Stryker had given him about Australia, as well as figuring out how his half sister could aid with the take-down of Itor.

Devlin had no qualms about murdering his biological father. He just had to decide if his sister would be part of the collateral damage.

CHAPTER
four

Beneath Melanie's feet, the floor vibrated, reminding her of the first time they'd met, when whatever power he possessed had ripped apart the jungle earth. She stiffened, her body rigid, her mind spinning. This man clearly hated her. Yet he wanted her. And she . . . Lord help her, she wasn't sure what she wanted. Her body was definitely reacting to his touch, and she was pretty sure her initial suspicion was correct, that it had been conditioned to like danger and roughness.

She was actually *turned on*.

God, what had Phoebe done with this body they shared?

She swallowed, her throat catching on a moan when Stryker's thumb smoothed over the sensitive underside of her breast. "Look," she rasped, "do you want to kill me, or fuck me?"

"Both. Neither. I don't know." His voice was impatient, guttural. "Where's Phoebe?"

"The earthquake . . . it scared her. She retreated."

Stryker bared his teeth and leaned in, even as his hand slipped beneath her shirt. "Get her."

"I can't. She's too deep. Why do you want her anyway? Why did you change your mind? First you want the drug to keep her suppressed and now you want her out. Which is it, because I'm about to get whiplash."

A muscle in his jaw twitched as he ground his teeth. Finally, he cursed and stepped back. "Forget it."

"No." It was a stupid move, but she inched closer to him. "You said this isn't personal, but that's bullshit. You want to kill her, you want to take revenge, but you need to keep me alive to use against Itor. That's it, isn't it?"

"You don't know anything."

She snorted. "I know the idea of ending me makes you hard. Is that how you do all your killing? Maybe strangle your victims while you're screwing them?"

His entire body jerked, the stark horror in his eyes actually making her take a step back. "*What?* I've never . . . Jesus!" He shoved both hands through his hair and kept them there for a second, as though he was trying to hold his head on. "Okay, yeah, the fantasies I have of putting Phoebe in the ground are pretty damned exciting, but not sexually."

"Then why . . . ?" She glanced pointedly at the enormous erection behind the fly of his pants.

"Side effect," he snapped. "Side effect of using my power. Or of anyone using a nature-based special ability."

Realization dawned, and suddenly things made sense. "That was why, in my apartment—"

"Yeah. You'd used your power, and I felt it."

Well, it was a relief to know that he wasn't some sort of sicko who got a sexual thrill from causing pain and death, but the fact was, he still wanted to kill Phoebe, which meant Mel would die too. Right now, he seemed to be walking a thin line between duty and revenge, and the best way to keep him on the side of duty would be to keep Phoebe as far from him as possible.

"We have to leave. We need to go to my apartment and get the drug—"

"We can't." He lifted the curtain with one finger and peeked outside. "Not until help comes to neutralize the guys who are after Phoebe."

"I can fight. I'm not useless."

"Right now you are."

His words struck at the heart of her, echoing those of her father and sister. *You're useless. Pathetic. No good to anyone.*

Resolve put steel in her spine, and she stripped out of her shirt and jeans, leaving her in only her underwear and a bra. She just wished her hands weren't shaking. "That can be fixed."

Stryker spun around, his eyes going wide. "Hell, no."

You're useless. Pathetic. "You afraid I'm going to hurt you once I get my powers back?" She stalked toward him, and though he stood his ground, his fists clenched at his sides. "Don't be. I need your help. You're my one shot at getting out of this hellish life."

The building shook again, just a tremor, and he groaned. "Put. On. Your. Clothes."

The command in his voice made her want to jump to obey. But the very obvious erection behind his fly told her she had a shot at this, maybe her only one, and she wasn't going to blow it.

"No. This is our best chance of getting to my place alive, and you know it." It occurred to her that he might be worried about unprotected sex, and she felt her face heat, which was weird, given that she was practically naked and propositioning him, but the thought of discussing protection made her uncomfortable. "I . . . ah . . . Phoebe, we take a shot to prevent pregnancy and disease—"

"Do you really think it matters?"

She blinked, and then what he'd said sunk in. Anger bubbled to the surface, obliterating any remaining nervousness. "Right. Who cares if you get me pregnant, since I'll be dead soon anyway. So let's get on with it."

A muscle twitched in his jaw, but other than that, he gave no reaction at all.

"Fine." He came at her, backing her against the wall. "You want it? We'll play." He ripped open his pants, and she nearly salivated at the sight of his cock as it sprang free, a thick, dusky column of hard flesh. Next, he tore her underwear and drove his fingers between her legs.

His handling was rough, but it wasn't painful, though she knew he could make it so if he wanted. The fact that he didn't, that he was actually taking the time to touch her, to concentrate the motion of his fingers right over her clit, told her he cared about her pleasure. Which was good, since Phoebe had said that the recharge had something to do with the chemical reaction that occurred when both she and her male partner climaxed.

Her hands were idle, she realized, and she reached for him, but he suddenly spun her around so her face was against the wall. He tugged her hips out, kicked her feet apart, and in one hard, powerful thrust, he entered her.

"Sorry," he said against her ear, "but I can't look into the face of the woman who killed my friend when I come."

For some reason, that stung. She got it, but she was so tired of being seen as Phoebe, and as long as Stryker saw only Phoebe when he looked at her, Mel would be in danger.

He pulled back and pushed inside again, and if she had ever thought she'd hate this, she'd been so wrong. Didn't matter that it was all so angry, as impersonal as if they were both masturbating. *She* had initiated it. *She* had gotten Stryker hard.

The rush of power brought with it a rush of wetness between her legs, and she moaned. The sound seemed to trigger something in Stryker, and he increased the tempo of his thrusts, began to pound into her with raw, brutal force. The erotic sound of skin slapping skin filled the room, and she had to bite her lip to keep from crying out with pleasure.

"How's this?" he gritted into her ear. "You like it rough? I hope so, because I can't give you anything else."

"I . . . no, this is . . . fine." More than fine. Sensation streamed through like lit gasoline in her veins. But still, she was plastered against a cold, hard wall, and though this wasn't an act of love, she felt a basic need for some kind of . . . what? Comfort? Connection? Wrenching her arm around behind her, she palmed his flank, loved the bunching muscles under her hand as he pumped his hips. "The bed . . . maybe we can move to the bed?"

"The bed is for women I like." He snagged her wrist and pinned it above her head against the wall so she couldn't touch him as he hammered into her. She cried out in a combination of pleasure and loss of control, but he must have taken the sound as pain, because his grip loosened, and the wild pounding of his cock inside her slowed. "Fuck."

The normally harsh word was soft, full of what she could have sworn was regret, and she was even more sure of it when he braced his forehead on the back of her head and let out a long, shuddering breath that whispered over her neck. Her skin prickled, and against her will she arched, taking him even deeper.

His thrusts gentled, and amazingly, the slower slide of his shaft over her sensitive tissues became even more intense. In no time, she was on the edge of detonation, her body quivering, her core clenching him greedily.

Mel didn't have a lot of—heck, she didn't have any—experience with this, but her body did, and it registered the sensation of skin on skin, as well as the rasp of Stryker's pants on her bare flesh. The combination of rough and smooth in addition to the slide of his hard shaft inside her slick softness made for a perfect storm of pleasure, and she couldn't contain the plea that escaped her.

"Please . . ."

"That," he said, "is only the first of the begging I'll get from you."

Though he meant it in the not-so-fun way, it didn't matter. The gruff, gravelly tone of his voice, the way his fingers dug into her hips, the slap of his balls against the fleshy lips of her sex . . . it set her off like nothing ever had.

Ecstasy shot through her core, spread to every nerve ending until even her skin popped with pleasure, and she let out a wail that was probably heard on the street below. The orgasm rippled, crested, and waned, and then, as Stryker barked out a pleasured sound of his own, his cock swelled, releasing a warm jet that triggered another intense climax.

Her pussy milked him, taking everything and squeezing until he began to jerk and grip her hips to still her as the sensations became too intense. Deep inside her, his cock twitched, and she shuddered, almost wishing he'd keep pumping . . . not because she wanted another orgasm, but because she didn't want to lose this connection.

Silly? Yes. But she'd never experienced the melding of a man and a woman, and given the way her life had gone, she doubted she'd feel it again.

But only a dozen heartbeats went by before he withdrew, stepping back as though he couldn't wait to not be touching her anymore. Weakly, she pushed away from the wall and turned around.

"Thanks," she said, feeling stupid, because were you supposed to thank the man who gave you an orgasm? Even if it was the best one you'd ever had? "I, um, need to go to the bathroom."

He said nothing, merely nodded and stalked to the window.

"Funny," she sighed, as she gathered her clothes off the floor, "but I always thought my first time might be more . . . well, not hateful."

Stryker's entire body tensed as he swung back around to her. "Your first time?"

Suddenly feeling exposed, she brought her clothes up to cover her nakedness, as if the flimsy things were a shield. "Yeah, I was a virgin," she said breezily, but when his expression only darkened more, she added, "I mean, I wasn't technically a virgin, since Phoebe has used the hell out of this body, but I've never had sex. You know, for myself." Phoebe had forced Mel out a few times while screwing, just to torture her, but she'd never initiated sex. How could she, when she didn't know anyone, and people she did know were Itor.

Something flashed in Stryker's eyes, but he turned away from her too quickly to see what it was. Right. So she hadn't expected roses and chocolate or anything, and sure, he only saw Phoebe when he looked at her, but he could at least try to act like she wasn't something he'd scraped off the bottom of his shoe.

"Okay. I'm just going to get cleaned up now." God, she was a babbling, nervous idiot. Did all women feel that way after their first sexual encounter? Phoebe had always played sex like a contact sport, using it as a tool to get what she wanted. Mel had never wanted any part of that, had hoped to someday find someone she could form an emotional attachment with. She'd dreamed about her first time . . . and this had been as far from it as she could imagine.

Oh, it had been good. Damned good. But it had also highlighted the fact that nothing for Mel would ever be normal. Even if Stryker's people could somehow help her—assuming they didn't kill her—normal was a pipe dream, and she might as well give up on it.

She cast Stryker one last glance before slipping into the bathroom. She really should thank him again, not for the orgasm, but for fucking her right into the real world. She'd never have a relationship or a family, she'd never get a degree or hold a job, and she'd never be free.

And now that Mel knew that, Phoebe was going to pay for what she'd done to her over the years. Whatever Stryker's people needed to bring her—and Itor—down, she would do.

Somehow, Mel would make sure Stryker got his revenge, and if it meant that she died, so be it.

"Phoebe," she whispered to herself in the mirror, "watch out, because you don't scare me anymore. You're the one who should be afraid."

* * *

Stryker was surprised he remained standing in the wake of Mel's innocent little announcement.

A virgin. A motherfucking virgin.

Maybe not in the technical sense—but in the sense it counted most.

If the entire thing weren't so goddamned serious, he would've been laughing at the absurdity of it all. Laughing, because he now understood the expression *If I didn't laugh, I'd cry.*

He shoved Oz's prediction to the back of his mind as he simultaneously shoved his cock back into his pants, where it should've stayed.

Oz, former ACRO employee. Seer of the dead. Predictor of future events, no matter how ridiculous they seemed at the time.

"Me with a virgin? Dude, not since middle school, and even then . . ." Stryker downed the rest of his JD on the rocks and stared at the dark-eyed man sitting across from him at the small table.

"I call them as I see them. You're going to marry a virgin."

"Well, that takes care of that, since I have no plans to marry." There were far too many willing women and his attention span was nil. No reason to make false promises like loving one woman and only one woman for the rest of his life.

Nope, not his bag.

He peered out the window, praying that he didn't see any major destruction. When he got into the sex haze, he wasn't ever sure that his powers were under control.

So far, everything looked fine outside. But he was far from fine, and from the look in Mel's eyes as she emerged from the bathroom, so was she.

"Did I hurt you?" he demanded, his words coming out harsher than he intended.

She shook her head, her cheeks colored, and he nodded like an idiot because what the hell else was he supposed to do?

She was supposed to be Phoebe. He was supposed to be able to kill her.

This whole ACRO agent, good-guy-versus-bad-guy used to be much easier.

"Let's go."

"We have to stop at my apartment before we do anything else—the shot, remember?"

"I remember. It's the only thing stopping me from killing you right now," he growled, and was surprised when she didn't flinch at his words.

"Trust me, I want to kill her myself," she told him. "Let's go."

Well, Mel was growing a pair right before his eyes. Interesting.

They left the hotel, and he kept her close as they walked down an alley toward a more open area—there would be less cover that way, but also less chance of the excedos attacking in public.

Of course, they had to get there first.

"Did you do that?" she asked as she looked up at the side of the building, which looked as if it had simply slid off.

He didn't answer her, just stepped over the large crevice where the road had split in two—no doubt also his handiwork—and hustled her along. There was no time to waste here. If she wanted to stay alive, she had to remain Melanie, because if Phoebe came out . . . he wasn't sure he could be responsible for what happened, no matter what he'd promised Devlin.

They made it to a bustling shopping district, and Mel slowed every time they passed a restaurant or food stand. He'd grab her hand, drag her away, and she'd be fine until the next one. Finally, at the window of a pastry shop, she refused to budge.

"I need food."

He stared. "Are you kidding me?"

"I guess sex makes me hungry. Do you have any money?"

Un-fucking-believable. And yet, he found himself buying her a damned chocolate croissant, which she happily munched as they threaded their way through the crowds. She looked around as they walked, often became distracted by the shops to the point that he'd have to nudge her and steer her in the right direction.

"Haven't you ever seen a store before?"

She trailed her finger along the glass front of a shoe shop, her gaze wistful. "I don't get out on my own much. Everything is done online and delivered. Even groceries."

"And clothes?"

"Phoebe buys those, since I don't usually go anywhere." She gestured down a side street. "This way."

"If you don't go anywhere, how do you know where you're going?"

"Alek made sure I'm familiar with all the cities where we have a residence, just in case anything bad happens."

He drew to a stop as four men approached from around a corner and two others closed in from the rear. "Like now."

"I hate these guys," Melanie muttered.

"Your powers—fully charged?" he asked, not taking his eyes off the approaching men.

"Yes."

"Good. I'd rather not start another earthquake if I don't have to."

"Let me take care of them this time," Mel said, and although he didn't like letting a woman take the lead in a potentially deadly situation, she did have the necessary skills to stop this from turning into a full-blown battle.

The men would never know what hit them.

"Back against the building. We want them in a group."

"Okay." The confidence in her voice was belied by the shaking of her hands, but she did as he ordered, and in one synchronized movement, they put their backs to the wall and allowed the men to close in.

These guys knew what they were doing, and at the far ends

of the street, they had cut off pedestrian and car traffic, which meant they were coordinating with more people—they might even have law enforcement on the take.

"It's payback time." One of the men, who Stryker fondly remembered as Dumpster Guy, gestured to his broken nose and fat lip. He was also walking with a limp, and Stryker couldn't contain a smile.

"I fucked you up pretty good—" Stryker broke off as an icy chill shot past him, blanketing the men in a freezing coffin of ice. Their faces froze in stark terror, bodies caught forever in motion . . .

Half a dozen men, who, in front of his eyes, began to crack apart, literally, into pieces. Body parts smashed to the sidewalk, still encased in their prison, and *holy fuck*, he didn't want to think about what this woman could've done to him, had she been given the chance.

You gave her the chance, asshole. She could've turned on him at any point. But she hadn't.

Probably saving it up. There was no way he could trust her. But he'd sure as hell use her until he could get her to ACRO.

"Stryker, let's go." At the urgency in her voice and the tug of her hand on his arm, they were moving at top speed down the alley. Two men loitered near an intersection, looking a little too interested, and when they began to follow, he whisked her into a recessed, shadowed doorway to what looked like an abandoned apartment building.

He kept his voice low. "How fast can you bring your powers to bear if we need to engage these guys?"

"I can't," she whispered. "I . . . well, I sort of drained my powers again."

"You drained your powers? What the hell kind of move is that?"

"You're angry at me because I saved your life?"

"I didn't ask you to go all Rambo ice on me." He heard the indignance in his voice and wondered if this wasn't the most ridiculous conversation ever. "Don't you know how to control the amount of force you use? Like, instead of full blast, how about half blast or something."

"I don't know how to do anything but let it all out," she said. "I can either do a big, widespread cold the way I did this morning, or I can fire a concentrated burst that comes out in a stream of supercold, like liquid nitrogen."

"You're going to tell me your power only has two speeds?"

"I don't get the chance to practice much because . . ."

"Phoebe. Right." His jaw clenched so hard he was sure he heard a pop. This Mel was up to something—no one with powers used them up like that . . . there was no way Phoebe would allow her to be so . . . vulnerable, was there? If they shared a body, Phoebe would want to make sure Mel protected herself.

You have no real way of knowing if Phoebe controls both sides . . . if this is all a goddamned act.

He couldn't stand here and try to figure all this out. She could totally be lying and he had no way to disprove anything. He tensed, ready to crack some heads as the men eased into view, but they turned down another street, giving Stryker and Mel an opportunity to run.

Which they did, all the way to her apartment. He did a quick walk-through to clear the place—looked like no one had been in here since they left, but he paced uneasily as she ducked into the bathroom and emerged with three filled syringes.

Uncapping one, she sank down on the bed. "I've never done this before."

Like a besotted dope, he nearly offered to do it for her, but thankfully his agent instincts kicked in—finally—and he stepped back, watched her carefully, waiting to see if she gave anything away.

She gave away nothing, not even a flinch as she sank the needle into her biceps and jammed down the plunger. And then the urgent slam of a fist against the front door made her jump in a way that seemed far too real for even the most seasoned actress.

"It's got to be Itor," she whispered urgently. "It's too late for the mail. We've got to get out of here."

"How? Unless you can fly, we're stuck fighting." He stared hard at her.

"They're going to kill you—you need to hide."

"Oh, sure, that's going to happen. I'll just let you walk back into Itor's hands. Not a problem."

"I'm trying to save you, Stryker. I'll get rid of them for you. I'll pretend to be Phoebe."

"Forgive me if I don't trust a damned thing you say." He took her arm. "We deal with this together."

He mentally calculated how quickly he could have sex with her, wondered if her power sparked instantaneously after an orgasm, like she could point and shoot right as he . . .

Ah, forget it. He drew his pistol, shoving Mel behind him in a gesture that struck him as oddly protective. Cursing himself as the biggest idiot on the planet, he eased toward the entrance just as the pounding stopped . . . only to be replaced by a hissing noise.

"What's that?"

He frowned. "I don't know." A chemical odor filled the air, and he whipped his head up to a vent in the ceiling. "Shit! The window!"

"I don't understand—"

He grabbed her hand, sprinted toward the window, and stumbled. He heard a thump behind him, turned, his vision going fuzzy, to see Mel, unconscious, on the floor.

His last thought as he joined her was that, seriously, only pussies used gas . . .

CHAPTER *Five*

Annika Svenson was now eight and a half months pregnant and kept saying that Oz's predictions didn't always pan out, that she was fine, that they'd been through so much shit together that the bad things between them had no doubt already happened.

As much as he wanted Ani's bravado and assurances about her pregnancy to wipe away his worries, Creed McCabe wasn't having it. He was pretty sure Ani knew she hadn't convinced him fully, but he wanted to keep her calm and so he pretended he didn't hear the death watch beetle ticking in his ear all the goddamned time. It was driving him crazy, and he was superstitious enough to tie the omen to Oz's prediction.

The thing was, Ani couldn't hear the tapping—when she woke in the middle of the night and found him staring at the ceiling, he'd tell her that the noise was driving him nuts. She told him he was hearing things.

Death watch beetles also tapped and ticked while looking for a mate, he reminded himself. He remembered his own long wait for Annika to decide to give him a chance, and for a moment he sympathized with the damned bug.

She didn't strut as well anymore—she had for the first eight months and now it was more of a strut-slash-waddle. And she looked damned cute doing so, and fuck, this should be the most joyous time in his life and instead he was walking around like Lurch with a hangover.

Even his own mother told him to *lighten the hell up, dear*. Only Kat, the spirit who had been bound to him almost since birth through the tribal tats that went from head to toe on his right side, seemed to understand. Hell, she shared his anxiety. She'd fought the relationship with Annika for so long, but both females—one ghost, one warm, breathing woman—had learned to respect each other, to even like each other. Kat didn't want to lose Annika either, and they both needed to keep their minds off even the remotest of possibilities.

And so he worked with ACRO's ghost hunters and took on jobs that wouldn't take him far away from Ani, went with her on every appointment, and enjoyed the fuck out of her hormones, which kept him really busy for many, many hours of the day and night.

She was excited and restless, and somewhere, deep down inside, he knew she was worried as well.

And the whole time, he kept the ring in his pocket as if it could possibly ward off all evil, twisted it like a worry stone, and stared at Ani's finger a lot when she was sleeping.

"*We don't need a piece of paper,*" she'd argued, and no, maybe they didn't, but he wanted it, wanted something between them to be goddamned fucking easy for once.

"You are seriously distracted."

Gabe stood over him, panting, and Creed realized the kid had laid him out flat.

"Fuck off," he growled.

"And now you sound like Ender." Gabe shook his head. "I need training, dammit."

Ever since he'd gotten back from that ill-fated trip in the Amazon where Akbar had died, Gabe had tripled his efforts in an almost superhuman way. Part guilt out of hurting Annika, part desire to prove himself to Devlin and the rest of ACRO, and if Gabe kept this up, he'd either burn out or save them all.

"Dude, you have got to chill every once in a while. More to life than training."

Gabe muttered something under his breath, and yeah, he was in the middle of relationship issues too. Devlin had always been obsessed with Itor's takedown, but it had morphed into something greater than all of them, a supersecret plan Dev wouldn't share with anyone.

God, they were all fucking pathetic when it came to intrapersonal shit, but put the fate of the free world in their hands and they managed just fine. "Come on," he told Gabe after he peeled himself off the floor. "You and I need a drink."

"I don't—"

"Trust me, you need several. You'll settle for one."

Melanie's head hurt. Her eyes burned. And the floor was really, really hard.

Floor? Groggily, she sat up, blinking in the dim light. There was metal all around her . . . a crate. She was in a metal cargo crate about six feet wide and ten feet long, and just high enough to allow Stryker to stand.

Which he was doing as he peeked through the air holes lining the side walls. Light streamed through them and the barred door, illuminating the dark space.

"What happened?"

Stryker turned to her. "We were gassed." He sank down to sit with his back against the wall. "I haven't seen anyone yet, but we seem to be inside a big warehouse."

Her stomach churned. "We need to get out of here."

"You think?"

Ass. "Can you use your earthquake thing?"

He shook his head. "I'll give away my hand if whoever has us doesn't know what I am, and even if I was willing to risk that, I'd bring the warehouse down on our heads. We need to wait until someone shows up." He shot her a piercing look. "Or you could freeze the metal lock to make it brittle, and we can break out."

She drew a sharp breath. Even if she could control it that well . . . she flexed her hand, testing her power, and though she felt a cool tingle, it wasn't enough to do something like freeze metal. She could maybe make some ice cubes for a drink, but that would be about it. "I'm . . . ah . . ."

"I know. We'll have to fuck."

"Shit."

"Yeah."

She glared at him. "You could at least pretend that having sex with me isn't the end of the world."

"Because you're acting so excited," he shot back, and she couldn't deny it.

Sighing, she rubbed her eyes. This was such a nightmare. The pounding in her head grew stronger, more like knocking.

Phoebe.

"How long were we out?"

Stryker shrugged. "About six hours. Why? Is your shot wearing off?"

"Yes." She was also hungry. Cursing softly, she patted her pockets, where she stuffed the two remaining shots. "They're gone."

"Over there." He cocked his thumb at a table on the other side of a thick, clear shield she'd bet was fireproof. Her syringes and his weapons were piled on the table.

"Damn—" Crying out from pain, she grabbed her head.

Stryker moved to her, put his hands over hers. "Hey." His voice was surprisingly gentle. "What's wrong?"

"She wants out," Mel gasped.

"Does it normally hurt?"

"Only when I fight it." All around her, the light faded, until she was in a tunnel of darkness. Distantly, she heard Stryker calling her name.

Then she heard nothing.

Phoebe took in the situation in one second flat. She was in a crate, held prisoner, with the ACRO agent known as Stryker.

Fucking great.

How in the hell had Mel gotten them into this? Whatever. She needed to get them out of it. Smiling, she tweaked Stryker's nose. "Hello, sexy. Did you miss me?"

Stryker swatted her hand away and scooted as far as he could get from her. "Shut the fuck up and send Mel back."

"I don't think so." She propped herself against the side of the crate and studied him. He looked the same as he had in the jungle—maybe more tan. And his eyes . . . those funky eyes. They were harder, as if life had bent him over and railed him for months. "Tell me, did you bury your friend . . . or scatter his ashes?"

"Shut. Up."

As if. God, she hated ACRO agents. Too many of her colleagues had died at their holier-than-thou hands, and she'd always been convinced that the earthquake that killed her mother had been caused by ACRO. Maybe not, but it was pretty damned coincidental that two Itor bodyguards assigned to keep watch over Phoebe, Mel, and their mother had died too, and yet civilians had been merely injured.

Continuing with the taunt, she ran her hand over the inside of her thighs to her crotch. "I think about him, you know? When I'm getting myself off. I think about how he screamed—"

Lightning fast, Stryker was on her, his forearm across her throat, his knee in her gut. She didn't react other than to smile as he bared his teeth. "You evil fucking bitch . . . I want your sister back, or I swear, I'll kill you right here, right now."

Phoebe feigned a frown. She was so going to mess with him, fill him with doubts about Melanie. "Sister?"

"Yeah. Sister." He narrowed his eyes. "She said you're some sort of Itor experiment."

She widened her eyes. "Oh, right. Sister. Yes, we were an experiment. While my mom was pregnant with me, Itor radiated her, and somehow our cells broke apart, and now we're two people."

"She said you were two embryos created in a petri dish."

She waved her hand. "Right. I forget. The radiation, you know. Messes with my head. In any case, I'm not letting her out. And you can't see Sandy or Jill either."

His head whipped back, and she knew he was now running through a multiple personality scenario instead of the truth. Good. He wasn't going to believe anything Mel said from now on.

"Wow. She really did a number on you, didn't she? I really hope you've taken everything she says with a grain of salt. She's got this sweet, innocent act down pat." She studied her nails. "I'll bet she said I'm mean to her. And that she knows nothing about Itor. That she doesn't work for them." She rolled her eyes. "She's the fucking best agent Itor has. So if I were you, I'd do whatever she says." She lowered her voice to a deep, sultry whisper. "She's even deadlier than I am."

A door somewhere slammed, and she reached deep for her gift. It sparked . . . then fizzled. Dammit!

"What's the matter?" Stryker's voice was taunting. "Can't get it up?"

"Fuck you," she muttered, which was funny, because that was exactly what would have to happen. She eyed him and decided that it wouldn't be a hardship. Biting her lip, she dropped her gaze to his crotch and felt her body warm up.

"Oh, hell no," he growled.

She raised her eyebrows. "You know what I need to recharge?"

"You could say that."

Interesting. "Did you and Mel do the nasty?"

"Just let her out."

"No," she purred, as she trailed a finger down his thigh. "We do this, and I get us out of here."

He grabbed her hand, squeezed to the point of pain, and shoved it away. "I wouldn't fuck you with someone else's dick."

She laughed. "See, that's funny. Because I've fucked several men who hated me. Best. Sex. Ever. Maybe not for them, but something about screwing a man who despises you is just . . . hot. I'll have you. I promise."

"I've met some scum in my life," Stryker said, "but you leave even the psychopaths in the dust. Now, if you want to get out of here alive, you'll let me talk to Mel."

Normally, Phoebe wouldn't back down. It wasn't as though she was powerless—even without her gift, she could hold her own in traditional combat. But right now they were sitting ducks, and if Mel could actually be useful for the first time in her life, Phoebe would roll with it. Survival was the first order of business, after all.

"Fine," she said tightly. "Tell her I said hi."

Mel blinked, her heart sinking when she saw that she was still in a cage with Stryker and that Phoebe hadn't gotten them out. Her heart sank even more when she realized that Stryker's eyes seethed with hatred. All the progress she'd made with him had been undone by Phoebe.

At least he hadn't killed her. That was something.

She sighed. "What did Phoebe do now?"

"Nothing. Take off your jeans."

"Ah . . ."

"*Now.*" His voice cracked like a clap of thunder, and she jumped.

"You know, you don't have to be a jerk. I think I've proven that I'm trustworthy—"

"Really, Mel? So there's nothing you've lied to me about? Nothing you're keeping from me?"

She swore under her breath. She hadn't lied to him, but there was something she was keeping from him, something she definitely didn't want him to know right now. Or ever.

"What did Phoebe say to you? Because you can't believe anything that comes out of her mouth."

"That's what she said about you, so at this point, I don't know what to believe. Stop talking. Start undressing."

"You really need to work on your seduction technique," she bit out as she wriggled out of her jeans, hesitating before slipping off her torn panties, but at the expression of amusement on his face, she jerked them off. Stryker unbuttoned his pants, and then suddenly he was on her, had her spun around on her hands and knees, one palm on the back of her neck to push her head down, which left her ass in the air and very little leeway to move.

"Hey—"

"Shh."

She felt the prod of his cock at her entrance, and then he was pushing against her. But she was dry, and each tiny thrust only stretched and abraded. When she cried out, he cursed and pulled back.

"Sorry," she muttered. "Guess being held by bad guys in a cage with a man who hates me isn't much of a turn-on."

He cursed again, and she heard a shuffling, felt a draft of air behind her, and when she turned, she saw him sitting with his back against the metal wall, legs stretched out in front of him. His pants were still unbuttoned, but he'd tucked himself back in.

Surprisingly, he didn't look angry. "Come here." He gestured with his fingers when she didn't move. "Come on."

She didn't understand, but she crawled toward him, hesitant but curious. Just before she got in range of his reach, she paused, her cheek an inch from his hand. For a long moment, they stared at each other, her unsure gaze meeting his half-lidded sensual one. She began to tremble. Slowly, he leaned forward until his palm came in contact with her cheek. His touch was light. Gentle.

And she trembled harder.

His fingers eased around her head and into her hair, and with an easy pressure, he nudged her closer. Was he . . . going to kiss her?

Mel's heart stuttered, and she reared back, but he caught her, and when she would have struggled, his whispered "Easy" settled her down.

But only a little. Her heart was pounding, her stomach was flip-flopping, and her lungs felt like shriveled little fists in her chest.

Their mouths met, barely. Stryker's lips were softer than she'd have guessed—silky, soft lips on such a hard man was an astonishing contradiction. But as he brushed them over hers, she found herself moving involuntarily closer.

His tongue was a warm, wet stroke along the seam of her lips, and little sparks ignited in her at the contact. She gasped, and he took instant advantage, increasing the pressure of the kiss, using his tongue to gain entrance. His hands drifted down her sides to her waist, and then he pulled her onto his lap. Her bare sex parted over the hard ridge behind his fly, and a strange, wonderful fever broke over her skin.

This was what it was like to be turned on. To *really* be aroused by a man.

A small voice told her she was stupid for feeling it, since Stryker hated her, they were imprisoned, and he was only doing this to make getting inside her easier, but her body didn't know any of that, and it was reacting to a powerful, attractive male.

A rough sound rumbled up in his chest as she writhed on his lap, needing to get closer to ease the ache that was starting to build between her legs. Her nipples tingled, and she was suddenly so hot, her body so tight that it was almost painful. A dizzying hunger swept over her, frightening in its intensity, and she jerked back.

Stryker caught her, drew her to him so his lips were grazing her throat, and a new rush of sensation rocked her.

"I'm . . . scared," she whispered. All she knew was that foreign feelings were overwhelming her, eating away at her control and leaving her vulnerable.

For a moment, he froze, as if what she'd said shocked him. And then he gave a quiet snort. "God, you're good," he breathed against her skin.

She had no idea what that was supposed to mean, but when he slipped his hand beneath her shirt and cupped her breast, she decided it didn't matter.

Truly, there were few lines Stryker wouldn't cross for ACRO—but forcing a woman into sex was a hard line drawn in the sand, even if Mel needed it in order to save herself.

And him.

In truth, he'd been so angry at seeing Phoebe, he'd been more than ready to punish *her* fiery ass . . . but not Mel, not this way.

As much as he wanted to, he couldn't shake the feeling that he was being duped. And still, he continued the slow seduction. He thumbed Mel's nipple, watched her shiver, and yes, things were different now than they'd been just minutes ago. Her cheeks were stained pink, her mouth dropped open, and small sighs escaped, enough to make his cock throb hard against her bared sex.

A hand on her back, and he pulled her closer so he could tongue a hard nipple, tug it between his teeth gently, feel her sex get wetter and hotter with every flick.

"Stryker . . ." Jesus, the way she whispered his name, was anyone that good when they were fucking? He'd been with Seducers, knew they were all trained in the art of sex and deception, but he also knew these physical signs of arousal.

"Thought I was cold . . . too cold for this," she murmured, her face buried in his hair, her body arched against him.

He ran a finger along her cleft and she let out a series of soft little moans that made him bite back a curse. Slid his thumb against the tight bud of her clit and she jumped as if the sensation was too strong for her.

He waited until she brought her ass back to settle on his lap, tried again, two fingers stroking her. When she moved her hips, he pushed a single finger inside of her and she stopped moving completely as he fucked her with it, and then another, opening her so their second time wouldn't hurt her as much as the first had.

Oz's virgin prediction threatened to ring in his ears and he pulled himself sharply into focus. "You're ready, Mel . . . so wet and hot for me. Let me in," he told her, heard the huskiness in his voice, felt the need driving him harder now because of the use of his powers earlier.

The push-pull of Mother Nature could be a real bitch.

He shifted her so she could let him inside. Her sex rippled around him, a sweet, torturous vise as she took him, inch by inch, winding her arms around his neck as she did so, keeping him as close as possible.

"Go ahead, take me," he murmured against her neck, wondering how she could feel so hot right now and still be able to freeze a man to death when she needed to.

Despite the fact that he knew she could kill him the second she came, his nonthinking head strained for more of her. It took everything he had not to slam his hips upward until she'd taken him in as far as she could.

For now, he couldn't rush it.

Finally, the length of him was settled inside of her and for a moment, he let her sit there, feeling the fullness. And then he couldn't hold still any longer, gripped her hips to rock her back and forth until a brutal groan ripped from his throat.

It wasn't enough, wouldn't be enough to satisfy the cravings that came with his gift, not until he threw her down and took her so hard, they'd both see stars.

This isn't about enjoyment—this is business.

But for his body, business most certainly equaled pleasure and there had never been any way for him to separate the two.

It wouldn't start now either, not when Mel told him, "Don't stop . . . please don't stop doing that."

She was moving on her own now, writhing, grinding, taking her pleasure, and he needed to do the same. But she was pinning him with her body and he nearly flipped her onto her back in order to take her the way he wanted to . . . on all fours would work too, and Christ, his balls jackknifed tight as she rode him faster and faster.

And then she froze, legs tensed, and oh, yeah, she was coming, her sweet little pussy milking him to his own climax as she did so. Her mouth formed an O and a small, surprised moan escaped, and then his cock spurted inside her in a blinding rush that made him glad he'd been sitting down.

He glanced over at the bars, wondering if anyone had walked by when they'd been deep in the throes of it. The corner was out of sight of most of the cameras, but it was obvious what they were doing. Clearly, whoever captured them didn't realize this could recharge Mel, or else they wouldn't have put them together in the cell.

And suddenly, he was oddly protective of them seeing more of her than was necessary, was glad she was facing him so they couldn't see the pure pleasure etched on her face.

"Is it always . . . like that?" she asked.

"Sex should always be good," he said noncommittally, didn't want to let her know that the orgasm had been, like, one of his top fucking five, could only have been made better if he hadn't been surrounded by cameras. And if he liked her.

She was staring at him. "Thank you."

"Don't thank me. Don't." He couldn't disrespect Akbar's memory like that, felt like he was already betraying his friend. "Just get us the hell out of here."

And still, he couldn't help but feel a twinge of . . . *something* at the look on Mel's face, disappointment mixed with content-ment.

She could fall in love with you, Stryker.

And she could also win an Academy Award.

Yeah, after this assignment he needed some downtime and lots of it. He'd tell that to Devlin as soon as he got out of this hellhole. "We need to get out of here. That's why I did this," he said dumbly, even though she was staring at him now like he was an idiot because he was repeating himself. And he was. Repeat-ing himself and an idiot. Idiot wrapped in a moron. An idiot bur-rito.

She couldn't get dressed fast enough. Neither could he; he checked his pockets even though he knew they'd stripped him of every possible weapon when he'd been passed out. Well, every weapon except the kind he'd been born with, and they had to know he was a danger.

Granted, an earthquake would bring the entire building down on them, so that wasn't an option. Still, he touched the walls as if testing the structure.

Mel fastened her jeans. "Most of these buildings can with-stand a small quake."

"It wouldn't stop at just this building," he said regretfully.

She was staring at him again and then she surprised him by saying, "Your gift—it's a tough one too."

He wanted to tell her that she didn't know dick about his gift, but dammit all to hell, she did. "Yeah, so? I don't need a therapy session."

"I probably do," she muttered.

"Can you just ice these assholes—just a little—and try to save something for later?"

"I doubt it."

"Try," he said fiercely. "Because you can keep making ex-cuses and feeling sorry for yourself that for your other half you've got a killer bitch who deserves to rot in hell, or you can try to be responsible for the powers you do control. Own your shit, Mel."

"Own my shit," she murmured with a half smile. "I might have that put on a T-shirt."

"I'll buy it for you if we ever get the fuck out of this place."

CHAPTER
Six

Oh, they were going to get out of this place. Damn skippy they were.

Mel eyed the door, and the steel-reinforced mechanism she assumed was the lock. She'd never used her power to freeze metal to the point of brittleness, wasn't sure it would even work.

But she had to get out of here, out of this enclosed space with a man who made her heart pound with both terror and desire, and how screwed up was that? She needed a shrink.

And a hamburger.

"Stand back," she told Stryker.

A muscle in his jaw twitched, as though her command grated on a nerve, but he moved to the rear of the crate, and wisely he didn't touch the metal.

His cheeks were still flushed from the sex, and for some reason, that gave her a neat little thrill.

Definitely needed the shrink. And really, a hamburger would improve her whole outlook and mood.

Taking a deep breath, she fired up her gift. Strangely, she always got hot when she used her power, though the few people who had touched her while she used it said her skin felt cold. That had been a long time ago, when she was a kid who had been too afraid of her father to argue about using her gift.

"You gonna do something," Stryker drawled, "or are we going to wait for the metal to rust out?"

"You're hilarious." Cheeks hot, this time from Stryker's smackdown, she put her hand on the sliding lock. Her heart pounded, and her mouth went dry. How much power to use? She hadn't been lying when she'd told Stryker she had little control. If she let loose, she could blast herself right out of juice and have none left to handle the bad guys. But if she tried to measure it, she could waste all her power without doing enough damage to the metal.

Nerves whacking out, she dropped her hand.

"Jesus," Stryker snapped. "What now?"

"Forgive me," she shot back. "I'm afraid I'll blow my wad on this one thing and have nothing left to fight the bad guys, and no offense, but I don't feel like getting fucked in a crate again." She spun around, marched up to him, and jammed her finger in his chest. "So unless you have some candles and wine in your pocket to at least make it a little pleasant, you'll shut the hell up and let me freak out for a minute."

His crystal eyes narrowed, and shit, she'd gone too far. She never acted out like this. But something about this man got her back up, and wasn't that the craziest thing about all of this? She was finally standing up to a man, and against the one person who would just as soon break her neck as breathe on her.

"It was pleasant enough for you to get off," he growled, "so don't play the injured party here."

"And you are? I didn't notice you having any difficulty getting it up."

He opened his mouth, but before he could respond with some cutting remark, the creak of a door opening had them both pivoting toward the sound.

Through the bars, Mel could make out a man in beige slacks and a long-sleeved black T-shirt approaching. He stopped a few feet short of the crate, stood behind the giant wall of Plexiglas-like material.

"Don't try anything, Phoebe." His thin lips quirked in a cocky smile. He had the upper hand, and he was damned proud of himself. "This shield is fireproof. And the metal in the crate is heat resistant. You're trapped."

Dammit. Mel had to let Phoebe out to deal with this guy. No doubt Mel would have to come back out to actually get them free, but she couldn't bluff her way through negotiations with someone she didn't even know.

"And you," the man said to Stryker, "I wouldn't expect ACRO to rescue you anytime soon. Yes, I know who you are. I just don't know what to do with you yet. Ransom you to ACRO or sell you to Itor." He shrugged. "I could also kill you."

"Try it, asshole." Stryker leaned against the crate, crossed his arms over his broad chest, and looked utterly bored.

Time to let Phoebe out.

They were still in the damned crate. Phoebe snapped her fingers, let a spark flick onto the floor, and okay, at least Mel wasn't a total dipshit. She'd screwed the ACRO agent to get their powers back. But they were still in the crate, and Maurice, that coward of an Itor agent, was standing behind what was no doubt a flame-proof shield. Clearly, her co-worker wasn't here to rescue her.

"What's this about, Maurice? I know Alek didn't order you to bring me in." Alek would have called like a normal person, and even if she was out of touch, he wouldn't worry unless she didn't show for the big event he had planned—one that was going to rock the world to its core.

Maurice laughed. Which made the wrinkles around his dark eyes even more pronounced. "Stupid bitch. This is about the arms deal. The one where you cheated the SN out of millions."

The SN—Solitary Nuclei—had their roots in Greek terrorism, but they were really nothing more than a group of ACRO, Itor, and TAG rejects who were desperately trying to be relevant. "And why do you care what I've done to the SN?" Before the words were even out of her mouth, she knew. Maurice was either working for them, or he was actually in charge of them. "You traitor," she bit out. "Why? After all Alek has done for you—"

"Done for me?" Maurice slammed his fist into the plastic. "I've been at his side for twenty years, and for what? So he can allow a conniving whore like you to take over the agency."

"So that's what this is about? Jealousy?" She'd known Maurice harbored resentment for the way Alek treated her, the way he'd groomed her with an eye for taking over Itor. But no way could Maurice claim that Alek showed her favoritism, because he hadn't. Not openly. He didn't want anyone to know—yet—that she was his daughter. Doing so would make her a target for his enemies . . . both outside the agency, and inside.

So no, with the exception of only a couple of scientists and trusted henchmen who had been sworn to secrecy, no one was aware that she was related to Alek, or that she had a pain-in-the-ass weakling of a twin. As far as anyone inside Itor knew, her father was a civilian one-night stand her mother'd had, and Alek had taken Phoebe in when her mother was killed, because she'd shown incredible promise with her fire-gift.

And no one inside Itor besides Alek knew how she had to recharge her gift. Everyone pretty much just figured she was a sex addict. Not that any of the men complained.

Maurice certainly hadn't.

"Jealous?" Maurice shoved his fingers through dark hair shot with gray. "I'm furious!"

"So you started up your little rogue agency? For what? You can't hope to challenge Itor."

"I don't need to challenge Itor. I just need to make life hell for Alek. Killing you will do that."

Stryker laughed. "Dude, stand in line. She's mine to kill."

Maurice arched an eyebrow. "Then why were you helping her?"

"My boss wants her. Preferably alive so we can torture information out of her, but either way, it's all good."

Maurice seemed to almost buy that. "And you fucked her . . . why?"

"Why not?" Stryker dragged his heavy-lidded gaze from her feet to her head, but not before lingering on her breasts, which tightened at his perusal. Damn, Phoebe had never coveted anything of Mel's, but for once, she felt a twinge of envy that her idiot sister had gotten Stryker between her legs. "Look at her."

"I've done more than look," Maurice said. "Several times." He shot her a lecherous sneer. "You still have those bite marks on your ass?"

"Why, yes," she chirped. "You still have a three-inch dick?"

Maurice's sneer turned into a furious snarl. "Where's the money, Phoebe? Tell me where the five million is, and I'll let you live."

She snorted. "No you won't. You can't afford for me to tell Alek about your double-cross. And with me dead, Alek will move you up in the agency."

"You'll tell me, Phoebe, if I have to torture it out of you." He spun on his heel and slammed out of the room.

"He's such an asshole," she sighed, as she turned to Stryker, who still wore that lazy, couldn't-give-a-shit expression, but his eyes drilled into her with utter contempt.

"I want Mel back."

"I'll get us out of this. I know Maurice, and I'm far more powerful than that simpering—"

"*Now!*" Stryker met her in the middle of the crate and clamped his hands on her shoulders. "The crate is heat-resistant, so only Mel can get us out of here. Do it before that psycho comes back to torture us both."

"Not into pain, huh?"

"Oh," he purred, "I'm into pain. *Your* pain, so send Mel back before I show you just how much I'm into it."

"And what's to keep me from roasting you like a pig on a spit right now?"

"If you fry me, you'll never get out of here. Melanie will listen to me, and she can get through the metal, but she needs me to help her do it."

He was probably right, but no problem. Smiling, she went up on her toes to brush her lips across his. "I can't wait to take you down. And I will."

Melanie was starting to despise this popping-in-and-out crap. She really hated how every time she came back into her body Stryker was staring at her like he wanted to rip her throat out.

"What . . . what happened?"

"Mel?"

"Yeah."

His hands tightened on her shoulders. "Do you have bite wounds on your ass?"

She blinked. "Excuse me?"

"Bite wounds," he ground out. "Do you have them? Bruises?"

"Ah . . . well, yes." They were hard to see, right at the juncture of the swell of her butt and the backs of her thighs. They'd hurt like hell, though. "I mean, they've mostly healed. Why?"

Stryker shoved away from her. "No reason. Get us out of here."

God, he was moody. "Yes, sir." She put her hand on the door, but before she could power up her gift, she heard him shift behind her.

"Does that happen often?" His voice was gruff, but quiet.

"Does what happen often? Bite marks? Bruises? Lash welts? Burns?" She shrugged. "I'm used to it." She thought he might have cursed, but she'd engaged her power full blast, the buzz zipping through her body and ears, blocking out all sounds. Beneath her palm, the metal began to develop a light skin of frost, and then thicker streaks of ice zigzagged out from her hand, until the entire door turned white.

Cracks split the frame, and little pops like gunfire filled the room. Quickly, she pulled back her power, feeling like most of her battery was drained.

"There's still some left, I think," she breathed. Excited that she'd actually been able to control herself—if only a little—she grinned and whirled around. "I did it!"

The expression on Stryker's face wiped her smile away in an instant. Sure, she'd kind of forgotten that he wasn't exactly an ally, so naturally, he wouldn't be as thrilled about her small victory as she was.

But what she hadn't expected was the tempest in his gaze, two thunderstorms, one full of loathing, the other full of hunger, and both battling as he stared at her. His hands were fisted at his sides, his thick arousal creating a noticeable bulge against the fly of his cargo pants, and yeah, she'd definitely forgotten that the use of elemental powers got him going.

Thing was, the way he was looking at her got her going a little too. Heat flooded her veins, her skin tingled, and despite the fact that they'd just had sex, she grew achy between her legs. When he came at her, she wasn't sure if he was going to kill her or fuck her, but she braced herself for either.

He did neither.

At the last second, he pivoted, roared, and shattered the door with a jumping kick that sent the thing blasting into a million pieces. He stood there for just a second, panting, his assessing eyes taking in the area, and then he fixed his gaze on her.

"Let's get the fuck out of here. And that Maurice asshole? He's mine."

* * *

Stryker's fists had curled as he spoke Maurice's name, the anger welling up inside of him in a way that would be deemed unacceptable by the National Earthquake Society, Devlin, and just about everyone else who liked their planet in one piece.

And then, with the elemental changes came the god-awful arousal that caused him to lose any and all train of thought.

Breathe, man, breathe and relax.

He did and his cock got harder. Yeah, the whole change-in-atmosphere thing was totally screwing him over—and badly—because all he could think about was screwing.

Mel's close proximity wasn't helping, and man, seeing Phoebe had sent him on a really not-nice trip down memory lane.

Phoebe.

He wanted to kill that bitch—and the more he learned about what she was into, the more his instincts to protect Mel kicked into overdrive. Which was ridiculous, because they were the same person.

Somehow.

"Stryker, we should go."

Mel was touching him—yanking on him, actually. And he snapped to, because they were nowhere near out of danger. The shattered door in front of him was a great reminder as well.

"Let's move out," he said, like it had been his idea all along. Mel shot him a *duh* look and started walking and he tried not to stare at her small, round, perfect ass . . . the one he'd held with a death grip while she'd moved up and down, impaled on his dick.

The perfect ass Maurice claimed he'd sunk his teeth into.

He ground his teeth and he swore he felt the building . . . shift. Mel felt it too.

"You've got to control that," she said.

"You're telling me about control? That's fucking rich," he muttered, and she yanked at him again, and dammit, the pull to her was much stronger now that they'd had sex twice.

Would it get worse after each time? Because that would be really not good.

"Stryker, come on," she said, and he was about to make another cutting remark when he saw the look in her eyes—it was couched, but the fear was there and he remembered what the fire-bitch of a sister put her through on a regular basis. Mel wasn't even an agent and she was doing a pretty decent job of holding it together.

But this was his show and he had to do better.

"We'll be fine—come on." He paused to grab her injections and his weapons, then took her by the hand, her cool palm in his warm one, and they traveled along the maze of basementlike hallways until they found the exit to the stairwell.

He put his hand on the door and the hairs on the back of his neck rose. He pushed Mel behind him as the door swung open away from him seemingly of its own accord.

Maurice stood on the small landing, waiting for them.

Fists curled. Uncurled. Building shook. Not good to bring it down on their heads. "Move out of the way and I'll let you live," Stryker said.

Maurice pushed his sleeves up, revealing wide leather wristbands, and Stryker froze.

Those bands hid wicked poison-filled spurs. That had been Akbar's power, and now Stryker's mentor's face swam in front of his eyes. . . . He remained locked up hard as Maurice unsnapped the bands and smiled, showing those damned, perfect white teeth.

Stryker swore he smelled smoke and he definitely saw red, but the emotion was too raw, too real, and pretty soon they were going to be covered in rubble.

Maurice threw out his arms and let loose a thin, caustic stream in Stryker's direction. Too late Stryker wheeled to the side; he was going to get nailed—*holy shit*.

The poison solidified in midair, the arc encompassed in a crystal clear coffin of ice, and it looked like some kind of avant-garde sculpture in its deadly beauty. Mel nodded with satisfaction as Maurice cried out in agony—the ice had not just frozen the liquid, but his arms to the elbows.

Excellent.

The building settled and Stryker's anger calmed sufficiently. He strode forward, asked, "You like biting helpless women?"

"Phoebe's not helpless," Maurice managed, his face white, his words pained.

"No, Phoebe's not," Stryker agreed, right before he cocked his arm back and punched Maurice in the mouth, shattering his front teeth.

He took immense satisfaction in making sure Maurice swallowed all the pieces before he pushed him aside, watching in fascination as the man's arms broke off as he fell.

"Do you want me to do anything else?" Mel stood to the side, gaze averted away from the semi-conscious Itor agent.

Stryker's cock throbbed, blood strummed, and he couldn't thank her.

Instead, he grabbed her and they headed up the stairs. They were one floor away from street level and they needed to make tracks to the safe house. From there, ACRO would send plenty of support, if they hadn't already.

He stopped at the door, peered through the glass at two hulking guards who seemed to have no clue that there'd been an escape.

"I'll take them—you back me up," he told her.

"I don't know how much control I'll have—when I'm scared, I lose it," she whispered urgently, and he thought about Akbar again . . . and about both their pain and fear.

"You're doing just fine, Mel." He needed to be fine too, dammit, and he willed it so as he slid through the half-opened doorway.

He loved the element of surprise, he thought as he slammed the men's heads together with a satisfying crack and let their bodies slide to the floor. At the same time, he felt the shift in the atmosphere and heard the now familiar whoosh of icy air rush past him.

Mel had frozen three other men who'd been rushing toward him, and by the quick, almost fearful look she gave him, he knew she'd shot her load. "I'm all out."

"It's all right. I've got you," he said, way more gently than he'd intended. He'd have to recharge her once they got to the safe house—and relieve himself in the process, because his cock was harder than before. It would make running . . . interesting.

First, he systematically stripped the unfrozen men of weapons, including a Taser, one of his personal favorites. He pressed a pistol into her hand, his fingers brushing the pulse on her wrist. His own quickened with that simple contact and he gritted his teeth and turned toward the doorway that led to their freedom.

Gabe was well beyond incoherent when Devlin asked him if he wanted to come. Spread-eagled, wrists and ankles cuffed to the heavy head- and footboards of Devlin's bed, Gabriel had very little choice in the matter, thanks to the leather strap Devlin had put around his balls before he'd buried his cock deep inside of him.

"Tell me," Dev murmured as he watched Gabriel carefully. Devlin was always careful when Gabe was tied, always made sure there was no panic or major discomfort.

Well, beyond the fact that his balls were tight enough to burst.

He opened his mouth but sounds jumbled together in a string of what sounded like low howls. Lately, there were always restraints between them, and while Gabe obviously liked it, he missed the way it had been in the beginning, with nothing but Devlin's hands on him.

He realized that he'd gone quiet, floated away, although his erection remained.

"Stay with me, boy." Dev's voice brought him back to the scene. "Where'd you go?"

"Sorry," he panted. "I was just . . . thinking."

For a second, the old Devlin was looking at him and Gabe almost told him what he'd been holding back. But then Devlin drove into Gabriel harder, slamming his prostate at the same time he released the leather strap.

Gabriel came so hard he was pretty sure he screamed . . . the orgasm seemed to last forever. And then Dev's nails scored Gabe's ball sac as he came himself, a heated rush that sent Gabriel into another orgasm.

The sensations rocked through him for a long while, even as Devlin unhooked the cuffs, rubbed the circulation back into Gabe's arms and ankles, checking his skin carefully.

All this shit was a not-so-clever way of Devlin trying to put distance between them. And he didn't even seem to notice he was doing it.

Gabe wanted to talk to Dev about that. Wanted to tell him about a lot of things.

Just this week, he'd found a rental available on the community bulletin board—a small house on the compound—and he'd checked it out. It was private, way bigger than his dorm room, and far more spacious than any place he'd ever lived in—and while it didn't have Devlin, Gabe still needed it.

But Devlin was quiet, lying on his side, staring into space. It had taken Gabe several minutes—if not longer—to come back to full consciousness. Dev tended to fuck him into the mattress on a good day, more so when he had something big on his mind, and tonight's problem must be damned near monumental, because holy good God, Gabe lost it twice in a short span of time.

But the sex was never the problem. No, it was always fucking mind-blowing. Lately, it was the before and after that had been severely lacking.

Because after sex, there was simply nothing. Dev would stare into space or at the ceiling and Gabe felt like he should be taking money off a dresser top and leaving without a word.

Gabe got Dev's distractedness—beyond being in charge of ACRO, his gift of controlled remote viewing often interfered with his life. Dev's CRV was kind of like being able to flip on a spy cam into the other ACRO agents' minds. Most agents—especially when on a mission—were more than willing to have Devlin as their backup.

No, the problem was the other big shit going on that Gabe wasn't privy to. There were secret meetings, conversations that stopped when he walked into the room—again, all normal, except normal typically didn't make Dev moody to the point of shutting down.

And fuck it all, Gabe was tired as hell of the walk of shame back to the dorms and the label as Dev's boy toy. Although he had gained respect—along with a great deal of well-deserved trouble—after his unauthorized mission to the Amazon, he still wasn't officially *with* Devlin.

Gabe remained in the excedo quarters, spending time at Devlin's when invited. He trained hard, tried his best to be friendly to the other agents, and he felt more and more unsettled on a daily basis, rather than the other way around.

He craved privacy. He craved Devlin in a way he hadn't thought possible. And all of that was taking a heavier toll than he'd imagined it would.

"*He's got a damned good job and a safe place to hang his hat. He's just young. Impatient,*" he'd heard Dev tell Marlena.

"*And you're old and impatient,*" she replied. Marlena had always defended him to Devlin, but even she couldn't persuade Dev to give Gabe what he wanted most—a home.

Another few minutes. He touched Dev's shoulder. Nothing. Cleared his throat.

Nothing.

Ah, fuck it. He shoved the covers aside and began to root around for his clothing.

Devlin finally woke from his reverie, turned on his back. "Where are you going?"

"Back to my quarters, the way I do every night." The words came out more harshly than he'd wanted, dammit. He'd been trying to show Dev that he was cool with this couple-times-a-week thing. That he didn't want to rush into anything more serious. That he wasn't falling in fucking love for the first time in his natural-born life and he was more scared of that than—

"Hey." Dev touched his arm and Gabe jerked like he'd been burned. "Gabriel—I wasn't trying to read you. I promised you I wouldn't."

"Yeah, okay," he muttered, shoved his pants on and grabbed his shirt. His shoes were somewhere by the front door. "I gotta go."

Dev didn't try to stop him.

The safe house was three miles from where they'd been held, but they'd gotten there relatively quickly even with Mel slowing at every café and asking if they could eat. The answer had always been the same, which was "When we get where we're going." Mel seemed to have no sense of self-preservation or she'd have put running ahead of her stomach.

At least her constant stops hadn't caused them any trouble, and they hadn't been followed, from what Stryker could tell.

Still, he couldn't afford to take any chances, and between that worry and the arousal clouding his brain, he pulled Mel to him the second he got the door secured.

She didn't fight him. No, she seemed to melt into his kiss, even as he yanked the shirt out of her jeans. She wanted him, and he wanted her to get the worried look off her face, liked when she responded to him like that . . .

Her attachment to him was not good. Sex would cure this touchy-feely crap by, well, touching and feeling. But that would be coming from a totally different head.

"You need this," he murmured.

"Stryker, wait—" She was pushing against his chest with her palms and he pulled back immediately because he wouldn't be one of those guys like Maurice. No matter that he had to have an orgasm soon or else he'd explode and not in the good way.

"Did I hurt you?" he demanded, and Jesus, so much for the no touchy-feely crap.

"No, no, it's not that. It's just . . . I was worried about you back there with Maurice. You froze and it had nothing to do with me."

It had *everything* to do with her. And it had been humiliating. He *never* froze up like that.

She looked so damned concerned that it pissed him off. He wasn't the one with the problems.

"Honey, pointing out my flaws right now isn't the best way to assure your orgasm."

Mel ignored him. "Your friend who died—he had the same powers as Maurice did, didn't he?"

"Akbar didn't die. He was murdered."

She blinked hard. Obviously waiting for him to add *by you*, but he didn't. He wanted to, but it wouldn't come out.

He'd been inside of Mel. There was no way Phoebe was that good at pretending to be innocent. The second Phoebe had taken possession of their body, his own had chilled. With Mel, despite the ice, he'd started to melt a little.

And he was really, really confused.

"I'm sorry, Stryker. You seemed upset. And you've been good to me."

He wanted to tell her to not talk, to shut up, to stop being nice to him. Instead, he took her into his arms again, did a slow grind of his hips to press his cock to her sex, and heard her gasp. "That's better." He slid his hand under her shirt, fingers around her nipple, and she moaned. "I don't want to talk."

His other hand went down her jeans and found her cleft. He

fingered the wet heat and she gripped his shoulders. Murmured, "Please . . ."

"Right. Please . . . want to—no, need to—fuck," he breathed into her ear.

She shuddered. "Yes. Hurry."

Hurry? Hell, yeah. There was no other choice. Bedroom? Probably a good idea, but since he couldn't see one from here, it would be too far away. The living room floor, the wall, hell, the kitchen table would do fine.

Stryker spun her, hooked his foot behind her calf to take her down to the carpet, but at the last second, his scalp tingled with warning, and he froze.

Froze to the click of gun safeties being flipped off.

CHAPTER
Seven

Not again. How many times could someone be captured in twenty-four hours?

"We got it, Stryker. Back away."

Mel blinked as Stryker straightened, keeping one hand on her arm. "Put down the fucking weapons. She's not going to hurt anyone."

Sweat dampened her palms when the three men fanning out in the room didn't lower their pistols—all of which were trained on her. "Who are they?" she whispered.

Stryker nodded at the two closest guys, who were both in jeans and T-shirts. "Wyatt and Ender. They're ACRO. The other one . . . TAG, I'm guessing?"

"Avery." His English accent was as crisp as his suit.

"Dev sent us to find you after you disappeared." Wyatt, his lanky, tall build lending the impression that he was always in motion, kept his gaze on Stryker, but his weapon never wavered from where it was aimed at Melanie's chest.

"Obviously," Stryker growled, "I'm fine. I assume you have a jet standing by, so tell me where it is, and get the fuck out."

Ender smiled, but it wasn't a nice one. "No can do, buddy. We have orders to get you both back to ACRO. So step away from the Itor agent, and we'll package her."

Package?

A rumble came from deep in Stryker's chest. "She's not dangerous right now——"

"Goddammit, Stryker!" Ender's blue eyes flashed. "You know the fucking rules. You could be compromised, so release her and let us handle it."

Mel swallowed. "Compromised? I don't understand."

Stryker's voice was grim. "If any ACRO agent suspects another of being under the influence of an enemy's psychic power, they can take control of the mission. Ender thinks I'm compromised, isn't that right?"

Another not-amused smile from the blond hard-ass. "Why else would you be trying to get into the pants of the bitch who murdered Akbar?"

The building rumbled, and Wyatt held up a hand in a placating gesture. "Easy there, man. You know we're just looking out for you."

"Fuck off," Stryker snapped. "I know what I'm doing."

"Do you?" That from Ender, who gave Mel a glare that could freeze lava. He was just looking for an excuse to shoot her. "I consulted with our TAG buddies on the flight over. Seems they've been looking for an Itor agent who matches her description for two years now. This agent seduced one of theirs, played the part of an innocent victim who needed help escaping the clutches of an evil agency. They found him impaled on the tines of a pitchfork."

For the first time since the agents arrived, Stryker looked uncertain. As if he was thinking of her goldfish and that maybe he'd been played or brainwashed or something. A thread of panic snaked its way through her veins. He was her only ally, and if she lost him now, she might die before she had a chance to either help them take down Itor or make Phoebe's life as miserable as hers had been.

Mel cleared her throat. "I'm on your side. I can help you—"

"Shut up." Wyatt's voice was utterly calm, but her voice box had seized up, painfully so, and she knew that somehow he was responsible. "Stryker, step away. Last chance to do this the easy way."

The building rumbled again. "Dev wants her alive."

"We know that," Wyatt said.

Stryker barked out a bitter laugh. "Yeah? And I know *accidents* happen."

"There won't be any *accidents* if you cooperate." Ender barely got the sentence out when all hell broke loose. Ender broke Stryker's hold on her as Wyatt threw her to the floor. She heard curses, shouts, and then Avery was thrown into the wall. The sound of fists hitting flesh rose above her scream, which cut off when Wyatt did whatever it was that affected her.

"I'm telekinetic and biokinetic," he growled into her ear, even as he wrenched her arms behind her back, "so I can do anything I want to your organs, your blood, your bodily functions. Cooperate, and this will go easily. Fight me, and I'll enjoy making you piss yourself before I explode your lungs, Phoebe."

"Leave her the fuck alone!" Stryker's voice cut off with an *oof,* and then there was more fighting, cursing, and finally, as some sort of icy-cold device closed around her wrists, silence.

She felt two pricks in her arm, knew exactly what Wyatt had dosed her with. "Nullox doesn't negate my power," she ground out. "And sedatives don't work either." Phoebe had undergone some sort of training or procedure that had made them resistant to many drugs and poisons. The trade-off, however, was that they were hypersensitive to other drugs, herbs, and some foods.

"Yeah?" he said. "My biokinetics *will* work."

Yep, they did, because the next hour or so passed in a haze— she might have blacked out, and at some point, she realized that she was no longer in the safe house Stryker had taken her to, but a luxurious private jet.

Where she'd been cuffed, including by her ankles, to a seat. Stryker was across from her, holding out a bottle of water.

"You okay?"

Nodding, she not-so-covertly glanced around for his friends. She found them, one behind her and one in front of her, both watching like hawks. "Yeah." She winced at the twinge in her throat. Wyatt's biokinetic gift was a killer. "Is that water for me?"

Stryker held it to her lips as she took a few swallows. "You were out for a couple of hours."

"I'm sure your friends were happy to keep you company." Jerks. Automatically, she reached deep to check the charge on her power, and though she was still nearly empty, the couple of hours she was out had given her a little juice. Not enough to defend herself, but maybe she could cool down the bottle of water.

"Didn't say a word to them," he muttered.

"Okay," Ender said. "She's awake now, and healthy as a witch, so stop with the tantrum silent treatment and tell us what the fuck is going on and why you're playing nursemaid."

"Because she's going to help us." Stryker spoke forcefully through clenched teeth, almost as if he was trying to convince himself.

Ender shoved to his feet. "Jesus Christ. Dev had better send you to the psychics for deprogramming."

Stryker's head came up, his eyes blazing, and before he did something that rocked the plane right out of the air, Mel spoke up. "Stryker's right," she said softly. "I want to take down my father as much as you do."

Stryker cringed, and she wondered if maybe she shouldn't have said anything. Ender's eyes narrowed. "Your father?"

When Stryker shot her a covert look that said to keep her mouth shut, she did exactly that. And how weird that twenty-four hours ago he'd been bent on killing her, and now she was trusting him to keep her safe.

"If Dev didn't fill you in, there's a reason," Stryker said, "so drop it."

Wyatt braced his arm over the back of a chair and leaned heavily into it. "You want to take down your father too. *Too.* Huh. Now, see, there are a lot of scumbags on this planet that ACRO wants to take down. But I thought it was really fucked up that Dev would want you alive, given what you'd done to Akbar."

Mel didn't bother explaining that she hadn't done anything to Akbar, because if Stryker had doubts, these guys would definitely not buy anything she said in her defense.

"I said let it go," Stryker growled.

Wyatt continued as if Stryker hadn't spoken. "So the fact that he didn't want you strung up like a butchered pig means that your father is someone big. Real big. Like, Itor big."

"*Fuck.*" A sharp inhale came from Ender's side of the plane, and when she looked up, she actually did a double-take at how pale the man had gone. "Alek. Your father is Alek Kharkov."

"Dammit, Ender," Stryker muttered. "I told you to leave it alone."

Wyatt whistled, low and long. "No wonder Dev wants her alive. Even if she doesn't give up intel, she's worth a mint in leverage . . . *damn.*"

Ender, who had been such an ass, who had been looking at her as if choosing the right size blade to slit her throat, was strangely silent, and watching her in a whole new, unnerving way.

"I'll help however I can," she said. "Phoebe is the Itor agent. I hold no loyalty to them. I'll do what's best for ACRO."

"What's best," Ender said, in a voice that was strangely sad, "would be to kill you before we land. Spare a whole lotta pain."

Stryker went taut, and though Mel couldn't move very far, she nudged his foot with her toe. "Hey." When he didn't react other than to glare at Ender, she nudged again, and he finally swung his gaze around to her. "I know you people don't believe that I want to help, but I'll tell you right now that I will not beg for my life again. If you have to kill me, do it. Please. Phoebe can't be allowed to go free."

Dev had been in the office since midnight, right after Gabriel left the bed. He'd been concentrating so hard on the pages in front of him that he barely noticed the office begin to come to life around him.

"The plane's a few hours out. The package is under control."

Marlena had coffee ready, and more important, the news of the day the minute she walked into the office, which was exactly the way Dev wanted it. No chitchat, no bullshit, just give it all to him straight, the good and the bad.

It was amazing how quickly things could go downhill. It was why, more often than not, he worked so late—it gave him the ultimate illusion of control, the feeling that he could ward off evil simply by remaining awake, aware, and in charge.

Of course, shit went just as badly when he was awake, but he found it easier to deal with.

"The house on the north corner's been rented," Marlena continued, knowing Dev liked to keep up with everything that went on in the compound, no matter how minute.

She slid the lease in front of him. He stared at the name on the dotted line and wondered how the hell he'd missed this. "What's this all about?"

"I figured you'd know." Her voice was mild but an eyebrow was cocked in a way that told him she was seriously annoyed with him.

"Well, I don't."

The boy wasn't trying to steamroll him, wasn't trying to worm an invite to live with Dev—he knew that for sure. Gabriel was guileless enough to ask if he thought it was in the realm of possibility.

It wasn't that Devlin didn't think it was—it's just he hadn't been doing a lot of thinking about his personal life.

"Well, maybe there's a problem you don't know about," she pointed out.

"He's pissed at me. Again." Dev drained his coffee and Marlena poured him more.

"You need to court him, Devlin," Marlena said. Obviously, Chance had been doing some courting of his own, because he'd never seen her happier.

"*Court* him?"

"Yes. Dinner. Movies. Not just overnights."

"I work late every night," he pointed out, and Marlena sighed and looked at the ceiling.

"You of all people know how to be creative. Make the most of that time so he stops feeling like a booty call."

Did Gabriel feel like that? Dev pondered for a few minutes, and yeah, okay, he guessed he could see what Marlena was talking about. "Has he said anything about it to you?"

"He doesn't have to say it. I lived it, Devlin, remember?" she told him softly. "You're giving him your body, but that's all."

"Maybe my body is all I have."

"That's crap and you know it. If you love him, you need to tell him everything."

"Everything is classified information."

"And you get to decide who has clearance," she shot back. "When we finally get Itor where we want them, you're going to be putting your life on the line. Asking him to do the same in the biggest battle ACRO's seen to date. Tell him."

Dev sighed deeply. He'd known the day was coming, told himself he didn't want to scare his lover. But in reality, saying all of it out loud to Gabriel could actually scare the shit out of Dev, more than he wanted to admit.

"Oz was the romantic one."

Marlena raised an eyebrow at that statement, shook her head, and left the room, and yeah, it was hard to believe that big, black, leather-wearing Oz was Mr. Romance, but it damned well hadn't been Dev.

More than once, Oz had lured him from the office with soft promises—and if Dev hadn't responded, Oz would simply throw him over the desk, fuck him until he was too tired to protest, and then take him home.

Now Dev scrubbed his hands through his hair and realized it was past ten in the morning, that he still had it in him to work all night and not break stride.

That he'd started working again all night because he was getting too close to Gabriel and it freaked him out.

Dammit.

"I could lose him, Oz." He tapped his fingers on the desk as if he was sending out a furious Morse code to the dead. "I could lose him the way I lost you, and then what?"

Oz, of course, didn't answer him worth a damn.

But right now, that was unfortunately the least of his problems, because the shit with Itor had been getting worse to deal with. ACRO's psychics might have built a protective shield around his mind, but the barrier didn't do anything to keep Devlin from thinking about his biological father. And now his half sister was being thrown into the mix—a two for one, since there was an alter—and he didn't know how the hell to deal with it.

Could he ever trust her? Would he have to kill her along with Alek?

Just then, the voices got louder—and he almost yelled out the office door to keep it down. Until he realized the voices were coming from inside his own head, and dammit all to hell, the arguing was enough to make him want to strangle one of them. He listened carefully to the angry male voices—and the worry, enough worry to make him nervous as well—and within moments had the who and where pinpointed.

Ender. Wyatt. Stryker. They were like extra-large children with enough testosterone among them to take down most of the free world.

Added to that, their goddamned posturing was making his

head throb. And not the good head in the good way either, dammit. Combined with this Gabriel thing, Dev was a far less than happy camper.

At least Avery was keeping his trap shut through all of this. But still, somehow, information that should've been classified was leaking out—and he knew for sure it wasn't from his mind being read.

And then, another voice, one he didn't know but it still made pins and needles shoot up his spine. *If you have to kill me, do it.*

"Call the plane," he barked into the intercom, and Marlena walked back into his office and calmly did so, keeping the phone on speaker as she said to the pilot, "Devlin O'Malley has a message for the men on board—can you please transmit over the loudspeaker for him?"

"Yes, ma'am. And yes, sir, Mr. O'Malley. Whenever you're ready," Captain Liskin said crisply.

"Which one of you assholes wants to tell me what's going on there?" Devlin paused to listen, heard Ender mutter, "Like you don't fucking know already," and that's when he lost it completely.

"When you get off that plane, your ass is mine, Ender. Yours too, Wyatt. And Stryker, I don't know what the hell's going on with you, but you've been out of contact—"

"I was detained," Stryker shot back with enough force to make Dev stop for a moment. But just a moment.

"You listen to me—all of you," he said with a growl. "Stop talking. Right now. And don't think about touching a hair on that woman's head, do I make myself clear?"

"Yes, sir," the men said in unison.

"And you, Melanie or Phoebe or whoever you are? Be careful what you ask for. Your wish might just come true."

CHAPTER
eight

"Oh, my God."

Annika Svenson stood at the threshold of Dev's office, her heart thundering madly. She probably wasn't supposed to over-hear Dev on the phone, but Marlena had learned long ago that trying to stop Annika from barging into the office was useless, and now that Annika was pregnant, the secretary made even fewer waves. In fact, everyone on base had suddenly become all kid-gloves with Ani. Even people who had always hated her. Which was kind of funny, and it took the sting out of being treated like an invalid.

Dev's brown eyes flashed with surprise, which was a rarity. "Clearly you forgot that conversation we had about you making appointments?"

"Which one?" She hurried inside, trying not to wince at how her boots pinched her swollen feet. "Dev—oh, my God, you got the bitch. You got that bitch who killed Akbar."

Dev nodded, but there was an uncharacteristic hesitance in the action. "Yeah. We got her."

Okay, so maybe he was having a bittersweet moment. Because, sure, they had the killer in their clutches, but the fact that Akbar was dead remained. Just as dead as the Phoebe bitch would soon be.

"Let me have her."

Dev leaned back in his chair, folding his fingers over his abs. Anyone else would have looked relaxed, but in his black BDUs, Dev managed to radiate authority and danger. "Annika, even if you hadn't lost your powers, you're the most pregnant woman I've ever seen."

"Oh, funny, Dev. It's these stupid maternity BDUs. Not flattering at all." She rubbed her very pregnant belly and ignored his smirk and his comment about losing her powers. That was one of the dangers of pregnancy among special-ability types like her; pregnancy often affected powers, and sometimes they didn't return after the baby was born. Annika was terrified of not regaining her electric shock ability that made her so lethal in the field, but she tried not to obsess.

Much.

"I told you months ago that you could wear civvies, and you should be on maternity leave anyway."

Whatever. She wasn't the sit-at-home-and-knit-booties type. "So. Who bagged the skank?"

"Stryker."

Annika's head snapped back hard enough to give her a sudden headache. "And she's still alive?"

Stryker had wanted Phoebe dead even more than Annika, had been consumed by the need to shove a blade into her black heart. No way would he have gone for the capture over the kill.

"She's alive," Dev said, "because I want her that way."

"You planning to torture her first?" Excellent.

"I'm planning to get her to talk. She can help us bring down Itor—"

"Bullshit." Annika eyed the couch and then decided that if

she sat, she'd be turtled and never get up again. "She won't talk and you know it."

"Phoebe won't, but Melanie might."

Okay, this was just bizarre. Annika didn't buy the whole multiple-personality thing, and she wouldn't believe anything the psycho said anyway. "And after you get what you want from her? Are you going to let Stryker have her?" The way Dev avoided her gaze put a lump in her gut, though it had to fight for room with the baby. "Dev?"

"Even if we can't get intel from her, I can't kill her. Not until Itor is dismantled."

A chill ran up her spine, feeding her dread and her anger. "*You* might not be able to, but *I* can."

"No," Dev said softly, "you can't. She's Alek's daughter."

"Then we send her back to him in pieces—" Annika broke off with a gasp. "Oh, God." She slapped her hand over her mouth and actually stumbled backward. Dev rushed around the desk to catch her, but she recovered and sidestepped him because, truth was, she didn't want to be touched right now. "She's . . . she's your sister."

He nodded.

Annika had to force herself to speak through a wave of nausea. "When did you find out?"

"Yesterday."

The baby kicked, probably sensing Annika's turmoil, and she willed herself to calm down. It didn't stop the swirling in her stomach, though. Poor Dev. He had such evil in his family. Just once, couldn't something be easy for him?

"I want to make one thing clear." His voice was hard, all business. "I'm not bringing her here for a family reunion. I plan to use her to get to Alek. Taking down Itor is my number one priority, and I will do anything to accomplish that."

"I know, Dev." She did. But she also knew that he sometimes gave people more chances than they deserved. Annika herself was a prime example.

He nodded in that dismissive way of his. "And just as no one knows Alek is my father, no one is to know that he's hers either."

Well, it wasn't "no one," since Dev had made Annika, Creed, Ender, and Marlena aware of his relationship to Itor's leader, but yeah, she got what he was saying. The fewer people who knew, the less pressure, speculation, and judgment would be on him.

"Goes without saying." She waddled to the door, the sudden urge to pee cutting through her worry that Dev might be in over his head with this Phoebe situation. "Call if you need to talk or anything."

"I will. Oh, and, Annika? You'd better decide on names. Soon."

She narrowed her eyes at him. "Are you being psychic or paranoid?"

"I'm not telling." He grinned, but damn, he looked beat. "I don't suppose you want to know if it's a boy or a girl."

"If I'd wanted to know, I'd have asked at my last ultrasound." She heaved her massive girth through the doorway, cursing when her belly brushed the doorknob. "This is all your fault."

"The baby?"

"Yes. You threw me and Creed together."

"Not like *that*."

"Still your fault," she grumbled as she shuffled through the waiting area, followed by Dev's laughter. It really was his fault, and though she gave him a hard time, she wouldn't change a thing. She might still doubt her ability to be a good mother, but she'd also once doubted her ability to love anyone. Yet here she was with her own little family she loved—Dev, Creed, and the unnamed life inside her.

And she'd do anything—*anything*—to protect them. Which meant that she didn't give a shit if Phoebe was Dev's sister or not. If the woman threatened Annika's family in any way, shape, or form, she'd pay. And Annika didn't believe in mercy. Or in second chances.

*　*　*

Mel had been in a lot of uncomfortable situations in her life, but hanging out on a plane with men who wanted her dead but who had been ordered not to kill her topped the charts.

Then there was Stryker. She couldn't figure him out. She got that he was confused, and that he was struggling to believe she was a completely separate entity from Phoebe, and that she was on the up-and-up when it came to wanting to help take down Itor.

So yes, he had some issues to overcome. Which would explain why sometimes he was nice to her, and other times, like now, he glared and snapped. At least this time, she wasn't the cause. His mood had been knocked around by Ender, Wyatt, and the man they'd called Dev, who had disconnected just a few minutes ago.

So now probably wasn't the best time to tell Stryker that she had to go to the bathroom. Maybe she'd start out with something that wouldn't require him to unchain her.

"This Dev guy . . . he's your boss, right?"

Stryker nodded.

"What did he mean when he said to be careful what I wished for?"

Stryker shrugged. Great. This was going well.

"Would I know him for any reason?"

Stryker's remarkable eyes narrowed, and she squirmed under the intensity of his stare. Well, that and because she had to go to the bathroom. "Why?"

"He sounded familiar." She frowned. "No, not familiar. More like . . . I don't know, like I felt him. Sounds crazy."

Ender, who hadn't taken his eyes off her, sat forward in his seat. "What do you mean, you felt him?" When she hesitated, he barked, "Answer!"

"Back off, asshole," Stryker snapped. "You're scaring her."

"Waa." Ender pouted mockingly. "I'm scaring the sweet widdle Itor agent. Maybe you can comfort her by trying to get into her pants again."

Stryker shot to his feet, and Ender met him in the aisle. Tension became a soup in the plane, but then Wyatt was there, shoving them apart. "Knock it off. I don't want another ass-chew call from Dev." No one moved, and anxious energy began to build again.

"Um . . . excuse me? I have to go to the bathroom."

"Too bad." Ender sank down in his seat and kicked his feet up on another. "You can hold it for a few hours."

"No," she said, "I can't. So unless you want me to ruin these really expensive seats, you'll let me go."

"I'll take her," Stryker muttered.

Ender swore. "I'll do it. She stays cuffed and the door stays open."

"You're not taking her anywhere." Stryker leaned over to unfasten her bindings from the chair. "And she can close the door."

"You aren't in charge anymore," Ender said, and once again, Stryker whirled to face the other man.

Wyatt slammed his palm on Stryker's chest. "Easy there, cowboy. Ender's right. The door has to stay open. What if Phoebe comes out while Mel is in the bathroom?"

"I'll go in with her." The expression on Stryker's face dared the other men to argue, and just as Ender opened his mouth to do exactly that, Wyatt finished unhooking the bindings.

"Go." Wyatt stepped back to clear the aisle. "But, Stryker, don't make us regret this."

Stryker yanked her to her feet, which were still shackled, same as her wrists, so she had to shuffle down the aisle like a prison inmate during a transfer. Behind her she heard someone mutter something about "compromised," and Stryker let out a series of nasty curses as he shoved her into one of the bathrooms. He came in behind her, and though she was grateful that it was about three times the size of a commercial jet's restroom and included a shower stall, it was cramped for two people.

"Thank you," she said softly.

"Don't thank me. I didn't do it for you. I did it for Dev. Hurry up."

She tried, but her fingers shook so badly that she couldn't unbutton her jeans. Finally, with yet another curse, he tore them open and turned away while she went. Between him and the cuffs, the whole thing was awkward and embarrassing, but she finished, stood, and once more needed his help.

"Jesus Christ." He reached for the buttons on her jeans. "You can freeze men so solidly they break into ice cubes, but you can't dress yourself."

Something inside her snapped, and she knocked his hands away. "Never mind. I don't want your help. If I have to go to the bathroom again, don't bother *helping*. I'll deal with Ender. At least with him, the hatred is consistent." She tried to shoulder him aside so she could get out of the tiny space that seemed to grow more cramped the longer she was in it, but he snared her wrists and pushed her against the shower door.

"You aren't going to get anyone else to help you." Stryker's broad shoulders filled her vision, and she did her best not to notice how his T-shirt stretched like a second skin over his taut muscles. "And you're definitely not going out there with unbuttoned pants."

"Oh, right. Because you can't have anyone thinking you tried to get in them." She struggled to get out of his grip, but his fingers only tightened more. "Do they know? Do they have any idea that you fucked me already? Maybe I'll tell them, just so I can see the look of disgust on their faces."

Fury lit his eyes, making the blues and greens swirl inside the crystal globes. "You do that, and I'll   "

"You'll what?" she spat. "Beat me? You can't even come close to what my own father did to me. Kill me? Big deal. It's going to happen anyway. How stupid do you think I am? Once you and your people are done with me, after you've wrung every drop of usable knowledge out of me, I'm dead. So stop with the threats."

His jaw worked, and she could hear the sound of him grinding his molars even over the hum of the jet engine.

"What's the matter," she taunted. "Can't find the words to convince me that you aren't going to kill me? As an ACRO agent, surely you've been trained to lie."

"Stop it," he ground out.

"Stop what?" Pent-up frustration put a sharp edge on her reply. "Stop being realistic? After I finally figured out that all my hopes for any kind of normal, *long* life were nothing but a silly fantasy?"

He lunged, his pelvis rocking into her, and she sucked in a sharp breath at the erection nudging her belly. Between her legs, she went instantly wet, as though her body was connected to his and knew exactly what they both wanted.

The space got smaller as he rolled his hips against her. "Stop *that*."

His breath hung like mist in the air. At some point, she'd engaged her power, and the bathroom had become a freezer. Just as she wondered if the rest of the aircraft had been affected, she got her answer.

"*Stryker!*" Ender's enraged bellow vibrated the walls, but Stryker didn't seem to notice.

Instead of responding, his mouth came down on hers.

Stryker was vaguely aware that Ender and Wyatt were in the background cursing, but he was more aware that his cock was rock hard and looking for a home inside of her like a heat-seeking missile set to strike.

He'd stopped before—he would not stop now. Not even if Ender and Wyatt tried to drag him off her, which he knew they wouldn't try. Once his elemental side was triggered, he was too dangerous to piss off further.

His tongue dueled with hers in a kiss that stole his breath and he didn't care.

He moved like lightning, because the need was too great, his body demanding satisfaction, his eyesight blurring. He slid the keys out of his pocket and leaned down, unhooking one ankle cuff. While he was down there, he yanked at her jeans, taking them down and off one leg.

When he stood again he unbuttoned and unzipped his own cargo BDUs and let them fall to his ankles. He didn't uncuff her hands, just slid his head between her arms and her hands sought quarter on his shoulders.

She didn't protest. His mouth sought hers again, his tongue slid inside in a blatant imitation of what he was about to do to her.

Hands on her ass, he hoisted her so her back was to the wall, her legs wrapped to his waist. His cock against her wet sex. And then he impaled her, driving in hard and fast.

It was only then he paused, the feeling of her hot flesh tight around him like a fist. "So hot, Mel. How are you so goddamned hot?"

Her eyes were wide from his penetration. "You," she managed to moan, and that's when he began to move again, his mouth capturing hers as he did so and everything else be damned.

He'd been holding back for too long.

He wanted more—his mouth on her breasts, his face buried between her legs to taste the sweet juice until she screamed, but that would have to wait. This was about instant gratification and it was still taking too damned long.

She gasped his name against his mouth, and yes, that's what he wanted. Wasn't sure where the hell this need to claim her came from, the need to protect her, but it was alternately turning him on and pissing him off.

And pissed-off sex was just as good as happy sex. Better, even, if the way she was meeting his thrusts was any indication.

She wanted to hate him as much as he wanted to hate her. And somehow, neither of them could get there.

It made it that much goddamned hotter, especially when her nails scored his back as he thrust deeply. She asked him to do that again, harder, and he could almost ignore the fact that the plane banked hard to starboard.

Of course, they banked along with it, but they didn't stop the motion. He ended up wedged into the corner with her half on top of him. All that mattered to him was that he was still inside of her.

"Fuck me, Mel," he told her, moved her hips up and down.

"Are you . . . doing . . . this?"

"I'm . . . doing . . . you."

"The plane . . . something's happening . . ." she managed, but then she was kissing him again and she was contracting around him, forcing his orgasm to shoot in a brilliant blend of color behind his eyelids.

The plane bounced wildly right along with his release, began to settle and straighten as he began to see clearly again too, and yes, it had been him doing something to fuck with the plane.

Best they untangle and face the music.

Mel's breath was warm against his cheek, her body bonelessly wrapped around his. She raised her head from where it had been against his shoulder, her eyes glazed.

"Hey, are you all right?" he asked.

"More than," she told him. She was rubbing his neck, massaging the muscles with her fingers, the clinking of the metal a reminder of who she was. Where they were.

What would Akbar say about all this?

At the thought of his name, Stryker sagged. It welled up inside of him, the anger that always threatened to boil over—that frequently did—changing to a pain so great he wondered if it would ever go away. "He's gone. Akbar. It's my fault."

"No, it's not," she said softly, tears welled in her eyes.

And it wasn't hers either.

"Your friend. I'm so sorry . . . you have to believe me . . . I'm so sorry . . ." she murmured as he struggled to breathe, to hold it together.

It wasn't going to happen.

Mel simply pulled him close, held him while he completely lost it, his head buried against her, his cock still inside her, and he mourned his friend with the woman who . . .

The woman he needed to save.

CHAPTER
Nine

They stayed in the bathroom for a long time. Stryker held Mel like she was a lifeline, and though she was confused as hell, she didn't complain. No one had ever held her like that, and she wanted to hang on for as long as possible. For a few precious minutes, she could feel what it was like to be normal. Cared for.

Which was silly. Stryker didn't care for her. He'd been horny, and the plane had been . . .

"Stryker? What was wrong with the plane? Was it your power?"

His heavy sigh shook his entire body. "Yeah. It's never affected anything but the earth before."

"Then why now?"

He shrugged. "Emotion. The fact that you used your ability so close to the sex." Gently, he extracted himself from her, lifting her arms from where they rested on his shoulders. "I think your elemental power affected mine. Since you turned the plane into a big ice cube, my power was able to hitchhike onto it."

She swallowed. "We're dangerous together."

His laughter was bitter as he tugged up his pants. "Yeah." He reached for her jeans to help her, but froze. "Fuck. You're recharged now."

"I'll be careful. I promise."

"It's not you I'm worried about." He checked his watch. "How long until we can expect to see Phoebe?"

"Anytime. She's been suppressed for a while, and she's not going to wait much longer. The plane jiggling probably kept her at bay, but . . ." She shook her head. "I can feel her stirring."

"Dammit." He shoved open the door. "I have the Itor meds, but I don't want to waste them if we don't have to. The guys will have a plan in place."

Oh, God. This was going to be embarrassing. And sure enough, when they stepped out of the bathroom, it was obvious that they all knew exactly what had happened in that tiny space.

Stryker didn't give them time to say anything, though it was clear that Ender wanted to. The rage in his eyes was like lightning, flashing over and over.

"What's the plan for containing Phoebe?" Stryker asked, as he settled her into her seat and fastened the chains.

"Why?" Wyatt stood. "Is she Phoebe?"

Stryker shook his head. "Not yet. But she could show at any moment, and trust me, if we don't have her secured and gagged, she'll either kill us or we'll kill her."

"Dev has pretty much everyone who can counter fire and ice on standby to be there when we land. They're also putting together some sort of fireproof thing to wrap her in, and preparing a chamber she can't melt."

"What about for now?" she asked.

Wyatt smiled grimly. "That's why I'm here. I can affect your heart rate, breathing . . . basically, put you to sleep once I get inside you."

Ender snorted. "Stryker has already done that."

"Would you rather have had the plane crash?" Stryker's voice was low, rough, and Mel had a feeling he was trying to keep from launching at the other man.

"I'd rather not have to think about you fucking the woman who murdered Akbar."

"Then don't." Stryker's fingers were gentle as he put the last chain fastener in place. "Because Mel didn't kill him."

Ender rolled his eyes. "You buying this bullshit, Wyatt?"

Mel expected Wyatt to say no, so she was shocked when he hesitated and then said, "I don't know. Look at Rik. Or Chance. They both have completely different species of animals living inside them. Totally unique beings. If it can happen with them, I don't know why it can't happen with Melanie and Phoebe."

Ender reached into a cupboard near his seat and grabbed a pack of peanuts. Mel's stomach, which had been simmering on low growl, began to make a serious protest.

"Um . . . could I have some?" She wasn't shy about asking for food.

Ender stared at her like she'd asked for a million dollars instead of a handful of nuts. "No."

"Give her the fucking peanuts," Stryker said, irritation putting an edge in his voice.

"It could be a trick. She could be allergic and trying to kill herself."

"I'm not allergic." She inhaled, catching a tantalizing whiff of the salty snacks, and her belly let out an embarrassingly loud rumble. "I'm hungry."

Slamming the packet on his little table, Ender shoved to his feet. "I'll get you water."

Water was not going to cut it. She needed food, and anxiety that they weren't going to give her any made her skin tighten. Without thinking, she lunged, grabbed the packet of peanuts, and dumped them into her mouth.

Ender moved like a snake, ripping the bag out of her hands, but not before she got a mouthful. "You damned thief."

Stryker studied her, his tawny brows arched high on his forehead as she chewed in blissful silence. "Okay, what *is* it with you and food?"

She swallowed and looked longingly at the cupboard where Ender had gotten the peanuts. "Can I have more?"

"Not until you tell me what's up with you." Stryker wasn't being cruel—logically, she knew that. But the part of her that freaked out at the idea of having food withheld took him seriously. And while physical beatings had never broken her, the threat of going hungry made her crack like an egg.

"Ever been starved?" she asked quietly. "I mean, like, you didn't eat for years?"

"That's impossible," Ender scoffed. "You'd die."

"Not if Phoebe is the one eating."

Stryker leaned forward in his seat, bracing his forearms on his knees. "So Itor—your own fucking father   didn't feed you? For years?"

She nodded. "I was around nine, I guess. I think it started as an experiment, and then became a way to control me. For eight years, they didn't let me have anything to eat. Only Phoebe got food."

God, the gnawing hunger still ate at her, and even the slightest feeling of having an empty stomach sent her into a panic, which was why she ate constantly. Food was both a comfort and a necessity for her own mental health.

"So you were always hungry?"

She blinked hard as the memories flooded back, because the thing was, the starvation was tied to a time in her life that was absolute hell. There had been so much experimentation, training, poking, prodding, and fear.

"Always." She looked down, not wanting anyone to see how much the food thing really bothered her, how terrified she was that Itor could do it all over again. "Now when I'm hungry, the memories . . ." Shuddering, she trailed off. She'd given them too much ammunition as it was.

Ender uttered a low curse, and Stryker disappeared to the back of the plane. He probably thought she was completely psychotic. He was probably right.

And then he was back, dropping the table from the compartment next to her and setting down a plate with a wrapped ham and cheese sandwich. Gratitude made her eyes swim, and she barely squeaked out a "Thank you" before digging in. In no time, the sandwich was gone, and he brought her another, plus more peanuts—which she covertly tucked into her pockets—and a carton of milk.

She inhaled the second sandwich and milk, and when she asked for a third, he gently put his palm on her leg. "You don't need to gorge yourself or hoard food. We don't starve people at ACRO, and what you told us isn't going to ever be used against you."

Oh, God, he knew what she was doing. He knew she was filling herself up to the point of discomfort because she didn't know when she'd get another meal. Stryker understood, and he was doing what he could to help her.

"It's so silly," she whispered.

Stryker shook his head. "I'd say that if the only issue you have after what you've gone through is a need to keep yourself fed, you're in damn good shape, and it's not silly. It's survival."

"Speaking of survival, are you ready to let me knock her out?" Wyatt cleared his throat and offered an apologetic shrug. "Sorry, man, but I hate flying anyway, and I'd feel a lot better if she was catching Zs and we didn't have to worry about the plane's engine freezing out or a fiery hole being blasted through the cockpit."

Mel didn't blame Wyatt at all. She was surprised they'd let her stay awake as long as they had.

"Can you give us a minute?" Stryker asked, though his tone said it wasn't really a question. He was taking the minute whether they liked it or not.

Ender hesitated, but then he moved to the back of the plane.

Avery turned to look out the window, and Wyatt took a seat a few feet away. Close enough that he could be there in a heartbeat, but far enough to give them a semblance of privacy.

"Look," Stryker said in a low, hushed voice, "I'm still not sure what to think about all of this. I don't know where my head is at, and I can guarantee that at ACRO you'll find few allies. Is there any way you can prove what you're saying?"

"You mean, can I prove that I'm a completely different person from Phoebe?"

"Yes."

She nodded. "A few genetic tests will do it. I'm a chimera. Two genetically distinct cells are in my body. Brain scans will show two different thought patterns when each of us is in control." She paused. "Those people Wyatt was talking about. Are they like me?"

"Sort of. Chance is more of a shape-shifter. He was infected by an animal bite, and now when he gets mad, he morphs into the creature. He's a little like the Hulk. He needs to be caged or sedated sometimes, but when he's fully human, he works for ACRO like everyone else. But Rik is two completely individual beings, so a lot like you, I guess. She was an Itor experiment too."

Mel's pulse picked up. She wasn't alone. "Is she . . . okay? I mean, how does she live?"

He shrugged. "Her other half is some sort of wolf thing her mate, Trance, named Cujo. Cujo was vicious when she first arrived at ACRO. Itor had tortured the shit out of both of them. But they're both fine now. Rik lets the beast out to run at night, and she works in the Cryptozoology department by day."

Hope sang through her. Maybe ACRO really could help her. If a way could be found to keep Phoebe suppressed or under control, maybe Mel wouldn't have to die. *If* she could convince them that she had nothing to do with their agent's death and that she was willing to do anything to bring down Itor.

"Thank you," she said.

"For what?"

"Being nice. I haven't had that since my mom died."

"I'm not doing anything special. Just talking."

She tried to touch his knee, but the chain jerked her back. "I know."

His throat worked on a swallow, and then he reached out and took her hand. Even though they'd had sex three times now, this was somehow the most tender, intimate gesture he'd made. That anyone had ever made to her.

Emotion trembled through her. She opened her mouth to thank him again, but the familiar tingle on her scalp and the tightening in the back of her neck cut her off. Damn her. Damn Phoebe for ruining this! Usually she was grateful for Phoebe to take over, letting Mel slip into blissful blackness, but for once, she was truly afraid. Phoebe would destroy every bit of progress she'd made with Stryker, and probably Wyatt too. And if Phoebe met Dev first . . .

"It's time," she gasped. "Get . . . Wyatt."

Instantly, Wyatt was there, and even as Phoebe began to claw her way to the surface, Mel felt her body go slack and her eyelids grow heavy.

The distinct bump of a plane's wheels hitting a runway was what jolted Phoebe out of sleep. She didn't waste time blinking and trying to figure out what was going on; she remained motionless, cracked her lids, and assessed the situation.

Which wasn't good.

She was chained to a seat, and a man she recognized from a file Itor kept on known or suspected ACRO agents—she thought his name was Wyatt Kennedy—was sitting across from her, hands clenched, his face pinched in concentration.

"She's waking," he ground out.

Someone with an English accent cursed. "Put her back to sleep."

"Can't. I'm about tapped."

Fucking biokinetic.

She heard that Stryker asshole talking to someone on a phone, heard another voice she didn't recognize as she reached deep for her power. She had a full tank. Excellent. She'd fry these fuckers the second the chains were unhooked from the seat.

The plane eased to a stop, and she played groggy as the engines powered down. The mid-cabin, rear, and front doors slammed open simultaneously, and a dozen men in black BDUs rushed on board with fire extinguishers and some sort of blanket. Anticipation gave her a rush as she lit up her power. She was going to turn the plane into a roaster oven. Stryker's thick arm came around her throat from behind, jerking her head back even as fire burst from her fingertips. The choke hold sent her flames into the seat in front of her, and then the men threw the blanket over her, and the fireball she summoned shot uselessly into it.

"You assholes," she snarled.

No one said anything as she was wrapped up like a damned mummy, blindfolded, tossed into the back of a truck, and whisked to God-knew where. There was more jostling, more chains, and then she was plopped into a seat.

Stryker—she knew by his scent—removed her blindfold. *And well, well, what do you know.* She was in a plush office, sitting across a desk from ACRO's head honcho.

"Devlin," she purred. "Nice to finally meet you."

He studied her, his shrewd, intelligent eyes so like Alek's. "I really wish I could say the same. Who are you right now?"

"Guess."

Devlin shifted his gaze to Stryker, who had moved to stand against the wall. "It's Phoebe." Stryker folded his arms over his broad chest. "You can tell by the horns and cloven hooves."

"You," she sighed, "are no fun." She turned to Dev and smiled brightly. "So we've met. What now?"

"Now I decide how long I want to let you live."

"Ouch. So ruthless. You really are our father's son. He'd be proud." In her peripheral vision, she saw Stryker's entire body jerk. The shock in his expression was priceless. Almost as much as the brief flash of *oh, shit* on Dev's face, which confirmed her suspicions that Melanie had already spilled the beans about Alek being their father as well. "You haven't told anyone about our happy family? I'm hurt. But I suppose if your people knew that your father is Itor's big dick, they'd have some serious doubts about you."

"I'm not worried about my people." He met her eyes, and damn, he was a good liar. She could respect that. "They know what I want."

"And what *do* you want, big brother?"

"For Itor to be dismantled from the ground up and for Alek to be nothing but a stain in the rubble."

Exhaling slowly, she considered her next move. Build on the family card, or antagonize him into making mistakes? Maybe both. "I can help you."

"And why would you do that?"

She sagged in her chair as though exhausted, and looked down at her lap, which was hidden by the damned fireproof blanket. "I only learned about you a few days ago. If I'd known . . ." She worried her bottom lip for a moment. "I didn't realize our father was trying to destroy his own son. I hate him for that."

"Why should I believe you?"

"Because I'm your sister. Our father deprived us of a life together. Give me a chance."

Stryker, still braced against the wall, looked like he was trying to keep his temper in check, and she got the feeling he wanted to yell at Dev, tell him not to believe her shit. "Did you give Akbar a chance?" he spat.

She summoned tears. So easy. "I was following my father's orders. I didn't know about my brother at the time . . . and if I could take it back . . . I'm so sorry."

There was a shuffling of feet, and then Dev was at her side

with a tissue, dabbing the tears off her cheeks. His voice was soft, understanding. What a sap. "Our father is a very powerful psychic, isn't he?"

She sniffled. "Very."

Dev's hand shot out and clamped around her neck. "So am I." His lips peeled back from his teeth as he got right in her face. "So don't fuck with me. I know when you're lying."

With a shove, he released her, and she resisted the urge to tell him how much she was going to enjoy killing him. Because she would. That idiot Maurice had been wrong—Alek might be grooming her to take over Itor, but what she really desired was ACRO. The organization was bigger, better connected with legitimate governments, but most of all, she wanted to take what her brother had. And she always got what she wanted.

Speaking of which, she slid Stryker a sensual smile. "Thanks for recharging me, by the way."

Stryker stiffened, and Dev scowled. "What are you talking about?"

"I normally don't tell people this, but since Stryker already knows . . . yes, my power runs down. And your helpful agent over there—"

"Shut up," Stryker ground out, and Phoebe feigned an innocent look.

"Oh, I'm so sorry. Dev doesn't know that you've been fucking me? Tsk-tsk. You people really don't communicate at all, do you?"

To his credit, Dev's expression didn't change, didn't give anything away, but she sensed strong emotion brewing in him. He was, no doubt, wondering what the hell his agent had been thinking.

Dev returned to his chair. "What are the extent of your abilities?"

"Duh. I can burn things. I can also sprout wings and fly, walk through walls, turn into a leprechaun, travel through time and space—"

"Enough!" Dev slammed his fist on the desk. "Are you psychic?"

"Maybe."

"She isn't," Stryker said, a little testily, though she had no idea why. "Paranoid fucking Ender told you I'm compromised, didn't he?"

Dev gave Stryker a sharp nod, and Stryker cursed but didn't say anything else.

"Let me talk to Melanie," Dev demanded.

"Ask nicely."

"I have no problem stringing you up until she surfaces, so you might as well save yourself pain and me time."

"And you should know that I have no problem with pain." She leaned forward in her chair—as much as the blanket and chains would allow anyway. "You don't scare me."

A long, tense silence stretched as Dev watched her, and as much as she hated to admit it, his stare unnerved her. It was so like their father's, and she wondered if Dev possessed the same tendency to go suddenly, unstoppably insane with rage.

"Does Melanie know about me?" he finally asked.

Oh, now here was where things would get really fun. "I don't think so. I hope you plan to tell her, though."

Dev's eyes narrowed. "Why?"

"Because our father hates her. I hate her. It would crush her little world to know that her only other family, her big brother, hates her too." She grinned. "How funny. Even funnier if you order her torture or execution. Priceless, really."

"You sick bitch!" Stryker's fists clenched. "Let Mel out. Now."

"I don't think so."

Suddenly, the room began to shake. Panic wrapped around her like a steel band, and she clenched her teeth, fought hard to stay calm. She couldn't let these fucks know about her one fear. *Don't give in, don't give in . . .*

The room shook harder, and a crack formed in the wall. She heard Dev's voice, Stryker's, and then it all became too much for her. She closed in on herself, but she'd be back. With a vengeance.

CHAPTER
Ten

Alek fucking hated sheep. Whether they were the animal kind or human kind, sheep were stupid as shit. He spurred his Waler stallion through the middle of the flock, kicking at one that was a little too slow. Dumb animals. The sheep station's resident animal whisperer, Barry, hadn't made the pea-brained things any more manageable, and Alek still cursed the day they'd lost the most powerful animal whisperer on the planet to ACRO. Kira Donovan would have been more than just someone to handle the sheep and dogs; she would have been an unbelievably powerful weapon.

Adjusting his wide-brimmed hat to shield his eyes from the hot sun, he put his losses to ACRO out of his mind, because ultimately, he would come out on top. The machine his scientists had just completed would ensure that.

Ahead, what appeared to be a run-down feeding station stood against the backdrop of a rocky hill. As he eased his mount to a stop, he heard the low buzz of an engine, and a motorcycle topped the ridge and dropped down, arriving near the rear of the feed shack.

Alek dismounted as Jordan, one of Itor's most powerful ex-cedosapiens, cut the engine. "Sylvia's plane landed. She has confirmation from our contact in London. The operation is a go."

"Excellent." Alek checked his watch. In exactly ninety-six hours and ten minutes, London would be rendered a ghost town, as the first phase of Itor's plan for world domination went into effect. "Has Phoebe bothered to check in?"

"No word from her."

Damn. She'd fallen off the grid, which wasn't unusual, but right now, when Itor was so close to striking a major blow to Western governments, she should be here. Phoebe wouldn't want to miss it. And truth be told, he didn't want her to miss it. She'd put so much work into the project, had worked side by side with him, and it had felt . . . good . . . to share something this important with his daughter.

He'd seen potential in her from the day he'd brought her home from Japan, but he'd despised Melanie and her weak, soft nature so much that for a long time, it had been hard to see through that to Phoebe. Eventually, Phoebe's strength had broken through the wall, and gradually, he'd become fond of her. As the years passed, he'd learned to love her, and that was something he never thought would happen with anyone.

A childhood spent in Ukrainian orphanages and on the streets had nearly sucked out his ability to care for anyone or anything other than himself. He'd once been diagnosed as a sociopath, and while he didn't disagree, he also didn't think the term should be applied so negatively.

Being a sociopath had worked for him.

"Put out the word through our satellite offices that she is to contact me immediately."

Jordan nodded. "Yes, sir." Dismissed, he mounted the cycle, and Alek entered the shack, an open lean-to with a hidden wood hatch in the floor.

He lifted it to reveal another hatch, this one metal, with a keypad. Quickly, he entered the code, and with a high-pitched beep, the door popped open. He took the ladder down the passage, where, at the landing thirty feet below, he had to enter another code into another door.

Alek would definitely be happy when they no longer had to hide Itor headquarters from the world. He stalked down the tubelike halls, his cowboy boots clacking on the glossy floor. He passed labs, break rooms, offices, and though everyone nodded in greeting, no one messed with him.

Finally, he made it through the maze of halls to the largest chamber, which housed the machine that would, very shortly, make Itor the most powerful entity on the planet.

Mathis, the physicist in charge of the project, met him at the door. "Are you ready to see the finished product?"

"That's why I'm here. Have you activated the security measures?"

"Not yet, sir. I was waiting for your permission."

Alek nodded. Once the security measures were in place, only he or Phoebe could activate or deactivate the machine, with a drop of their blood. "Do it."

Mathis opened the door and gestured. "This way."

Alek followed the tall German to the 2012 device. The thing was monstrous, filling a chamber the size of a football stadium. At its heart was the Izapa crystal, which Phoebe had procured as the last necessary piece. The thing was designed to capture the radiation that would be funneled toward earth on December 21, 2012, when the Milky Way's dark rift struck the perfect position. The catastrophic effect of that radiation would be devastating to living things, but if the device could capture it, focus it strategically, Alek could destroy only populations he wanted to kill off. He would hold the planet hostage.

He'd be a god.

And now they were ready for a test run. The crystal had been absorbing and collecting the less powerful radiation that occurred naturally on a daily basis, and now they had enough stored to fire at one city. London had drawn the short straw.

By this time next week, the world was going to be a very different place.

Mel came to in a room that was shaking. Stryker was next to her, teeth bared, that familiar expression of hatred on his face.

"Stryker," she gasped. "Stop."

He blinked, and almost instantly, the shaking ceased. "Mel?"

She tried to stand . . . but she was wrapped like a mummy and chained to another seat. "Guess you had to scare Phoebe?"

"Yep."

The man sitting at the desk scrubbed his hand over his face. "Couldn't have done it without bringing the building down?"

"It's still standing."

"Fuck," the man muttered. His gaze cut to hers, and she got the same eerie feeling of familiarity she'd experienced on the plane. "You're Melanie."

It wasn't a question. "Yes. Are you . . . Dev?"

He nodded. "I need to ask you some questions." His words were clipped, hard, and she had a feeling Phoebe had pushed him to his limit of tolerance.

She glanced at Stryker, who inclined his head, reassuring her. "You might not have long. Phoebe will want out soon."

"That's fine," Dev said. "I'm having you transferred to a fireproof cell in a few minutes. It's basically a big stone chamber. That's where you'll stay while you're here."

"Sounds lovely," she muttered.

"Your comfort is the least of my concerns." He flipped open a file of handwritten notes. "While you were sleeping on the plane, Stryker filled me in on everything, well, almost everything"—he shot Stryker an annoyed look that Mel didn't understand—"that happened in Rome, and all he knows about you. So let's cut straight to it."

"Um . . . okay. But did he tell you that I didn't kill your agent? You have to believe me—"

Dev cut her off with a sharp slice of his hand in the air. "I don't have to believe anything. We'll get to the truth, and Akbar will have justice, but right now I need to hear everything you know about Itor and Alek Kharkov."

Mel's sense of self-preservation kicked in, and she steeled herself for negotiations—which she really wasn't good at. "I'll help," she said slowly, "but I want something in return."

"You aren't in any position to make demands."

"I have something you need," she pointed out.

"And I have people who can extract information against your will. So this can go easy or hard. Your choice."

"Dev." Stryker's voice was calm, reasonable, and it made her stomach knot, because it was the kind of tone one would use when trying to talk down a vicious dog. "She wants to help. This isn't Phoebe—"

"If you can't handle this," Dev said sharply, "you can wait outside."

No! She couldn't be stuck in this office alone with a stranger who seemed ready to start pulling out fingernails to get what he wanted.

"Mr. . . . um . . . Dev." Her breath shuddered out of her as she summoned her best argument. "Please. I just want a chance. You have that Rik person who is living here with her other half. I was hoping you could help me. Itor developed a drug that keeps me or Phoebe suppressed . . . so what if you could modify it? Make it so gradually I have control all the time. Or most of the time."

"You're serious."

Stryker slapped the two syringes on Dev's desk. "She's serious."

Mel swallowed, wished she had some water. "Like I was saying, I've been wanting to find you ever since the jungle . . ." Wrong thing to say. Dev's eyes darkened, and storm clouds rolled in on Stryker's face. "Um . . . I just thought we could help each other."

For a long moment, Dev sat there. Finally, he nodded. "Okay, I'll play. We'll see what we can do for you. Now, where is Itor's main base?"

Oh, not so fast. She didn't doubt that Dev would research the suppressant drug, but she did doubt that it would be a priority, and she was pretty confident her life was still in jeopardy once Itor was gone. Somehow, she had to make sure she was safe, and the way to do that was through Stryker. He was her one ally, and if she could stay close to him, she might have a chance to convince Dev and everyone else that she wasn't a danger to them.

"I'll tell you, but I'm not telling you everything. Not all at once."

"We don't have time to fuck around," Dev snapped, "and I won't play games with you."

"All I want is to not be locked in that cell."

"Not negotiable."

Desperation was a buzz in her head, and she felt her icy gift start to spread through her marrow. *Calm down.* The last thing she needed was to drop a display of uncontrolled power, which would only reinforce Dev's position.

"If I use the suppression drug, I can promise you that Phoebe won't come out. I could use it during the day, and then at night go to the cell and release her. That'll mean she'll only be using our body at night, and she'll be exhausted, so she'll sleep for a lot of it, which means you won't have to deal with her as much."

"I said no." Dev's voice was tight, the set of his mouth even tighter. He wasn't going to budge, but she couldn't stop pushing.

"Stryker could keep track of me. Phoebe is terrified of his power, so you'd never have to worry about her somehow breaking loose. I just . . . if you lock me up, you could forget about me. Not bring me food. I can't do it."

Dev shoved to his feet. "This goddamned conversation is over."

"Please." She couldn't be stuck in a tiny little cave made of stone, with nothing to do and no one to talk to while she sat around waiting either to be tortured or to die. And what if she got hungry? Stryker said they wouldn't use what she'd said against her, but . . . God, she'd been stupid to say anything.

"What part of *no* are you having trouble with?"

"The no part," she snapped. "Even Itor let me have an apartment."

He went taut as a bowstring. "Do not compare us to Itor."

The battle was lost, and she knew it. With nothing left to lose, she didn't bother to contain her temper—or her power. The temperature in the room dropped at least forty degrees.

"Why not? You're going to keep me in a stone cell, force information out of me, and probably kill me when you're done. From where I'm sitting—all tied up—the comparison is right on."

Dev hit a button on his desk. "Security team, get her out of here." He jabbed a finger at Stryker as men burst through the door. "You. Take a seat."

Melanie didn't fight the men when they hauled her from the chair and out the door. She should have known that Phoebe would poison Dev against her. Maybe Stryker was still on her side, but at this point, she was afraid to hope.

CHAPTER
Eleven

Devlin remained standing—as always—and Stryker tried not to squirm in his chair like an errant schoolboy.

The first time he'd been summoned to this office, the pose had been the same, only it had been Devlin's father looking at him sternly and Stryker had been seven years old. His temper had set off a minor earthquake that managed to swallow up a small auditorium, which, thankfully, had been empty at the time.

Stryker now knew that the man had been Devlin's adoptive father. A fact that shook him to the core, only because Devlin was nothing like Itor's leader. It certainly proved the nature-versus-nurture theory Devlin was always so ferociously preaching.

He wondered how long Devlin had known about Alek, wanted to ask him, but Devlin wasn't in the mood to answer Stryker's questions. No, Dev had crossed his arms in his I'm-waiting-so-let's-give-this-your-best-shot-at-an-explanation-before-I-rip-you-a-new-one pose.

God, this was going to hurt.

Some guys got off on being in constant trouble. Stryker wasn't one of them. "I like Mel."

There, nice and goddamned fucking lame.

"Gee, I hadn't noticed," Dev said.

"You never said sex was off-limits on this job," he snapped, and then realized with a stunning clarity that he'd slept with the boss's sister. See, that was almost enough to make him light-headed, if the anger at being kept in the dark about the exact nature of this mission didn't break through. "And how long have you known that your father is the head of I?"

Devlin's stance didn't change, nor did his expression. "I didn't think you needed a checklist before a mission this danger-ous. You didn't have the clearance to know about Alek—and the information you've learned goes no further than this room."

"How are you going to keep Phoebe's mouth shut?"

"Since you seem to know Mel so intimately, I guess that's your job," Dev snarled.

"You have to make sure Phoebe doesn't come out. Don't you get it, Dev? I still want that bitch dead. But Mel . . ." He shook his head. "No one deserves what she's been through."

"Is it true Phoebe's afraid of your power?"

"Yes. She ran away from me in the Amazon after I started an earthquake. She got so scared she retreated her personality and let Mel come out. That's when I first met her, although at the time I thought she was just a damned good actress."

Dev narrowed his eyes. "You understand how much is riding on your ability to tell them apart."

"Of course I do. And I do know her better than anyone." Maybe even better than she knew herself, if that was possible.

"If you take this on—"

"I am taking this on," Stryker interrupted. As he got up, the walls began to shake and he stood toe-to-toe with Dev, and yeah, bad idea, because Devlin's temper flamed as effectively as Phoebe's.

Within seconds, Dev slammed against him, pinning him to

the wall with a surprising strength for a man who wasn't an ex-cedo. "Shut it down and listen to me, you dumbshit. You got too close. Sex on the job works when it's for intel. You got your intel and you continued screwing around with a woman who is the enemy."

Stryker remained with Devlin's arm across his windpipe, knowing full well he was putting his life in Dev's hands. "Phoebe is the enemy, Mel isn't. Don't you dare insinuate that I insulted Akbar's memory," he croaked.

"I didn't do anything of the sort," Dev said quietly as the pressure increased on Stryker's throat. "I guess that was your guilty conscience whispering in your ear."

"Fuck you, Devlin." Stryker growled the words through gritted teeth because it was better than breaking down again. Doing so once—and in Mel's arms, no less—was enough.

"If you're unsure at all about Melanie—"

"I'm not."

Devlin's nostrils flared, but he didn't say anything else when he moved away to let Stryker breathe again.

Stryker coughed, drew in a full breath, and then pushed away from the wall. Devlin spoke before Stryker had a chance to say anything.

"Obviously, Melanie has trouble controlling her temper flares as well," Dev commented. "You seem to know about that."

Stryker ignored the well-deserved dig. "Phoebe knows how to control her powers. Mel doesn't. She can shoot and score, but she can't stop herself from using it all up in one or two shots. She improved in a short amount of time—and under pressure—when she helped us escape from the underground prison in Rome, but she'll need a lot of training before she's consistent."

"Then you'll work with her in a safe location. You can teach her as well as anyone. And you can practice your self-control at the same time," Devlin said. "I realize that her powers pulled at your elementalist side, but now that you recognize the problem, you can fight it. How long does it take her to recharge her powers?"

"Twenty-four to forty-eight hours for a full recharge, although with every hour, she gets a little stronger."

"But there's a way she can charge fully—and fast—right?" Dev asked. "One you've gotten a little too much pleasure out of."

"Yes." Stryker wasn't about to give the man any more fodder.

"Since she won't need to recharge her powers quickly, she can let it happen the old-fashioned way—with time and rest. Better that we never have her at full charge anyway, correct?"

Stryker felt himself tense, knowing this was—and would continue to be—a giant test of his self-control. Already he was uncertain, but Devlin was leaving him no room for choice.

Still, he didn't answer and Devlin didn't push. The man would simply assume that an order given was an order followed.

"If what Melanie's saying is true—that she wants a chance at a new life with ACRO—she'll play an integral part in Itor's takedown." Dev's gaze drilled into Stryker, as if daring him to argue. "We have a once-and-for-all shot at destroying them. We need to take that opportunity. But she has to know she's putting her life on the line, no matter which agency she chooses. She might not make it out of this alive."

"None of us might," Stryker added. "And we're all still willing."

"That's good to hear." Dev paused. "The science lab will verify and reproduce the shots Melanie brought with her. Check on them in the morning. For tonight, let Melanie sleep off Phoebe in the cave. You can pick her up tomorrow, take her to medical for some tests I want done, and then keep her with you until nightfall. She's not to leave your sight for any reason."

Stryker nodded. "I'm sorry, Devlin. Learning about her must've been hard."

When Devlin didn't answer, Stryker took that as a sign he'd been dismissed. He was at the door when Devlin spoke again.

"Stryker?"

Stryker didn't turn around—didn't want to—but he paused with his hand on the doorknob. "Yes?"

"For the record, Akbar would be damned proud of you for trying to help an agent in need."

Stryker rested his forehead on the door frame and closed his eyes. "Would he forgive me, though?"

"He'd tell you that you need to forgive yourself first."

"Easier said than done," he mumbled, and heard Devlin saying "I know that too" as Stryker exited the office.

"You're pushing too hard."

Dev gritted his teeth as he pushed the weight bar off his chest, an inhuman sound escaping his throat. "You saying I'm old?"

"You're not young." Ender cocked an eyebrow. "What are you trying to prove—that you could take down Itor all by yourself if you wanted?"

"Yes." Dev grunted out another rep with a weight Ender could no doubt lift with his dick, his arms shaking so badly the bar only made it halfway before it began to come down toward his chest.

"'Kay, s'long as we're clear on you setting realistic goals." Ender leaned over as the weight forced the bar to crush Dev's throat. "Want me to take that now, big guy?"

"Fuck. You."

"I'll leave that to your young man," Ender said with a smile, and, yes, Dev would find a way to make the excedo pay. Having children had only made the man more of an asshole, if that was even possible—and Ender seemed to relish the title.

Ender took the bar off him, finally, and Dev lay there limp, panting. "Get the fuck out of here. Now."

At least Ender knew to quit when he was ahead, sauntered out of the semi-private excedo gym as if he didn't have a care in the world. Devlin remained prone, catching his breath and stewing about what lay ahead.

He had Alek's daughter in his possession. Whether or not Alek knew—or suspected—was a subject of much debate among the psychics at ACRO. They were hard at work, as was the IT department, trying to figure out if there was chatter about Alek's missing prodigy.

Stryker believed in Melanie, enough to agree to shadow her. Devlin couldn't read either Phoebe or Melanie's mind, a fact that bothered him immensely. He'd lied to Phoebe when he said he could read her, but truth was he'd have to rely on his other senses to see if he was being bullshitted.

He scrubbed his face with his palms and wished his plan was taking better shape. He'd always been good at coordinating strike attacks—it was one of his strengths. He wasn't sure if he was simply too close to the target this time . . . but something was off.

He was about to get up and head to the showers when Gabriel strolled in, wearing sweats and a tank top, and Devlin wanted nothing more than to fuck him, right on this bench. His reaction to the boy was that instantaneous.

Gabe stopped short when he saw Devlin. "I thought this gym was for the excedos only." Yes, Gabe was still pissed, even though he sported an erection as hard as Devlin's own.

"Excedos and the man who runs the place," Devlin pointed out, and Gabe shrugged like that didn't impress him at all.

Correction, Devlin's job didn't impress him—not in a starfucker kind of way. Devlin knew that Gabe wasn't with him because of who he was.

Actually, these days, Dev had to admit he wasn't sure why Gabriel was with him at all. Marlena was right—Dev hadn't given him much reason to hang in there, beyond the sex.

"That still doesn't answer the question," Gabe pointed out.

Breathe, Devlin. Just breathe and keep your temper. "I was training with Ender."

"You could've asked me, you know."

He could have. Probably, he should have. "I didn't think you were speaking to me."

"You don't ask me for anything even when we are speaking."

"Christ, when did you turn into a girl?"

Yes, that certainly did it. Gabriel punched the wall, collapsing the cement in a nice, round circle and proving he was not a girl, and then he left, stalking out in a way that made Dev horny.

Gabriel always made him horny. All the training, the testosterone, was just making Dev want him more. Want it more.

"What are you going to do, order him to come back?" he muttered to himself.

"You could try asking."

Dev shot up, because that was Oz's voice. And when his dead lover finally deigned to talk to him, Dev was sure as hell going to listen.

That didn't mean he was going to take Oz's shit lying down. "Fuck you, Oz. What? You want to watch?"

"I do, sometimes."

"Asshole," Devlin muttered, still refusing to turn around to the place Oz's voice was coming from.

"You never minded that," Oz said. "And you're really fucking things up."

"Thanks for pointing out my shortcomings. Always a pleasure to have you visit."

"I sent Gabriel to you because that's the way it was always meant to be. I can't force things to happen, but I can move them along in the right direction," Oz told him. "But Gabriel's meant to be here, at ACRO, as more than just your lover. You know that. And you're holding back, hurting yourself and him and ACRO, by not sharing information because you're embarrassed by your heritage, and you're afraid he'll be repulsed enough to leave you. You're holding him at arm's length to protect *yourself*. Not him."

"Why are you lecturing me?"

"I'm not telling you anything your own conscience hasn't, Devlin. That was quite a pot-calling-the-kettle-black conversation you had with Stryker earlier."

Devlin turned to see Oz sitting on one of the weight benches in his black leather, looking completely real and not at all corporeal.

Goddammit, he hated that Oz knew him so well.

"I know. It's why you don't want Gabe to know you—why you keep shoving him away. But when I'm gone, who's going to call you on your shit?"

Gone? "What do you mean gone?"

"Ah, Dev, come on. We've known each other too long to play games. I'm not hanging around forever. I'm not part of a soul posse. I bought some extra time, but that's all." Oz's voice was gentle but his words weren't. "Gabe's a big part of your plan. Tell him everything. Let him help you."

Dev turned away. "How is he going to help me?"

"You'd be surprised what happens when you let someone inside, Devlin. But you already knew that."

When Devlin turned around with a retort, Oz was gone.

CHAPTER
Twelve

Stryker could keep track of me . . . Phoebe is terrified of his power.

Melanie had asked for him. Wanted to be with him. And he was fully aware that this could all be a well-executed plan to cut his balls off and take ACRO down from the inside.

Could be. But it wasn't.

Going over all of it in his mind made Stryker sleep restlessly, if he could even call what he did sleep. Frustrated, he threw the covers on the floor and paced around his house on the west side of the ACRO compound, the one he'd moved into when he'd turned twenty-four and completed his first solo mission. He'd lived here ever since, in the three-bedroom, two-story house with the big deck and the hot tub and various other amenities he'd put in over the years.

There was no need to ready a guest room. Dev had all but ordered Stryker to stay with Mel, which meant if she needed a nap she would sleep in his bed and he would stay in a chair watching her.

The thought of being around her and letting her arouse him

by using her powers made his throat tighten. It wasn't that he wasn't used to keeping a tight rein on himself . . . but something about Mel stirred him in a way that seemed to make control impossible.

What if control *was* impossible around her? Was he supposed to choose between fucking and an earthquake that could take out the compound?

Thinking about sex while knowing he couldn't have sex was making him too damned grumpy. He watched TV for a while. Used the weight room at two A.M. and saw Gabe slam in a few minutes later.

Guess Dev was still pissed as hell and Gabe was bearing the brunt of it, from the way he viciously slammed the weights around.

Stryker had been doing his own slamming, trying to get rid of the nervous and angry energy that had built up over the past hours. The two men wordlessly spotted each other through a brutal workout and then Gabriel went for a run, while Stryker used the sauna and showered.

Sometime after six, he grabbed breakfast to go from the cafeteria and headed to the fireproof cave they'd locked Mel in last night.

Mel, because he refused to think of her as the same person as fire-bitch. They might share one body but they were two completely separate people.

He moved past security by showing his ID—Devlin had put his name on the list and the guard had been waiting for him.

Stryker walked up to the stone structure, which was fronted by a single fireproof pane of glass.

She was sleeping. They'd kept her in the fireproof blanket for safekeeping, which couldn't have been comfortable all night. When she woke, she'd be Mel, and she'd be looking for him.

"I'm taking her with me," Stryker told the guard. "I just need to wake her up and make sure everything's fine before you open the door."

He looked through the window and tapped lightly. Mel's eyes opened and she looked around, half startled. He tapped again and she looked up and saw his face through the glass, gave an unabashed smile before she pulled it back.

The natural, unguarded reaction tugged at him.

"You can open it now," he told the guard, who still hesitated. "Give me the keys and I'll do it."

The guard did as he asked. Stryker couldn't blame the guy for worrying about being deep fried—Phoebe's threats had been detailed and extreme.

Stryker unlocked the heavy door and pulled it open. Mel watched him enter the room as she struggled to sit up with the weight of the blanket around her.

"Are you all right?" he asked.

"Phoebe took over a few minutes after I got here, so I don't remember much. I'm fine, though." She paused. "Do you have the shots I need?"

"We're going to pick them up from medical when I take you there for some tests. But we'll do that after you eat breakfast," he said, and saw her face light again.

"You mean—I can leave here, go with you?"

He stood over her. "Devlin agreed. And now my ass is on the line, Mel."

"I understand."

"I hope you do. Because I'll be put down if this gets out of hand." He undid the lock around the fireproof blanket and pointed to the narrow doorway that led to the bathroom. She practically ran there, the poor thing, and when she came out, she looked much calmer.

He motioned for her to follow him out, which she did. The guards kept their distance and Stryker motioned for her to sit at the table outside the cave, next to him, where he'd laid out her food.

She didn't hesitate, dug into the breakfast enthusiastically.

"We'll grab more on the way back from medical," he told her

after seeing her demolish the eggs and bacon and pancakes. He remembered how she was on the plane at the thought of not being allowed to eat—he never wanted her to feel that fear again. She nodded, leaned back for a second with her hands over her tummy as if letting everything digest.

"After that?"

"We'll go to my house," he said, more gruffly than he intended to. "Let's get moving."

As they walked out of the security section and through the compound, Mel was brimming with questions. Innocent ones about the different units, and the different badges on the BDUs, but every answer he gave could arm Phoebe, so he was careful.

Once at the medical facility, he waited while Mel was run through a battery of tests—MRI, EEG, blood draws . . . all of which she handled without a single complaint. Afterward, they headed to the pharmacy.

"Everyone seems . . . happy," she said as they sat in a small room, waiting for the injections to keep Phoebe at bay.

"Well, not all the time, but yeah, this is a really cool place," he agreed.

"When did they recruit you?" she asked, but before he could answer, the cool voice of the nurse interrupted.

"Stryker was born here." The nurse, Kylie, smiled at Stryker as she handed him the bag full of hypodermics. "We think we successfully duplicated the formula, but you might want to be alert after the first injection to be sure it works. This is a week's supply. Just call me if you need more—you know my number. Make sure to inject her every—"

"I know when to give myself the shots," Mel said, slipping Stryker a sweet smile—and okay, then, this was . . . weird. "Come on, I'm hungry."

She tugged his hand possessively, with an assurance that made Kylie turn away with a pout.

They walked along, hand in hand, to the caf.

"An old girlfriend?" she asked.

"Not exactly," he muttered, and she didn't press it. He wondered if it was bad that her possessiveness turned him on, so much so that he found himself fantasizing about stripping her of her clothes and taking her in an open field.

Well, it was bad since he was forbidden to take her clothes off at all. Fuck. He took his hand out of hers to open the door to the caf and followed her inside.

"Those are the men from the plane," she said, right before they got in line, and yes, Ender and Wyatt and Avery had strolled in together, no doubt fresh from a debriefing. "I'm sure they're okay guys."

"Wyatt is. I don't know Avery well, but Ender's an asshole and really proud of it," he told her. "Grab your food to go. We'll make a trip to the store later . . . if you can cook."

"I can," she said with a touch of playfulness in her voice that suited her. "I don't mind playing with that kind of fire."

The last time Mel had been happy was when she was a little girl, living in Japan with her mother. Somehow, Greta had given Mel a normal existence—at least, as normal as possible, given the circumstances.

"You have a great gift," her mother had said, and though she sounded wistful and sad, there had been a spark of hope in her green eyes. "You must always fight for yourself. Even if all your fighting is done behind the scenes, prepare yourself for the day when you can break free and chase your dreams."

Mel hadn't understood what Greta was saying at the time, but at some point in her teens, when she finally realized that her father would never love her and that he and Itor wanted only to use her, she decided to spend her moments of control doing something for herself. Thanks to her mother, she truly believed she could be happy.

"I lost my powers, but I'm free. I always had a backup plan."

Mel had always had a backup plan too. Which was why she'd

taken college courses when she could. Why, when she'd finally had the opportunity, she'd tried to find people who could help her.

And now she was with them. Oh, she wasn't dumb enough to believe she was completely off the hook; they needed her, would use her, and if Phoebe pissed them off, they might kill her. But right now, she had a chance to prove herself useful.

And to breathe easy, if only for a little while.

Stryker took her to his house, which was on the outskirts of this amazing base, where people seemed so . . . content. Sure, they'd thrown some harsh words in her direction, but she could handle both those and the hateful looks. She understood them, but if Stryker could come around, so would they, in time.

Stryker's house was bigger than she'd expected, and a typical bachelor pad. There were clothes draped over chairs, a few dishes in the sink, and when she wandered into the bedroom, she found the bed unmade.

Looked like he'd had a rough night. Or like he'd had a woman in there.

The thought made her queasy. All that breakfast she'd inhaled stirred in her stomach, and she rushed for the sliding glass door that led to a remarkable deck outside.

"Hey," he said. "What's wrong?"

"Nothing." She looked out at the trees behind his house. "This is all a little overwhelming." And she really could use a shower and a chance to brush her teeth. She watched him brace his forearms on the railing and stare out into the woods. "Do you share this house . . . I mean, do you have a, um, girlfriend?"

He snorted. "No. And could you maybe dial it down a little?"

For a moment, she frowned, and then she realized her power was seeping out, and a skin of frost was forming on the railing beneath her hands.

"Dammit. Sorry. I've never been like this." Then again, she'd rarely been in situations that emotionally compromised her. She spent the majority of her days locked in one of Phoebe's residences with no contact with anyone other than the odd Itor person.

"We'll work on it after you get a chance to eat and clean up."

"So you're going to be my trainer? Is there anyone else here who can work with ice? Or fire?"

He swung around to her, braced his hip on the railing, and crossed his arms over his chest. "We have some pyrokinetics, yes. But none are as powerful as Phoebe. And we don't have anyone who can work with ice. That's an extremely rare ability."

"No wonder my father worked so hard to get me to come on board with Itor. Well, that and the fact that I used to be the dominant personality."

"When was this, exactly?"

"From birth. I had complete control for twenty hours a day. Phoebe couldn't barge in no matter what until about the eighteenth hour. There has always been a two-hour period where whoever is in control weakens, and we have to fight to stay. And then, once that period is up, the other person comes out, and they can retreat only voluntarily."

"So what happened to make Phoebe dominant?"

She shrugged. "Itor. I told you that after my mom died, we were taken there. Once Alek figured out that I was useless to them and that Phoebe was more than willing to sell her soul, they developed the drug that allowed her more time in our body. By giving her tiny amounts, and by making my life hell so I didn't *want* to be in control, they gradually lengthened the amount of time she was out. Took a couple of years, but eventually she was able to keep control for twelve hours without the drug. She still needs it to hold on longer, but yeah . . . she's worked her way from four hours to twelve."

"Which is why you mentioned to Dev that you wanted help getting to the point where you were in control most of the time."

"Exactly. Because it used to be that way, and I know it can again. And," she said with a smile, "Itor is developing some sort of weapon or device or something that can destroy a pyrokinetic's ability permanently. It's meant to be used against the enemy. I only know about it because I saw some paperwork that Phoebe left out in our apartment. If ACRO can get hold of that, we could render Phoebe harmless."

Stryker's breath hitched. "Why didn't you say something sooner?"

Guilt made her skin tighten. "I probably should have. But I can't spill everything. I trust *you*. But your people all want me dead, so I need to have some sort of insurance policy."

"Shit." He thrust his fingers through his hair, and then suddenly, she was in his arms and he was holding her tight. "You shouldn't have to fear for your life in good-guy territory. This is bullshit."

"It's okay," she whispered. "I understand. Your boss has to do what's necessary to protect his people . . . and pretty much the entire world."

Stryker pulled back, just a little, so she had to look up to see his face. His palm cupped her cheek. "You're remarkable."

Hardly. But she didn't argue. "Do you . . . do you still see the woman who killed your friend when you look at me?" Probably a stupid question, one that would totally ruin the mood, and when his eyes darkened, her heart sank.

"How's this for an answer?" His voice was a husky murmur, his body hard as he hauled her against him and put his lips to hers.

Instantly, her body flared to life. She kissed him back, aggressively, hungrily, and she felt his surprise in the hitch in his breath. No, she wasn't letting him take the lead this time.

Their tongues met, swirling and tangling together as his hand lifted to cup her breast. She nearly sobbed at the exquisite sensation that fired hotter when he squeezed gently while nibbling at her lower lip. Tiny, stinging bites met delicate, feathery caresses and sent curls of honeyed pleasure through her veins.

Somehow, Stryker had taken command of the kiss after all, his skilled mouth and hands distracting her from her own goal . . . which had been to show him how much she wanted him. All the intimacy before had been about need in the face of danger. This was about want.

She let him know with a rolling grind of her pelvis against his. A hum of appreciation broke from his lips, and his hand dropped to the curve of her butt to press her more fully against his arousal.

"Stryker," she murmured against his lips. "Make love to me."

A low, throaty groan dredged up from his chest. "You want me?"

She arched against him, practically begging for it. "Yes."

"You want my cock inside you?" His kisses drifted up her cheek to her ear. "Right here? Now?"

She shuddered with desire as his words turned to erotic pictures in her head. "God, yes."

His mouth captured hers again, his kiss turning desperate, hot. Aching for him, she slipped her hands between their bodies and fumbled with the button on his BDUs. And then, abruptly, he pushed away with a curse. "I can't. I'm sorry, Mel, but . . ."

Dazed, she stepped back awkwardly, and his hand shot out to catch her elbow. She jerked away, her unslaked lust mixing with confusion to create a caustic mood. "It's okay to have sex with me when you need to, but not when you want to? Or maybe you don't want to?"

Stryker tensed, becoming a wall of taut muscle as he whirled to slam his palms down on the wood railing. "Trust me," he said hoarsely. "I want to."

She eased up behind him and touched his shoulder. "Then why can't you? Is it because you're worried about what your friends will think? No one needs to know."

"I'll know." Dev's deep voice from behind her put a knot in her gut. Both she and Stryker swung around to face ACRO's boss and another man beside him.

"Dammit, Dev," Stryker growled. "You could have knocked."

"And you could have answered your cell. Oh, wait—you

couldn't, because your tongue was down Melanie's throat." As Mel's face heated, Dev turned to her and gestured to the dark-haired man standing next to him. "This is Ryan Malmstrom. He was a spy inside Itor for a while, but the information he's got is spotty. I was hoping we could ask you some questions, and between the two of you, we can get some holes filled."

Still hot-faced and stinging with embarrassment, she agreed, and they all sat at the patio table. Stryker brought out some beers and chips and salsa, but somehow, what looked like a relaxed atmosphere . . . wasn't. She felt like a mouse dining with cats. At least Stryker sat down next to her, and she slid him a grateful smile.

"First," Dev said, "I need to know where all Itor bases are."

She took a handful of chips and covertly pulled the bowl a little closer. Blue corn, her favorite. "I'm not sure I can identify all of them, but I can tell you what I know."

Ryan slapped some papers on the table and clicked a pen. "Go."

"There's a large base in Kiev. A major station on some island in the Pacific. Smaller offices in Madrid, Rome, Gaborone, Botswana, Karachi, Pakistan, and Tokyo."

There was a fierce intensity in Ryan's brown eyes as he unfolded a large sheet of paper and pushed a blueprint at her. Revenge, she thought. He wanted revenge for something, and though she couldn't be sure, she didn't think Akbar's death was all of it.

"Which facility is this?" he asked.

Frowning, she traced her finger over the lines. Some of the areas were marked—laboratories, living quarters, etc., but many were followed by a question mark. "I don't get to see inside the facilities very often . . ."

Her finger began to shake as it went over one of the rooms. Alek's office, which held nothing but bad memories . . . and her blood. As if Stryker knew how much she'd hated every second in that room, his palm came down on her back and rubbed in slow, soothing strokes. Dev's keen gaze didn't miss the gesture, but it was impossible to tell whether he approved or disapproved. And when Stryker's eyes met Dev's, instant tension flared up, as if Stryker was daring his boss to say anything.

"It's the Australia compound," she said quickly, hoping to disperse the friction in the air. "Headquarters. How do you have this?"

"When I was inside Itor, I was able to pull up some vague blueprints, but none of them were labeled." Ryan twisted the cap off his beer. "From memory, I've put this together, but since I was only inside one—the island compound—I didn't know which this belonged to. Is it accurate?"

"Mostly." She popped a chip in her mouth.

"What can you tell us about it?" Dev's voice was firm, as if he expected her to answer, and she supposed he had every right, seeing how he'd given her everything she'd asked for.

"Do you have a map of Australia?" While Ryan pulled a laptop computer out of his bag and fired it up, she munched on a couple more chips and followed them with a swig of beer before she continued. "It's in the middle of nowhere, disguised as a sheep station. A sheep ranch. It's a profitable enterprise, run entirely by Itor personnel. There are barns, a huge house, outbuildings, all of which are part of the ranch, but are also used for Itor business and housing agents. The main Itor facility itself is underground."

Stryker let out a low whistle. "Damn. No wonder we were never able to find it."

"We assumed there was no true headquarters," Dev said. "We were looking more at the multiple facilities as heads on a hydra."

Mel nodded. "Alek does make sure that agents and resources are spread throughout the facilities so that if one is taken down, Itor isn't crippled. But if you struck the Australia compound and maybe one or two of the others simultaneously, you'll wreck them." She fingered the computer screen until she found the area she was looking for. "Here. There's a town twenty miles from the ranch. It would be a ghost town if not for Itor. There's a gas station, a small store, a pub, and a diner. On the outskirts are a few houses. Phoebe keeps a residence there. We could use her place as a stage."

Dev appeared to consider that, his gaze shifting between the map and her. "Can you get us inside the facility?"

"I'll have to pretend to be Phoebe . . . but yes, I can do it. And if you can convince her that I'm not giving up information, she'll be easier for you to handle, and we might be able to trick her into cooperating."

Dev exchanged glances with Stryker, and she recognized the look. He was wondering if he could trust her, or if she could be leading them into a trap. She nearly kissed Stryker when he gave Dev a single, fierce nod.

"Tell me about Alek," Dev said. Commanded, really. "What's he like?"

"Ruthless. Cold. Scary." Sort of like Dev, actually, except people seemed to respect Dev more than fear him.

"Does he travel much?"

"I don't know. I've rarely seen him outside headquarters. I think he doesn't like to leave."

"Is he married? Kids?"

"I don't think he's ever been married." She pulled the bowl of chips even closer, since no one but her was eating them. "No kids except me and Phoebe that I know of."

Dev cocked his head, and she squirmed under his penetrating gaze. "What's your favorite food?"

She blinked at the sudden change of subject. "Food?"

"Yes. What do you like to eat?" He glanced at the nearly empty bowl and his tone became laced with wry amusement. "Besides tortilla chips."

"I . . . ah . . . love pasta. And hamburgers. And pizza and ice cream. Chocolate ice cream. Hate fruit-flavored ice creams, but I'll eat them if I have to. And I love donuts." Oh, God, she was so rambling, but food got her all excited. More than a coping mechanism after the years of starvation, it truly had been one of the few joys in her life, one of the rare pleasures in which she could indulge. She loved to eat. "Do you have a donut place nearby? One that makes good crullers? Because it's really hard to find good crullers."

"I love crullers," Dev murmured. "And I hate fruit ice cream. And walnuts."

"Me too!" She smiled, and was shocked to see one corner of Dev's generous mouth tip up too. "And strawberries. I love them, but they make my lips swell."

"They do the same to me," he said softly.

"I've never met anyone else who had a reaction like that." She shrugged. "But I haven't met many people. And it's not like when I do meet them I ask if they have an allergic reaction to strawberries." Really, could she ramble any more? No, not likely. But Dev made her nervous, while at the same time he made her feel like she *should* be comfortable. It was an odd combination, and really unsettling.

Dev stared at her for so long that once again, she began to squirm. Finally, he stood, and Ryan with him. "I'm having some clothes and toiletries delivered for you. If there's anything else you need, Stryker will handle it."

He left, and she breathed a huge sigh of relief as she sank back against Stryker's chest. It was weird to have someone to lean on, even weirder to have them circle their arms around you and hold tight because they knew you needed it.

"I can see why he's your boss," she muttered.

"Why's that?"

"Because," she said, as she stared at Dev's empty chair, "something about him reminds me a little of Alek."

Mel's life history nearly broke Stryker's heart. He knew a lot of the men and women at ACRO had shitty family backgrounds, but watching Mel struggle to talk about her food issues on the plane . . . that had almost been too much for him.

Hearing that Devlin was like Alek was probably the scariest thing he'd heard in a long time—and in some way, the most comforting. They'd be an even match. But Devlin needed to be better than Alek.

Stryker thought on that while Mel showered and dressed in the jeans and T-shirt Dev had sent over. When she finished, he allowed himself an indulgent, admiring gaze before speaking. "We should go practice now. Devlin wants me to help you try to control your power."

"I'd like that."

He collected a few things covertly—including the fire blanket, plus a couple of injections—and they drove over to a spot a few miles from his house.

It was a perfect area—a big field with a small waterfall on one side.

She smiled when she saw it. "It's so pretty. Is this ACRO property?"

"Yes. We do a lot of impromptu training here." He looked around—it was early afternoon, which left them plenty of time to work. "It's quiet today, which is good."

They got out of the SUV and walked a couple of yards to a spot that was close enough to some trees.

"Do you really think I can gain control of my power?" she asked.

"Yeah, I do. And you get to practice, which is great. With my power, I couldn't really practice, you know?"

"Ah, that's true."

"When I was younger, I had to learn control fast. If I didn't, I'd kill people. That's how it was explained to me, and you know, I got it together fast."

"That's a lot of guilt to put on a kid."

"A dangerous kid," he corrected her. "Let's try this with you aiming for those trees. They're used to upstate New York winters. They can take it, if you don't go full force with the ice."

"If I do, I'll be out of my power anyway. But you can help me get it back quickly, right?" she asked, the shy note in her voice matching the pink in her cheeks.

He put his head down and said, "I can't. I'm under direct orders not to touch you like that."

"From who?"

"Devlin."

"Is that why he seemed so angry when he walked in on us kissing?" she asked, and he nodded. "So it's not about keeping me a secret from your friends?"

"What? No—not at all. I don't give a shit who knows I like you, that I'm dying to kiss you. That I'd take you right here in the middle of the damned field if I could."

She inhaled a shaky breath. "It's because I could be the enemy, isn't it? No one wants to risk a breach of security."

"Could be. But I think it's part punishment for arming you in the first place. Dev's a strict taskmaster as a boss." And then there was the sister thing, which Stryker didn't want to think about.

She gazed at the copse of trees, and just as he began to wonder where her thoughts had gone, she spoke. "When I engage my power, how exactly does it affect yours?"

"You haven't noticed that when you work your powers, you turn me on?"

She blinked. "Oh. I meant like how it was in the plane, how mine seemed to make yours sort of unpredictable. But now that you say it . . . I'd hoped the turn-on stuff wasn't only my powers . . . but you know . . . forget it."

Damn, this new relationship stuff was hard. No wonder Gabe always looked like his nose was out of joint. "Mel, I'm attracted to you. I would be, whether or not your powers pulled at mine. The arousal isn't what makes me fall for you, okay? The fact that I want to have sex with you when your powers turn me on is an added bonus."

"Really?"

"Yeah, really." He shook his head. Thought about Oz and his damned prediction. Thought about telling Mel what Oz had said and decided against it. "Look, let's just get to work."

"But it's going to be . . . painful for you."

"More so if Devlin finds out I didn't teach you anything," he said. "Just give me a little ice, okay?"

"Yes, sir." She faced the forest. "Brace yourself."

She shot out a blast of ice shards that stripped the bark off a tree, and Jesus, what that would do to a person . . .

She cut herself off as quickly as she could.

It hadn't been quick enough for him, though.

He took a deep breath as the rumble started inside his body, which he tamped down by sheer force of will.

His cock didn't pay any mind, remained obviously rock hard. And painfully so.

"Stryker?"

"Don't worry about me. Try again. Think refrigerator instead of freezer. Think soft-serve ice cream."

"Right. Got it. I'm starving for ice cream now, by the way."

"Concentrate," he said through gritted teeth. Thought about her naked, splayed for him. Thought about driving into her wet heat until she was screaming his name . . . wondered if he could find a place to jerk off where she wouldn't notice.

She was staring at him and he pointed in the direction of the woods. "Ice. Now."

She complied then, sending a cold cone of air whistling toward the trees in a powerful stream that he'd seen kill a man back in Rome.

He nearly doubled over. "Again."

Throwing out her hand, she somehow made snow swirl over the green canopy of trees.

It was like someone was yanking his nuts out of his body through his throat. "Again," he rasped, because said testicles were lodged in his esophagus.

A massive wave of cold coated all the trees in frost.

He was on his knees at this point. He ached—his body was one giant throb of need; this was the most effective torture Devlin could have ever devised for him.

"My powers are almost out."

Thank fucking God. "Keep going."

"I don't want to do this anymore," she murmured. "I'm killing you."

"No one's ever died from blue balls," he said through gritted teeth. "I'll be fine."

"You don't look fine."

Well, no, he wasn't fine at all. And as she let off the last of her icy blasts, his body was rocked with the most painful urges he'd ever felt. He clawed the ground and tried to breathe, looked anywhere but at Mel, and his eyes fell on the waterfall.

His erection was a steel rod and fucking painful. Hell, maybe this would be the best thing for him—a cold shower times a million.

He took off at a dead run, not stopping until he hit the water. Kept going until his body was under the freezing wash and he was shivering.

Bye-bye, erection; hello, hypothermia.

"Stryker—are you okay?" Melanie was asking, from directly in front of him. She'd stripped naked, her skin glistening with crystal water droplets, but she didn't seem affected by the cold at all. Well, her nipples were pert, hard little buds . . . and this wasn't helping anything.

"You'll freeze."

"Um, no. Cold doesn't affect me. At all." She glanced down. "Doesn't appear to be doing you much good either."

"Fuck. Mel, please, just give me a few minutes."

But she was in his arms then, her mouth on his, so damned warm and willing, her legs wrapped around his waist. His body felt right against hers, his body continuing to beg for mercy from his arousal in an all-consuming way, until he couldn't think straight . . . couldn't see straight.

That wasn't from hypothermia either.

Her fingers wound through his wet hair and his hands held her hips, moved them back and forth, wanting nothing more than to be inside of her, right here and now.

But fuck, he couldn't. He promised Devlin, and he did not go back on his word.

He pulled back, rested his forehead against hers. "Sorry, Mel," he said over the slight rushing roar of the water, his voice raw.

"I'm not." Her blond hair was slicked back from her face, accenting how goddamned beautiful she was, her eyes bright and clear. "I won't play a part in torturing you anymore. If we continue to do this, we have to work together, no matter what it takes. And I'll tell Dev that, right after I make you feel better."

"Can't," he said through chattering teeth.

"You have to. It's as much a part of your needs as breathing, Stryker. You can't be expected to fight your nature."

"I have to be strong."

"You are," she told him. "You're the first person not related to me to stick up for me, in the face of your friends and fellow agents. Your boss. If that's not strong, I don't know what is."

He allowed her to lead him out of the water and toward the car. She opened the hatch of his SUV and helped him tug off his clothes. He crawled inside while she started the car and put the heat up to full blast. And then she got in, shut the hatch, and cuddled next to him.

She grabbed the fire blanket, spread it over them, and that, combined with her heat, warmed him. Her kisses covered his neck and then drifted lower as he groaned, and yeah, so much for Dev's order.

Stryker might have been cold at one point, but right now, all Mel felt emanating from him was heat and the promise of raw, erotic sex.

Sunlight streamed through the windows and spread over Stryker's tan skin, highlighting his ropey muscles, chiseled features, and broad warrior build as he reared up over her to adjust their positions in the cramped space. God, he was a sight to behold when he was aroused, and she doubted there was a female alive who wouldn't feel her hormones shift into overdrive if she was in Mel's shoes. Or out of her shoes, as it were.

As the blanket fell away, she caught sight of his cock, jutting upward so the head tapped against his carved abs. She dragged her gaze down, following the thick veins to the tawny nest of springy curls, and then lower, to the heavy sac beneath. She couldn't tear her eyes away, realized that for all the times they'd had sex, she'd never actually taken the time to explore him.

Or taste him.

Stryker shoved one half of the split backseat forward, creating more room, but when he started to lower himself next to her, she gripped his hips and stilled him.

"What are you doing?" His voice was beautifully gruff, and his eyes darkened as she leaned in, mouth watering.

"Something I've never done." She closed her palm around him and caressed, long strokes up and down.

Lowering her head, she put the tip of her tongue to the tip of his cock. His breath hissed, and she loved that. Loved *this*. The texture of his tight skin was like nothing she'd ever had on her tongue, and his flavor was incredible. Clean, yet smoky, and she wanted more.

Slowly, she swirled her tongue over the head of him, and then took the entire cap fully in her mouth. His sharp inhale filled her with satisfaction, and experimentally, she added a little suction.

"Jesus," he moaned. "You said you've never done this before?"

A sudden flare of doubt had her lifting her head. What if she was bad at this? He'd probably been with plenty of women who knew what they were doing, and while the very idea of some other woman doing this to him made her ill, so did the thought that she'd be so inept he wouldn't enjoy it.

"Hey," he said, his hand coming down to pet her hair. "You okay?"

In her palm, his shaft jumped as if complaining about the lack of attention. "I'm fine. But what if I'm terrible at this?"

"Are you fucking kidding me? What you've already done affected me like no one else has."

She melted a little . . . and then went back to her task with a vengeance. The moment her lips slid over his cock again, Stryker groaned, his fist tightening in her hair. He let her play, exploring everything about him, from his flavor to his reactions when she touched different areas or changed the pressure or speed of her strokes.

"That's so good," he breathed, as she dragged the flat of her wet tongue down the underside of his shaft, pausing at the very base to place a lingering kiss there. The sound of his breathing changed, becoming raspier and faster, and when she went even lower with her mouth, his thighs trembled. He liked that.

The knowledge made her smile as she licked him, lapping at the tight skin. Gently, she opened her mouth and sucked one ball inside to bounce it on her tongue, all the while keeping up the fist action.

"Mel," he gasped. "I need to . . . move."

She nodded, and as he started to pump his hips a little, she realized why his thighs had been shaking; he'd been trying to hold still, maybe so he didn't frighten her. Oh, he couldn't do that. Not with sex.

She worked her way back up, fascinated by the way he rolled his hips into her touch, her lips, and when she took him deep in her mouth, the thrust of his pelvis brought the head all the way to the back of her throat.

"Sorry," he rasped. "Fuck . . . better . . . stop." And yet, he continued to pump, and she was fine with that.

Totally fine. She was practically shaking with excitement, and her own arousal had become so consuming that she was rubbing her sex on her heel, working herself to near orgasm.

The SUV rocked with his motions, and she offered up a quick prayer that no one was in the area to see it, especially since, in the afternoon heat, the windows hadn't fogged up.

Shifting because her knees were digging into something lumpy beneath the carpet, Mel gripped the hard globe of Stryker's ass cheek for leverage, increased the tempo of her strokes, and flicked her tongue over his head as she sucked.

"Stop." He tugged on her hair, but no way was she stopping. Instinct told her he was close, and she definitely sensed a change in him. His cock swelled, throbbed, and he even felt hotter.

"Mel . . . shit . . . I'm going to come." He tried to scoot backward, bumping his head on the roof, but she dug her nails into his ass and held him in place. He hissed, and then shouted as his orgasm took him.

Warm, salty fluid jetted into her mouth, and she moaned at his wild, musky essence. The pumping of his hips became jerky and irregular, and she thought maybe it was a sensitivity thing, if men were anything like women. Slowly, she drew her mouth up, sucking the last drops from him as her mouth popped free.

"Damn," he breathed. His head was back, eyes closed, and he was panting as he came down. "Damn." And then his head dropped forward, and the wicked smile on his face made her heart thump with excitement. "Your turn."

Before she could even gasp, he grabbed her, flipped her around and over the back of the seat so she was hanging with her butt in the air. She cried out in surprise, and then she cried out in ecstasy when he spread her thighs and buried his tongue in her sex from behind.

"You're so wet," he said against her, and the vibrations almost set her off. "I love this."

She did too. His tongue plunged in and out of her twice more before he licked her valley from clit to core over and over, never lingering in one place long enough to let her detonate. His thumbs spread her wide, allowing this clever tongue to get everywhere.

"Do you like this?" He swirled his tongue around her entrance. "Do you like the feel of my tongue tasting you? Or . . ." He latched his lips onto her clit and sucked, and she cried out with the beginnings of release. "Do you like me to suck you off?"

"B-both," she gasped.

"Not done with the options," he said. And he proved that by penetrating her with his tongue. "Do you like me to fuck you with my tongue? Or . . ." He put his entire mouth on her core and did some sort of combination lick/flick/suck/swallow that made her scream. "Oh, yeah, you like that. You like it when I go down on you so hard that's all you can feel while I'm swallowing your juices."

He did it again, and this time, he let her have what she wanted. The climax rocked her from her feet to her scalp, and she shouted into the seat as she clawed at the leather. The ripples were seismic waves that set her off again and again, helped along by the lashing of his tongue.

As the fourth climax peaked, he dragged her from over the back of the seat into his lap, impaling her on his cock so her spine was against his chest. He fell back, planting his fists in the carpet as she grabbed the seat and pumped, working herself through the orgasm that was intensified by the scrape of his cock against her sensitive tissues inside.

"Faster, Mel," he breathed. "Fuck me. Fuck me hard."

There was no other choice. Her body demanded more and had no trouble following his order. Her silky arousal coated him until they were gliding like they were on oiled rails, and the wet sounds of skin slapping skin filled the vehicle.

"Yeah, oh . . . *yeah*." His hips came off the floor, bucking her upward so she barely missed banging her head, but it would have been worth the bump. Would have been worth a damned concussion, because as he filled her with hot come, she blasted to another orgasm in an explosion that made her see stars.

Gasping, trembling, she fell back on top of him. His breath sawed in and out as he gathered her in his arms and rolled so they were tucked, spooning, together. Gradually, her thundering heartbeat slowed, and a beautiful, bone-melting exhaustion set in. They'd had some intense sex, but that just beat everything. Because this hadn't been sex of need. This had been sex of *want*, and for the first time, she understood the power of it.

And for the first time, she felt sorry for Phoebe, because Melanie had no doubt that her sister had never known anything so wonderful.

* * *

The stinging tickle in Mel's scalp was what woke her up. She sat up with a startled gasp, unsure where she was, and she jumped when Stryker's hand came down on her leg.

"Hey, you okay?"

She blinked, bringing him into focus as he lay on the floor of the SUV. He'd pulled the blanket over them, and at some point, the sun had gone down, leaving them in dusky twilight.

"Yeah." She scrubbed her hands over her face. "Yeah. I need a shot, though."

He patted the floor behind him and came up with his pants. After digging around in the pockets, he handed her a syringe. Quickly, she injected the contents and snuggled down in the blanket with Stryker again.

"This is nice," she said on a yawn. "I've never done this before."

"Sleep in the back of an SUV?"

"Sleep with a man, silly." She feathered her fingers over his cheekbone, taking what was probably an inordinate amount of pleasure from the simple act. "What was it like to grow up with your family?"

His hand swept up and down her back. "I guess the best way to put it is that no matter what, I always had someone to turn to. My parents were there when I needed them, but they also had the guts to stand back and let me make my own mistakes."

That sounded so . . . perfect. "Where do they live? Are they nearby? Are they like you?"

He smiled fondly. "They're like me. Mom can manipulate water, and my dad is an empath. They're in England right now. Dev sent them to The Aquarius Group in an agency exchange thing. I talk to them about once a week."

"Brothers? Sisters?"

His toes curled against hers playfully, and she wiggled them back. "I'm an only child."

"Was it lonely?"

"Sometimes, I guess. But it also taught me a lot of independence."

"Do you ever wish you had siblings?"

"Nope. Can't imagine that with your evil twin you really miss having them either."

She'd thought about that a lot when she was younger. "I would love to have a brother or sister who isn't hell-bent on destroying me." Stryker tensed, a very subtle hardening of his muscles. "Don't worry. Phoebe won't win. I won't let her. It would just be nice to have family. Someone to call on Christmas day, you know? An overprotective brother or a sister I could shop with. You know, normal stuff."

"Trust me," he muttered, "you don't want an overprotective brother. *I* don't want you to have an overprotective brother." He tugged her securely against him. "And besides, a family is what you make. The people you choose to surround yourself with. Blood doesn't make family."

"You're very wise for an only child," she teased, and then, suddenly, she found herself flat on her back with Stryker on top of her.

"I'm just plain wise. And don't you forget it." Bending his head, he kissed her playfully, little pecks that tickled her jaw and neck as he peppered her with attention. "We should head back to my place. I want to spend time doing this right. Slow. In a bed."

"Mmm . . . sounds good."

He pushed himself up, just as his cell rang. "Shit. Hold on."

As he scrambled around to find his phone, she hopped out of the vehicle, fully naked, and just stood there. The night was cold, which didn't bother her, and the stars were like glitter against the black sky. On the horizon, a full moon rose up behind the trees, and somewhere close by, a howl broke the silence.

"That's Cujo," Stryker said, as he fished around in his pants pocket. "Rik's other half." He finally got his phone out and open. "Yeah."

Mel didn't stick around to eavesdrop. The outdoors called to her, the sense of freedom a beacon. She'd always been stuck inside a room or apartment or house when she was in control, and when she did get away to shop or take the occasional stroll through a park or something, she hadn't been able to relax, had been too paranoid that one of Phoebe's enemies was going to grab her.

But now she could walk through the grass and savor the velvety texture on the soles of her feet as the cool breeze caressed her bare skin. The waterfall was a rush in her ears that vibrated her entire body. In the glow of the moon, the water rippled, and the fine spray became fluid beads of light. It was the most beautiful thing she'd ever seen.

At the edge of the water, she stopped, opened her arms, and threw her head back. A sense of peace flowed through her, and for the first time in her life, she almost felt . . . alone. Not alone as in no one was near, because she'd always been lonely. This was an airy, calm wholeness. Like she owned her body completely. There was no Phoebe in the background.

She didn't know if this was a result of the suppressant drug or of something else, but it didn't matter. Her eyes stung with the purest, most intense joy she'd ever known.

She was going to be happy here, and that was something Phoebe couldn't take away.

As if she could relate, the Rik-creature howled, and there was no mistaking the elation in the sound. Rik and Cujo had obviously found a balance and mastery over their abilities. It gave Mel hope, which piggybacked on the success she'd already had with Stryker earlier. Now, if she could use her powers in a steady, slow stream, she might be able to create the same effects while not burning herself out.

She might also ease the effects on Stryker. Reaching deep for her newly banked powers, Mel kneeled on the river's shore and dipped her fingers in the water.

Go slow, go slow, go slow. She kept up the mantra in her head as the tingle of her gift rose up from her chest and streamed down her arm. At her fingertips, the surface of the river began to harden, until a thin sheet of ice had spread to several feet. A bead of sweat formed on her brow as she struggled to keep control. Her natural instinct was to fire everything she had, in part because restraint was painful. Agony was a wave of fire that sizzled over her skin. Her muscles felt like they were pulling away from her bones, and stabbing bursts of pain were railroad spikes in her brain.

Slow, slow, slow . . .

She couldn't. Crying out, she let loose in a focused stream of power. Instantly, the water, which had formed a crust over the surface for twenty-five yards on each side of her, solidified. Ice cracked as it overtook the rushing river, and suddenly, absolute silence filled the night as the waterfall became an ice sculpture. A beautiful splash of crystal pouring down on a river of glass.

"My God." Stryker stood behind her, eyes wide as he took in the sight. He was wearing his pants now—no shirt, and behind his fly, evidence of what her gift did to him drew her gaze. "It's amazing."

"Well, I am an art history major," she teased as she stood and stepped out onto the ice. "And I could totally get a job at an ice rink." Her nakedness didn't bother her, and in fact, it felt natural to be out here with her creation, with Stryker's eyes glued to her. Slowly, seductively, she padded toward the waterfall, feeling his hot gaze on her ass. As she got closer, she heard the soft gurgle of running water beneath the thick sheet.

"How strong is the ice?" His voice was low. Husky.

She reached for one of the icicles that had formed at the base of the waterfall. "It'll support your weight," she said over her shoulder.

"Good." The ice creaked and groaned as he moved carefully

toward her. "Because we're going to do something new for your next lesson. You're going to discharge during sex."

"During?" Oh, now, that sounded interesting. She broke off the shaft of ice and turned, drew a sharp, appreciative breath at the sight of Stryker standing there, his eyes burning with raw need. He didn't give her time to say anything. He dropped to his knees, palmed her thighs, and buried his face between her legs. God, she would never grow tired of that.

Pleasure swamped her, and she cried out at the exquisite sensation of his tongue lashing her clit and pushing inside her. A tiny bit of her power remained, and she called on it, channeled it into the stick of ice in her hand. Stryker groaned as the effect gripped him. One hand left her thigh, followed by the rasp of his zipper. When his hand didn't return to her leg, she peeked, nearly came at the sight of him working his cock as he feasted on her sex.

A blush heated her cheeks as she handed him the ice. "I made a toy."

His eyebrows climbed high on his forehead. "Damn," he breathed. "You made an ice dildo."

It looked exactly like a hard cock, complete with veiny ridges and a mushroom cap. With a wicked smile, he slid the tip between her folds. Moaning, she threw her head back against the wall of ice behind her, and when he pushed the dildo inside her, she arched into his hand, taking it deep. His tongue went to work as he fucked her with the ice, and when he latched onto her hard knot of nerves, the climax took her with such force that she nearly lost her footing.

Stryker caught her, held her steady with one hand as he continued to pump the melting ice in her core. It scraped over tissue still sensitive from the earlier sex, and she came again, this time with a cry that rang out in the chill night. A howl joined hers, and distantly, she wondered if Rik communicated with her wolf, because it would have one hell of a story to tell.

Suddenly, Stryker was gripping her hips and pulling her down to her hands and knees. His mouth met hers in a deep, wet kiss, and then he spun her and brought her ass up against him. The ice slid from her and was replaced by his hard, hot flesh, the contrast making her moan.

"You're going to come when I do," he said thickly, each word punctuated with a pump of his hips. "And I want you to use your power. Fucking turn this place into a winter wonderland. It'll probably trigger my ability, but it'll be a good practice for me to keep it under a four-pointer."

"Yes," she whispered. "Hurry."

He moved against her, powerful, hard thrusts that slipped them both forward on the ice. The erotic slap of his balls hitting her sex joined the sound of their panting breaths and the occasional snap of ice as it thawed and the water moved beneath it. Stryker's fingers dug into her hips, a biting pain that added to the rush of adrenaline and pleasure that warmed her all the way to her marrow.

"God, this is good." He pushed deep before drawing back so only the head of his cock was inside her. For a long moment, he stilled, his entire body quivering. "Not yet. Shit . . . not . . . yet."

Feeling naughty, she rotated her ass and pushed back, swallowing him with her core. His hiss accompanied a tighter grip on her hips, and then he covered her so his broad chest was a blanket on her back, and his teeth sank into her shoulder.

An orgasm built swiftly, hovering dangerously out of reach. He had complete control, and as he held her like that, unmoving and completely dominating, it was she who began to quiver.

"Please," she moaned.

He released her, licking the place he'd bitten, and then his mouth was at her ear. "Come now. Let your power rip."

He sliced his hips forward, and the climax that had been smoldering lit like a torch. His name fell over and over from her lips, and then he joined her. The pleasure was as intense as burning gasoline flowing through her veins. Through the ecstasy, she reached for her power, and even as her well filled, she let it loose.

The result was beyond anything she could have imagined. The temperature plummeted. Grass froze. The earth turned to frost. Crystal flakes formed in the air and spiraled around them like they were in a snow globe. And all the while, she orgasmed, one long, constant climax.

"Fuck . . . oh, fuck . . ." Stryker's moans were barely audible over the rumble of the earth shaking beneath them. "God . . . *damn.*"

Minutes later . . . had to be minutes . . . many of them . . . Stryker stopped moving. Her bones turned to gel, and she fell over. Stryker eased down onto the ice with her, his cock still inside her, sweat sticking them together. The insides of her thighs were wet, evidence of his orgasms—several, or maybe, like hers, one incredibly long one.

They lay like that until their breathing became normal and he began to shiver. "That was . . . wow," she murmured.

"Ah . . . yeah." He helped her up, and she noticed that his legs were as wobbly as hers. "It was like your power fed mine, and both fed my damned orgasm. I've never . . . Jesus." He wiped the back of his hand over his forehead. "Best sex I've ever had. By a long shot."

Awesome. She was grinning like a fool as they wobbled and stumbled their way back to his car. "Food. I need food."

"Let's get you some." As he gathered her clothes from the car, his expression turned glum. "Then I need to take you to the cell."

Yeah, that sucked. But she'd be out again in the morning. "It's okay. We'll gradually lengthen the time I'm in control, and soon, I'll only need to be there for a few short hours."

His smile was terse, as if he didn't believe it or didn't like even that option. A sickening thought sank to the pit of her gut. Maybe he didn't want to be tied to her like that. She could certainly understand, given what Phoebe had done to him. But now wasn't the time to freak out about it. Making it through the coming days and weeks . . . that was priority.

Because she knew that Phoebe was going to do her best to destroy everything, from Melanie to ACRO. And if anyone could do it, Phoebe could.

CHAPTER
Fourteen

Stryker hated taking Mel to the cave, hated the thought of her being alone there.

But if she did switch over, the last thing he wanted to do was be around Phoebe. And so he forced himself to leave her there with the guards, and he walked around the ACRO compound aimlessly.

Missing her. Feeling that it wasn't fair he could go back to his house and she had to share a body—and everything—with fire-bitch.

She'd had to share everything her whole life—and with Phoebe, so it didn't constitute sharing. Mel literally got the left-overs, the scraps.

She had nothing of her own. She deserved something to call hers.

And he realized what he could do to rectify that, at least in a small way, for right now.

He spent the rest of the evening and into the dawn working nonstop on the small guesthouse on his property—about half a mile from the main house, it was a two-bedroom, one-bathroom, one-story house with a decent enough kitchen. And no furniture.

He spent time cleaning it out . . . fixing the electricity. And the heat, even though that didn't really matter to her. Hauled a couch and a rug and some other things from his own house over to hers.

He had nothing to put inside the bedroom besides the clothes Dev had sent over, but he'd rectify that today—maybe he could take her shopping for furniture or something before they practiced. Because the time to leave for Itor's compound was coming closer—Stryker could feel the battle brewing in his bones, the place was practically vibrating with nervous energy. Training for everyone had been ramped up and even support staff had been working overtime.

He cleaned the kitchen, put in some of his own dishes and pots and pans, and wondered if he had time to go grocery shopping before she woke up.

But no, the sun had risen and he knew she would worry when she didn't see him first thing in the morning. So he jumped in the shower and then dragged on fresh black BDUs and got to the cave in time to stop a meltdown.

She'd been trying to keep it together, but he saw the start of tears when he went inside to take the fire blanket off her. He let her rush to the bathroom and then hugged her when she came out.

"You were late. Sorry, I just got nervous," she whispered against his chest.

"I had a good reason. Come on, I'll show you after you eat some breakfast, okay?"

He knew taking her back to the house where there was no food wasn't the best idea, waited while she ate a huge breakfast at the cafeteria, picked at his own food impatiently.

Nervously. Like he was about to propose or something, and God, he was an idiot. *Here, I made you a house.*

Maybe he needed to rethink this.

"What's wrong, Stryker? You're distracted," she pointed out as she put down her fork, the food in front of her having been demolished.

"I am, a little. It's just . . . I have something to show you." He didn't say much more than that and she didn't press as they walked back to his house.

When he guided her past it instead of heading inside, she looked at him curiously.

"Come on—don't worry, it's a good thing." At least he hoped it was. And when they got to the guesthouse, he unlocked the door and let her step inside.

And then he handed her the key. "This place . . . it's yours," he said finally.

She stared between him and the key. "Mine? You want me to stay here?"

"I'm not . . . it's not that I *want* you to stay here. Unless you want to. Shit." He stared up at the ceiling for a second to get his bearings and then looked back at her. "I wanted you to have something of your own while you're here. You said you always had to share. And the cave's no place to call home. So while I want you at my house, you can stay here too. Get some privacy. Fix it up any way you want. And then later, if you want a bigger place, ACRO has other houses . . ."

She cut him off with a kiss, wrapping herself around him like she'd never let him go.

"You need to help me christen this place," she told him after she'd kissed him breathless. "I can't think of a better way than this."

"No food . . . so I'll have to eat you," he murmured.

"I like . . . that thing—with your tongue," she said shyly, and oh, yeah, he liked that too. A lot. And in a matter of seconds, he was hoisting her onto the kitchen table, tugging her jeans off . . . throwing them across the room. He peeled her top off too, just because he loved seeing her naked.

And then he pulled one of the chairs as close as possible to her.

"I know the kitchen's one of your favorite places," he murmured right before he buried his face between her legs; her calves were thrown over his shoulders and she was so open to him. Tasted like heaven as he licked and laved until she was practically writhing off the table for him.

Her moans alone could make him come all over himself. But he held back, reveling in her orgasm as he continued to tongue her through the contractions.

When she was quivering, tugging at his hair, he moved back, kissing his way up her belly to her breasts. She leaned toward him and collapsed into his lap and he held her for a few minutes.

"I don't think we're done," she murmured, her hand sneaking between them to stroke his cock through his pants.

"We're definitely not done, baby," he groaned, letting her work him for a while, until his balls tightened and he knew he wanted to come inside her. He tugged her hand away gently and then stood with her against him, kicked the chair away and turned her toward the higher counter. Bent her over it and spread her legs. "Yeah, just like that. Beautiful."

She looked over her shoulder and wiggled her ass at him.

"Wench," he growled, and reached for the spatula on the counter near her. Spanked her with it lightly. When she responded, he continued until she was telling him she could come like this.

He wanted to feel that.

"I've never used one like *that*," she said breathlessly.

"I like introducing you to new things." He spanked her until her ass was a pretty shade of pink and she was squirming and her sex was glistening and then he knew he couldn't hold on any longer. Unzipped his pants and didn't bother to step out of them.

Took her quickly, filling her deeply, and then both groaned together when his cock was buried in her to the hilt. "Don't use your power," he rasped. "I don't want to bring down all that hard work on our needs."

She spread her legs wider, arched back into him while he stood there, trying to breathe. And then he began to move against her, hips slapping the back of her thighs, their moans mingling together, and yeah, this was definitely the most fun he'd ever had in the kitchen.

Stryker had fallen asleep almost immediately after they'd made love. He'd muttered a sleepy "Sorry to be a typical male, but . . ."

And then he'd conked out. It was no surprise, given that he'd been up all night working on this incredible house, and then the sex had taken the last of his energy. She'd shaken him awake and urged him to the couch, where he'd collapsed, falling right into rattling snores.

She'd wandered around the house, exploring, touching, and tearing up whenever she thought about what Stryker had done to give her something of her own. Something that would never be tainted by Phoebe. Mel didn't deserve any of this, and to be honest, she wasn't sure why Stryker had given so much of himself, but she needed to give back.

Somehow, she needed to do something for him.

She showered, found lots of new clothes in the closet, and dressed in the green-and-white sundress, paired with strappy white sandals that sat among the twelve pairs of shoes lining the floor. Dev had certainly kept his promise to send things to wear.

Then she needed to go shopping, but even if she knew how to drive, she doubted she'd be allowed off the base. So, in what was probably a highly insane move, she took Stryker's cellphone from his pocket, cycled through his phone book, and dialed the one person she knew hated her and would have no problem breaking her neck if Phoebe somehow broke loose.

Ender arrived, all scowls and curses, waited while she left a note for Stryker, and then drove her to the grocery store. She tried to make small talk, but the man didn't make it easy.

"Are you married?"

"Yes."

"Do you have kids?"

"Yes."

"Boys or girls?"

"Yes."

Okaaaay. She gave up, did her shopping, and then, to her horror, at the checkout she realized she didn't have any money.

"I got it," Ender said, and he didn't even sound grumpy, to her amazement. "Dev said to buy you anything you wanted."

"Really?" she teased. "Because I saw a sporty little BMW on the way here that I'd love."

"I'll have to call in for authorization on that one," he said, without missing a beat. And holy crap, he was actually serious. Ender was fully prepared to buy her an expensive car. Why in the world would he believe that Dev had included a new vehicle in the order to give her what she wanted?

When they got back to the guesthouse, Ender helped her bring in the groceries—Stryker was still sleeping like a log— and as Ender set down the last bag, she turned to him. "Thank you."

He swung around to her, his tawny brows coming down to form a serious line over his eyes. "You know how you can thank me? Don't fuck with Stryker or Dev."

"I know you don't believe me, but I'm telling the truth when I say I would never do that. I care about Stryker, and I plan to cooperate with your boss."

Ender's voice was cool, but not unkind. "Good. They're both rock-solid guys. Don't hurt them."

Though he could mean physically, she got the impression he meant not to break their hearts, which made no sense. There was definitely something going on between her and Stryker, but Dev . . . he was interested in her only because she could help him. How in the world could she break his heart?

She didn't get a chance to press, though, because Ender stalked out of the house, started up his GTO, and tore out of the driveway. Sighing, she unpacked the groceries, including a bag of powdered sugar donuts she'd grabbed to munch on, and began cooking.

She was nearly finished when Stryker came into the kitchen, his tousled hair lending a boyish appearance that was at odds with his markedly rugged facial features and body. He was shirtless, shoeless, and the only reason Mel didn't jump on him right then and there was that her hands were covered in garlic.

"Hey." His voice was a lazy morning-rough drawl, and it reached right inside her. A weird, primal vision of her fat with his child and lying in bed with him, his powerful arms holding her possessively, fed her starved fantasies far more than food ever had.

It was also nothing but a fantasy, and she needed to remember that. Even if she and Stryker managed to eke out some sort of relationship, they couldn't ever bring a family into the mix. Who knew what Phoebe would do to sabotage a pregnancy, and she definitely couldn't be trusted with a child if she emerged at the wrong time. And how could the situation ever be explained to a kid?

It couldn't. So back to food it was, and she smiled as she popped the French bread in the oven and removed the pan of filet mignons she'd finished off in the dry heat. "Hey."

He inhaled deeply. "God, something smells good."

"Filet mignon with blackberry sauce, sautéed broccoli with almonds, and spicy garlic bread with jalapeños and artichoke hearts." She lifted the lid on the sauté pan to stir the broccoli.

Stryker let out a long whistle of appreciation, which made her smile even bigger. "Where did you get all the food?"

"Ender took me to the store."

"I can't believe I slept through all that," he grumbled. "Do I have time for a quick shower?"

"If you hurry."

He moved toward her, his gait loose, shoulders rolling. He wore his smoky sensuality like a second skin, right down to his heavy-lidded gaze that held her captive as he stopped in front of her. One finger came up to hook her chin and lift her face to his. When his lips came down on hers, she was more than ready, and hell, she wouldn't care if her dinner burned if he wanted to do some heat-making of his own.

Instead, he kissed her, a leisurely meeting of lips that might appear tame to someone watching, but from where Mel stood, it was a carnal promise of more to come. Just as the broccoli pan began to hiss with steam, he pulled back, winked, and sauntered off to the shower.

The bastard. She'd gone weak in the knees and he was swaggering away like he knew it.

Well, she might not be able to make a man swoon with the skill of her kisses, but she'd make him moan at the first taste of her meal.

By the time she'd plated everything and placed all the food, plus two glasses of wine, on the table, Stryker was dressed and looking better than the main course. And sure enough, he moaned at the taste of the beef.

"Jesus," he said. "Where did you learn to cook?"

"I watch a lot of cooking shows and experiment with recipes." She shrugged. "When you don't have much else to do, you get real good at the things you *do* do."

"You aren't *real good*, babe. You're freaking fabulous."

The compliment was food for her soul, and she grinned so broadly her cheeks hurt. "I'd love to be a chef, but I can't exactly enroll in cooking school or get a job, you know?" Which was why she'd gone with studying art history. The first couple of years could be done with online courses. She might even have been able to find some sort of online work.

Stryker took a sip of his wine. "At the waterfall, you said something about being an art history major?"

Dabbing her mouth with her napkin, she nodded. "Well, I haven't declared a major yet, but that's what I'm aiming for." She tucked the napkin in her lap. "My mom had an extensive collection of art, and some of my favorite memories of her were when she explained their origins to me or took me to a museum. I learned to appreciate the art in all the places Phoebe takes us, so it just made sense to take online classes while I could."

"Was your mom also an awesome cook? Because this is amazing." Stryker cast her a smoldering, seductive glance. "*You're* amazing."

Cheeks heating, she stabbed a broccoli floret. "I wanted to do something nice for you. You've been so good to me . . . it was the least I could do."

"I'd make you a house every day if I knew I'd get fed like this afterward."

She waggled her brows. "We're not done yet either."

Leaning back in his chair, he rubbed his belly. "I don't think anything else will fit."

"This will." She went to the kitchen and grabbed the handheld immersion blender and two bowls in the fridge. When she placed the bowls on the table, Stryker frowned.

"Bowls of murky water is dessert?"

"Just wait." She dunked the whisk attachment into one of the bowls and turned on the mixer. Then she turned on her own power, and keeping a tight hold on it, she channeled a trickle of her gift into the ceramic bowl, ignoring the twinge of pain in her head that came with her restraint. The mixture in the bowl, which had been lukewarm, since it had been made with boiling water and then placed in the refrigerator, chilled quickly. It set up within seconds, and thanks to the whisk, it whipped up into a light froth. When it was the right consistency, she removed the whisk and repeated the procedure with the other dish.

"Voilà," she said, as she pushed one bowl in front of Stryker.

"Foamy blancmange. Light, sweet, and tastes like vanilla. It's art and food combined."

"That. Was. Awesome." Stryker's crystalline eyes fixed on her with something akin to admiration, and she warmed from the inside out.

"Wait until you taste it. It melts on your tongue."

He kept his gaze on her while he dipped his spoon into the foam and brought it to his mouth. "That's good." His eyes darkened dangerously, and her spoon froze halfway to her mouth. "But you know how it would be better?"

She gulped. "N-no?"

The wicked smile that touched his lips made her mouth go dry, and then he was on his feet, she was lifted onto the table, scattering dishes everywhere. She squealed, and then gasped when he flipped up her dress, tore off her panties, and used one palm to push her back on the table.

"Close your eyes."

"Why—"

"Close. Your. Eyes."

Right. Okay. She obeyed, and was rewarded with a curious sensation between her legs. The foam. Stryker drizzled the foam over her sex, and she groaned with pleasure. It was like soapsuds, except cooler, with the bubbles popping and tickling her sensitive flesh. She'd never felt anything like it, but she made a mental note to keep the ingredients handy for future erotic play, because damn . . . *amazing*.

A warm, wet stroke brought her hips off the table as Stryker licked right up her center, catching the sweet froth. He licked again, added more, and kept the lick, foam cycle going until she was writhing, panting, begging him to let her come.

"You're ready?" he said against her core. "You want my cock in you?"

"Yes, God, yes."

He rose above her, palmed her thighs, and tugged her butt to the very edge of the table. Reaching down, he unzipped, released his erection, and guided it to her entrance. But before he penetrated, she scooped some froth out of a bowl and placed it strategically so he'd feel the cold effervescence with her. His sharp inhale through clenched teeth was followed by a slice forward of his hips, and he was seated fully inside her slick heat, his balls rubbing against her ass.

There was nothing leisurely about this session, and that was fine with her. They'd sated one hunger but fueled another, and this was a main dish of raw need with a side of naughty.

He leaned into her and went at it with wild, uncontrolled strokes. The foam crackled between them, the bubbles bursting on her clit with every hammering thrust. Her orgasm struck like a thunderstorm, crashing over her with such intensity that she threw her head back and screamed. Distantly, she heard his answering shout, felt the hot, rhythmic pulses of his come as he spilled inside her.

When it was over, she was trembling with post-orgasmic exhaustion, and Stryker was hunched over her, fists planted on the table on either side of her head, eyes closed.

"You're going to kill me," he breathed. "Damn, Mel . . . you're going to kill me."

He meant it in a way that should have given her warm fuzzies. Should have made her grin from ear to ear, and maybe it would have if she didn't feel Phoebe starting to stir and knew that it was almost time to head to the cave.

Instead, she closed her own eyes so he wouldn't see the fear in them. The fear that what he'd said might actually happen.

CHAPTER
Fifteen

"Baby, maybe you should sit down."

If there was any way to get Annika to *not* do something, it was to suggest she do it, and she shot Creed a glare as they strolled around ACRO's little park. Darkness had closed in, and the duck pond was quiet, the ducks having settled in the grass with their beaks tucked into their wing feathers.

"I need to walk," she gritted out. She'd been restless all day, had been cleaning like a madwoman, grocery shopping, and now she wanted to work out. Obviously, spending two hours in the gym wasn't an option, but she could wear out the ACRO sidewalks.

"Why don't we go home, and I'll give you a backrub?"

"I'd rather you gave me an orgasm."

"Another one?"

They'd been screwing like rabbits for the last couple of days—her obstetrician had given them the green light, and as a plus, it might trigger labor. Excellent. Because she was so ready to not be pregnant anymore.

Creed, on the other hand, seemed to want to plug her up and keep her fat, as if maybe the kid could just grow to adulthood inside her. He never said anything, but she was pretty sure he was still freaked out by his brother, Oz's, prediction that if she had Creed's baby, she'd die. Or something like that.

Oz was so full of shit.

Someone was walking toward them from the direction of that ridiculous cave Dev had built for Phoebe, his gait clipped, stiff, and Annika's temper surfaced. She'd talked to Dev a couple of hours ago, and when he told her about the deal with Stryker and that murderous bitch, she'd come uncorked.

Annika marched—well, waddled—right up to Stryker. She must have looked as pissed as she felt, because when he saw her, he halted, his stance wide, shoulders back, and his expression shuttered.

"Annika, no!" Creed grabbed her arm, but she jerked out of his grip, closed the distance between her and Stryker, and struck him hard on the cheek. His head whipped to the side, but other than that, he didn't react.

"You bastard," she snarled. "How could you? How could you be fucking the woman who murdered your best friend?" Next to her, Creed's presence was a comfort, and she felt him go taut, as though he expected Stryker to react badly, maybe violently, to what Annika had just said and done. Creed was so overprotective lately. Not long ago, that would have driven her nuts, but she'd sort of grown to enjoy it.

"It's not that simple," Stryker said softly.

"It seems pretty simple to me," she snapped. "I get that she's Dev's sister, so he has an excuse to be a little mush-brained when it comes to her. But you? You saw what she did. You heard Akbar's screams." Annika still heard them sometimes.

Stryker swallowed, his gaze tripping away for a second. "It wasn't Mel—"

"Yeah, yeah. It was Phoebe. Whatever. I don't trust either

one of them, and what are you thinking, letting her run around loose?"

"Only Mel gets to be free. We're locking up Phoebe."

Annika snorted. "You can't contain someone like that. Trust me." The baby kicked, and she winced, pretty sure a foot was lodged in her throat. "How old was she when she started training? When she went to Itor to be their product? Because I'm telling you, she doesn't think the same way the rest of you do. She's a machine. A cold, hard killing machine. She's hardwired for two things: killing and survival. She will *not* be contained."

Annika knew, because she had been raised that way, and it was a miracle that she'd turned out okay. The fact that she'd still been a teen when Dev saved her was probably a factor, as was the fact that although she'd practically been born to be a trained assassin, the CIA hadn't been particularly cruel. She could only imagine what Itor had done to Phoebe . . . Mel—whoever the hell she was.

"Rik was a killer when she came here too," he pointed out, but she shook her head.

"Not the same thing. Rik was forced to do the things she did. Phoebe does it willingly. And she enjoys it. You can't cure psycho."

"We've taken precautions," Stryker said. "It'll be okay."

"Okay?" She jabbed him in the chest with a finger. "I promise you, this will not end well. She *will* get out, and she *will* end up killing someone. God help you if she kills someone I care about."

"Ani." Creed's voice was low, soothing, and it brought her down a notch. Maybe half a notch. "We should go."

"Oh, no. I'm not done with him—" She broke off with a gasp, as a sharp, stabbing pain ripped through her belly.

"Annika?" both men said simultaneously as they caught her arms.

Fuck, that hurt. She'd been shot, stabbed, beaten, run over by a car . . . and yeah, this kid was kicking her ass. Wetness bloomed between her legs, and then became a gush down her legs.

"Annika!" Creed's voice was as panicked as she'd ever heard it. "What's wrong?"

"It's time," she groaned. "Get me to medical. Baby's coming."

Stryker was finding it hard to breathe. Annika had been ushered off by Creed and he'd uselessly sat down on the nearest steps and buried his head in his hands and wondered how things could be so damned good and so damned shitty all at once.

Trance was sitting next to him. Stryker had no idea when the man had arrived, but he'd been apparently waiting patiently for him to pull it together and stop hyperventilating.

Probably why the man's hand was on the back of his neck, holding his head between his knees.

"You all right?" Trance asked as he peered down at him.

"My neck hurts," Stryker growled.

Trance snorted and let him up. "You were hyperventilating."

"Thanks for saving me," Stryker said, with more than a tinge of sarcasm in his voice. "I'll have to owe you one."

"You can come work out with me, then. Ender was supposed to train with me but he's, ah, busy."

Stryker raised his brows. "Kira's in heat already?" Ender was mated to Kira, an animal whisperer who literally went into heat every spring and needed to be serviced, quite often. Usually, halfway through the season, Ender cried uncle and Kira's needs were satisfied with the sperm he banked for that express purpose.

But that didn't stop him from trying.

"No. But he's practicing. Asshole's determined to do it without any help this year." Trance stood, and yeah, just what Stryker wanted now, to practice sparring with an excedo who could literally throw him through a wall with no effort.

Still, it would keep him sharp.

After a quick walk to the excedo gym, Trance and Stryker suited up. Rather, Stryker suited up so he wouldn't be beaten to a fucking pulp while Trance trained.

"Want to tell me what's wrong?" Trance asked as Stryker deflected a hard blow to his gut.

"No." Clenched teeth. Sweating already, and goddammit, this was the worst idea ever.

"Have it your way." Trance slammed him across the back, sent him flying face-first into the mat, and stood with a foot on Stryker's back.

"What the fuck? Is this humiliate Earthquake Boy day?" he grumbled.

"Don't make me beat it out of you," Trance told him.

Stryker thought back to the day before last, with Rik's howls ringing in his ears . . . the way Mel looked under the waterfall.

He'd never look at an icicle the same way again. And the guesthouse . . . the smile he'd gotten when she realized she had a place of her own. He'd thought the warmth of that moment could hold him through anything. But the look on Annika's face, her accusations . . .

Just then, Trance moved, and Stryker bounded up. Got a good slam or two across Trance's face before he spoke.

"I put Ani into labor," he panted as he ducked Trance's blows. Or tried to anyway. But Trance had him in a choke hold, and suddenly Stryker didn't feel like playing this bullshit game any longer.

The ground rumbled slightly, enough to make Trance pull back from Stryker and stare at him. "You've been able to control that shit before."

"Yeah, well, maybe I can't anymore." Stryker sank to the mat and leaned back with his palms down.

Trance walked over to the fridge to grab a couple bottles of water, tossed one to Stryker, who caught it one-handed.

He drained the water and hoisted himself up, but Trance stopped him from leaving the gym. "We're not done."

"Yeah, we are." Stryker flung the empty bottle in the trash and swung back around to Trance. "How do you do it?" he asked suddenly, almost viciously. "You live with a killer. You love one. How?"

Trance had him on the ground and pinned by the throat, a sound dangerously close to a growl Rik would normally emit ringing in his ears. "Don't you ever call Rik that. Understood?"

Stryker managed to nod. Trance let him up and then said, "Besides, the woman you're currently fucking has the same reputation. So maybe I should ask you what it feels like."

Those words made Stryker see red. The floor rumbled again and he went headfirst into Trance's gut. And Trance let him. As the men slammed to the ground, Stryker willed himself to stop before the gym collapsed on his head. If that didn't kill him, Devlin would.

"So you're falling for her," Trance said as though it was the most natural thing in the world.

And it was. But nothing seemed natural about Mel and her dual personality.

Mel. "Yeah," he admitted. "And I thought I'd reconciled everything that happened with Akbar. So why do I sometimes still feel like I've betrayed him?"

"It's not going to go away all at once. And you know as well as I do that everything comes at a price. Especially love." Trance shook his head. "It was a battle, Stryker. It could've easily been you instead. Akbar knew he was in danger every time he went out on a job."

"But I've fallen for the woman who killed him—sort of, anyway."

"I thought you said they were separate people," Trance said.

"They are. I know they are. But Ani . . ."

"Fuck Annika," Trance said. "I mean, come on, she's suspicious of everyone. She's almost as bad as Ender."

"I think she's worse."

"She's also hormonal and terrified of losing her powers forever," Trance pointed out. "Mel is dual-natured, just like Rik. And Annika still calls Rik a werewolf experiment or some shit like that." Trance grimaced.

"How the hell did you do it, Trance?" Stryker heard his voice crack and yet he couldn't look away from the man who was married to a woman whose other half had killed his father.

Trance looked up at the ceiling, his face betraying the emotion he felt. "It wasn't easy. But in the end, I loved her more than I hated what she'd done."

"So you don't hold her responsible?"

"No more than I hold you responsible for something that's not your fault," Trance said, broaching an always sore subject with Stryker. "Just because you can't predict disasters in time to save people doesn't make you responsible for their deaths. Some things are out of your control. Some things were out of Rik's control too. And it sounds like Mel would do anything to get her life together, even putting herself in the hands of people she knows want to kill her for what she—her sister—did to their friend."

"What can I do?"

"Love her. Help her. Believe in her. Because you'll be doing it when no one else can. And you're the only one who really counts."

Creed held the baby girl in his arms and felt his knees shake. Kept staring between her and Annika as if he feared this could all crumble and disappear at any moment. Because Oz was so rarely wrong—if ever.

But Annika had come through the labor and delivery just fine; in true Annika fashion, it happened quickly, with a minimum of drama and a great show of strength.

She hadn't asked for—or seemed to need—any drugs or an

epidural. But in the end, that was a good thing, because the baby came in record time—under an hour from the minute she'd felt her first contraction.

"I told you I'd be fine," Annika said softly. She looked tired but happy. Glowing, actually. "And she's great."

Creed still didn't believe it, but the proof was right in front of him.

Dammit, Oz. Why did you feel the need to scare me half to fucking death during her pregnancy? "I guess we're just one big, happy family, then."

But Ani was frowning a little.

"What's wrong?"

"Do you think . . . I mean, you were given the tattoos as protection," Ani said. "Maybe?"

They stared at the tiny girl with the perfect skin and saw nothing out of the ordinary. "Mine didn't come out right away," Creed said, not sure if he wanted his daughter tatted up the same way he'd been.

Granted, he didn't think she'd have much choice in the matter. That was up to Oz's magic and whatever kind of deal he'd struck with the powers that . . . tattooed.

He placed the baby on Ani's bed and she gingerly unwrapped her. Her skin remained unblemished on her front. Creed picked her up and held her so they could both see her back. And, as they watched, the tattoo began to form, a light, delicate swirl of ice blue and white along her back, a design as unique as a snowflake and one that offered her protection from the big bads of the world . . . but that would offer its own set of challenges she'd have to deal with later.

"I guess that answers the question," he said quietly. Kat, the ghost who'd been his guardian since birth, was behind him, chatting away in his ear that she was now an aunt, and it didn't bother him at all. Today, nothing could.

It had been a long road with Kat. She'd helped him hone his abilities as a ghost hunter and she'd been so protective for most of his life that he hadn't been able to truly form any relationship—not until Ani, and even that was hard won. Now Kat was as protective of Ani as she was of him. And, he assumed, Kat would also take on that same role of guardian with his daughter.

At one time—hell, a lot of the time—he'd wished Kat would leave him, go into the light and free him. But now he realized he couldn't imagine life without her. She was as much a part of him as his tats and his abilities. As much a part of him as Ani and the baby—both of whom had taken his heart.

He cradled the baby girl against him and said, "Any idea about names? I'm guessing Creedette is out of the running."

She snorted. "As if." And then she grew serious, nibbled her bottom lip. "I was thinking . . . Renee."

"Renee." He tried it on for size. "That's nice."

"It was my mother's name," Ani said quietly.

He held the baby against his chest with one arm and reached his free hand out to grasp hers. "Then I think it's pretty damned perfect."

Devlin was at his door. It was one of less than a handful of times he'd come to the dorms and the gesture wasn't lost on Gabe.

"I'm here to apologize," Devlin said after Gabe moved aside to let him in.

"I get it, Dev. Oz sent me or whatever and you weren't ready and that's all right."

"You weren't ready either," Devlin reminded him.

"It was, ah, cool while it lasted."

"So you're going to run again?"

Gabe shook his head. "No, I'm done running. But I won't be the one you have to worry about hurting you. I get self preservation. I understand your need for it. But I can't keep doing this—whatever it is—without shredding myself up inside. And I'm not that self-destructive anymore."

He'd come a hell of a long way in a short period of time. The fact that he'd allowed himself to attach to Devlin so easily told him so much more than anything else. Whether or not Devlin's old lover had a hand in it, Gabriel felt things for his boss, his lover, he'd never thought he'd be able to.

And right now it could be crumbling beneath his fingers.

But instead of saying good-bye, Dev said, "Please. I'd like to invite you to my house. I've got dinner ready. I'd take you out, but there's something I need to speak with you about in private." He looked around the room at Gabe's packed bags with a frown and then nodded. "Right. The rental house."

"Is there anything you don't know?"

"Yes. I'm apparently quite rusty in the relationship department," Devlin admitted as he took Gabe's bruised hand in his and looked it over, running his fingers over it gently. "Come. Dinner's getting cold."

It was still Dev—arrogant and self-assured enough to not think or worry about the fact that Gabriel might've had other plans.

On the drive to Devlin's house, the man held Gabriel's hand in his, but he was still majorly distracted.

And it was majorly annoying.

They didn't speak until they arrived at Dev's place and sat down to dinner, and then Gabe was surprised at Dev's words.

"Next time I train, I'd like to do so with you," Dev said as he poured Gabe a glass of wine.

"You don't have to pity train with me."

"So stubborn. I have a cure for that, you know."

"Yeah, fucking me blind." Gabe finished the wine in one gulp, something that always made Dev wince. "Tell me what you brought me here for."

"There's so much, Gabriel. I don't know where to start."

"Start anywhere. I'll ask questions if I'm confused. But please, Devlin, share something with me." Gabe was aware he was close to begging, and he never did that outside the bedroom.

But it triggered something in Dev, because he leaned forward and hooked Gabriel's legs with his under the table, and he started talking.

"There are things you need to know. Things I've kept from almost everyone. Hell, if it were any other time in ACRO's history, I'd keep you in the dark indefinitely too," Dev started. His eyes drilled into Gabe's. "We have a chance to take down Itor."

Gabriel stood and kicked his chair back into the table. "Jesus, Dev—you sound like you're giving a goddamned presentation to new clients. It's me. Cut the shit and tell me something. Anything beyond your ACRO versus Itor rhetoric."

He turned his back on Devlin, something he should've realized was always a mistake. Gabe was down on the floor in seconds, Devlin half on top of him.

Devlin's hand inside his pants.

Gabe gasped as Devlin's hand found his cock.

"You have more to say to me? I thought you'd just learned to keep your mouth shut," Dev mused.

"Fuck talking," Gabriel murmured as Dev ripped open his pants. "Talking is overrated."

Devlin stroked Gabe's erection, hard and fast, and Gabe found himself burying his head against Devlin's chest, wanting—needing—that closeness. Asking for it, even as his balls tightened and Dev dipped his head down so he could take Gabe's cock in his mouth.

There was no precursor. The second Devlin took him in, Gabe came, shooting in a hot rush that made his hips come off the floor. As he lay there, not wanting to come back down to earth, he was aware that Dev was stripping him. His bare legs opened wantonly for Devlin—they always had, there was no way he could deny this man anything.

That scared him. But he let Devlin claim him on the floor, coming again as Dev pounded him, leaving Devlin with a dark, welted bruise on his neck.

Laying his own claim to Devlin made him smile.

As they lay there in the aftermath, wrapped around each other on the expensive-as-hell rug, Devlin said, "I was adopted."

"Okay. Well, at least you had a cool family."

"That's not why I'm telling you." Devlin shifted so they faced each other. "My real father—my biological father—is the head of Itor."

It was only then that Gabe understood the true weight of Devlin's confession—and his distractions of late. All he could do was touch the man's face, which was contorted with pain . . . all he could do was listen as Devlin filled him in on how he discovered this fact, how his biological father had used Devlin as a mole . . . mind-rape.

How Melanie and Phoebe, the alter-ego woman who killed Akbar and was currently fucking Stryker, was Devlin's half sister.

What the hell do you say to someone after he's told you that?

"I love you, Devlin," he said, and yeah, that probably wasn't it. But Devlin smiled, rubbed the back of Gabriel's neck. "You don't have to say it back to me."

Devlin stared at him for a long moment. "Not now, Gabriel. I will say it, but not until this is all over."

Gabriel didn't quite understand that logic and wondered if it was just a way for Devlin to escape saying it back ever. But Devlin had shared one of the most important secrets of his life with him, and that was not to be discounted. "So what's the plan?"

"That's the problem—there is no plan." Dev's voice was tinged with frustration.

"You need to utilize everyone. And I mean everyone."

Dev blinked hard. Gabe waited for him to say that was out of the question. But all he said was "That puts ACRO at complete risk."

Gabe stared at him steadily. "ACRO's at complete risk if you don't. Either way, you need to shit or get off the pot. And I don't think getting off's going to be an option for that much longer. You can't go in alone."

"You and what army's going to stop me, boy? I don't re-member needing your approval to go on a ground op and I can't see that starting now."

Gabe shoved him then—*shoved him* against the floor. "Guess what—you *can* see and it *is* starting now. You putting yourself on the line is bullshit and you know it. There's no one else who can run this place like you—no one's ready to do it. So before you go out and get your ass fried, you might want to think about shit like that, *old man*."

Devlin tried to shove the boy off him, but Gabriel had the upper hand this time. Devlin grabbed his arm in a last-ditch ef-fort to get out from under him.

"Go ahead—read me. Like I give a shit," Gabriel snarled. "I still end up on top."

Gabe gave him no quarter, spread his thighs, and Dev re-mained helpless beneath him, his palms around Gabriel's wrist, reading emotions that he didn't need to be a goddamned psychic to see at all. "You can't do this alone, Devlin."

Gabriel's cock brushed the crack of his ass and Dev was achingly hard. The last time someone held him down like this . . .

"Oz," Gabriel said as though reading his mind. "It's always going to be about Oz."

"Not always," Devlin breathed. "Not right now."

Would Gabe take him? There would be no stopping him if he really wanted to . . . and from the look in Gabriel's eyes, he wanted.

So did Devlin. Which was why he didn't stop Gabe from searching in his pocket for the lube, didn't do anything but close his eyes and relax as Gabriel's fingers entered him, one, then two, and then a third, opening him up.

"So tight, Dev."

"Been a long time," he murmured back as a knuckle brushed

his prostate and the jolt of pleasure nearly sent him through the ceiling.

"Want to make you relax. Want to make it all better for you," Gabriel said as he withdrew his hand and replaced the fingers with the head of his cock. As it breached the ring of muscle, Devlin heard himself groan, loudly, felt his legs spread unconsciously, bucking his hips up to take in more. "That's it, Devlin . . . just let me in. Let me in all the way, dammit."

Devlin did, for the moment, let his boy take him and fuck him and love him until they were both coming, Gabriel's lips brushing his when they were able to move again.

The words *I love you* nearly slipped from Devlin's mouth then, but stopped when his cellphone rang—the special tone he had for Ani.

Dev cursed and Gabriel handed it to him, resignation in his eyes.

"Text message," he told his lover. "From Marlena . . . shit, Annika's had the baby."

CHAPTER
Sixteen

There was something really fucked up about going from holding a sweet-smelling infant to standing in front of one of the most evil women Dev had ever met.

But that's what he'd done, and instead of rocking two-day-old little Renee, he was confronting Phoebe and having a hard time reconciling the seemingly genuine Mel with this psychotic fiend.

"Hello, bro. Nice of you to grow some balls and finally come see me." Phoebe's voice grated on every one of Dev's nerves. "Maybe you feel guilty for shoving me in this wet, stinking cave?"

"There are a lot of things I feel when it comes to you, but guilt isn't one of them." Annoyance was a big one, though that was aimed more at Stryker, who had decided, after a few days of working with Mel and putting her back here at night, that they no longer needed to wrap Phoebe up in the fireproof blanket. Apparently, he was making sure she was discharged, leaving Phoebe powerless for the few hours she was here.

Stryker had better be fucking right about that.

"Why are you here?" Phoebe had been pacing back and forth in the twelve-by-twelve cell, but now she sank down on the stone bench to peer at him through slitted eyelids.

"Tell me about Alek."

She appeared to consider that. "Tell me about Melanie."

"What about her?"

"What's she told you?"

He snorted. "Nothing. Yet." He put on his best liar face. "Seems that you and our father have terrified her to the point that the harder we are on her, the more she clams up."

Phoebe's lips peeled back in a silent snarl. "You're hurting her?"

"You care?"

"It's *my* body. Of course I care."

"You a little sore?" If she was, it would be because Stryker had used her hard and not because of torture. Oh, Dev knew what was going on, but since things were going well, he'd hold off chewing Stryker's ass for disobeying his order. And yeah, he really didn't want to be thinking about his agent boning his sister right now. Putting the thought out of his head, he slapped his palm against the fireproof glass. "You haven't seen anything yet. She'll talk."

Phoebe yawned. "Won't matter. If Alek couldn't break her, you can't. Besides, in about thirty-six hours, it'll be too late."

"Why's that?"

"Let's just say that our father is going to make a very big statement."

We've got chatter. Something big's going down. City in Europe, probably Great Britain. Within days.

The email from a source at the CIA earlier in the day had set off Dev's alarms, though he wasn't sure why. Then Wyatt's wife, Faith, who was in charge of TAG, had come to his office with intel from her agents . . . credible information that London could be a target for a terrorist attack. The warnings were too vague for anyone to do more than put law enforcement on alert, which meant that either the chatter was just that—chatter—or whoever was planning an attack was running such a tight ship that no one would know anything until it was over.

Itor could pull off something like that. But how?

"You look worried. Same frown Daddy Dearest gets when he's freaking out about something." Phoebe's eyelids drooped, and she leaned back against the wall. "He authorized me to kill you, you know. How's it feel to know your own father wants you dead?"

"I don't know. How's it feel to know your brother wants you dead?"

Phoebe didn't hear. Before he finished the sentence, she was asleep.

"Mel will come out if you call for her." Stryker's voice came from behind him, and Devlin didn't bother to turn around. Instead, he kept his gaze on the woman, who looked so deceptively innocent while sleeping.

"Has she said anything about Itor striking a big city?" Dev's voice was rough. God, he was exhausted. Maybe Gabe was right. Maybe he needed more help than he thought. Set the ego aside and all that shit.

"If she'd brought up something that important, I would have told you." Stryker's voice was as rough as Dev's, but for a different reason.

Dev shouldn't press. But he did. "If she knew about a pending strike, would she say anything?"

"I don't like what you're implying."

"I don't like implying it."

Stryker palmed Devlin's shoulder, yanked him around. "Dammit, Dev. You need to give her a chance."

"No," he said, "I don't. You want to? That's fucking great. Real sweet. But you don't have hundreds of people relying on you. People who could die if you trust the wrong person just because they share some DNA with you. My own father broke into my head and fucked me. So why should I think that a sister who grew up under his thumb would do anything different?"

"Because Melanie *is* different."

"I want to believe that." He lowered his voice, willed himself to calm down. "But I can't afford to. Not yet." Though he was a little closer—he'd had Faith come in to dig around in Mel's brain a little . . . the agent couldn't read thoughts, but she could probe psychic centers and read brain waves. She'd come up against a boxlike section in Mel's brain that she couldn't access, an area she assumed contained Phoebe. Later, when Phoebe was in control, Faith had repeated the procedure, this time able to get inside the formerly locked section but finding an identical area she couldn't access on the other side, confirming Mel's story that each sister controlled a section on opposite sides of the brain. It seemed that whoever's box was open was in control of the body.

He'd also had Samantha, ACRO's most powerful psychic, try to get a read on Mel and Phoebe, but she'd gotten nothing.

"Does that mean you're not going to tell her the truth about you being her brother?"

"That's exactly what it means. And you aren't telling her either."

Dev could practically hear Stryker's teeth grinding, and damn if he thought it was good or bad that his agent had fallen so hard for Melanie. If Stryker was right, she needed him, and Stryker needed her. But if he was wrong . . .

Fuck.

"Wake her up."

With a curse, Stryker barked Mel's name. She sat up, blinking, and Dev was sure it was Phoebe until Stryker smiled. "Hey," he said. "You ready for breakfast?"

Her eyes lit up. "Mmm . . . food." She blinked again, her gaze shifting to Dev, and she lost the happy expression even though Stryker had entered the cell to bring her out.

Well, if that didn't make him feel like a shithead. "Mel, I was just talking to Phoebe. She said something was going down soon. I'm guessing we're looking at an attack of some sort. Do you know what she was talking about?"

"No." She yawned. "They never tell me anything."

"Do you know if Itor has been working on a special weapon?"

"Weapon?" She took Stryker's hand and allowed him to pull her to her feet. "They're always working on something. But . . ." She bit down on her lower lip.

"But what?"

"Just before we went to the jungle, we were in Mexico. Phoebe and some Itor people spent weeks searching through some old ruins. I heard one of the guys talk about something called the Izapa crystal. Later, when I was at Itor, I overheard Alek discussing a device that the crystal completed. He was eager to test it."

A chill went right up Dev's spine. "Test it? When?"

"I don't know. The end of the month, I think."

The chill turned to ice, and he couldn't blame Mel for that. The end of the month was thirty-six hours away.

"Pack your bags," he told Stryker. "We're heading to Australia."

CHAPTER
Seventeen

They arrived at Phoebe and Mel's Australian house as four different groups in the middle of the night, using the cover of darkness to move all the agents inside—but only after Ryan, who possessed some sort of ability to manipulate electronics, ensured that all surveillance bugs and cameras in the town had been disabled.

By the time everyone was in the house, it was packed to the gills with forty ACRO and TAG agents. And still more were already moving to the ranch, where they would use their unique skills to hide until the attack went down.

Now that ACRO was poised for an early morning raid, and everyone was in place, Dev asked Mel to take a seat at the kitchen table and discuss details with the agents on an individual or team basis. Everyone had a specific job, and it was up to Mel to instruct them about the most advantageous way to handle it.

So she sat there with Stryker on one side, his hand on her thigh in a comforting gesture, and Dev on the other, all serious and stiff. She'd love to see him relax, but she had a feeling that would never happen around her. Not unless Phoebe could somehow become a non-issue.

The dream was nice, but not very likely.

First up was the animal whisperer in charge of ACRO's Animal Division, Zach Taylor. Apparently, Ender's wife, Kira, had wanted to be the one to come on this mission, but Ender had put his foot down. According to Stryker, he didn't do that often with Kira, but Ender hadn't wanted his wife, the mother of his three kids, to be anywhere near the kind of battle they were facing.

So Zach was there to ensure that no animals were injured in the taking of Itor and that the guard animals were kept from harming agents.

"Guard dogs are kept here"—Mel pointed to positions on the map of the ranch—"here, here, and here. There are six more that patrol either on their own or with handlers. I can't tell you where they'll be, but nearly all of Itor's working dogs are either German shepherds or Belgian sheepdogs that can pull double duty as herders or guards."

"Any other animals I need to know about?"

"Besides the sheep and horses, no," she said. "Get the dogs on our side, and we should be clear."

Next up was Ender, who still eyed her as if she was going to spring a trap, though he seemed more sad about it than angry, and for the millionth time, she wondered what had prompted his change of attitude.

Then came a dark-haired ex-SEAL named Remy, whose ability to manipulate the weather was going to give him a major role in the initial assault. As he sat, he bumped fists with Stryker and then got right to business.

"I'll roll in a storm from the west," he said in a thick Cajun accent. "The wind and rain will drive everyone inside and allow for us to approach the main ranch house without being seen."

Stryker studied the map. "It'll also herd everyone into groups and make them easier to take out."

"Hell, yeah." Remy fingered a sketch of one of the outbuildings. "What's this?"

"Agent quarters," Mel replied. "To outsiders, it appears to house ranch hands."

A slow, lazy smile at once softened the hard lines of Remy's face, and gave the impression that the guy enjoyed his job maybe a little too much. Which was scary. "I'll take that out with a tornado. Any other buildings I can demolish?"

She pointed to another building that housed agents, a guesthouse, and a storage barn. "These, but the guesthouse is really close to the main building . . ."

"No problem." Remy's slow molasses voice dripped with confidence. "I'm pinpoint accurate."

"Even at a distance?" Mel hoped her skepticism didn't come through, but his situation was odd. He and his meteorologist wife, Haley, had left their son with Kira so Haley could be here—even though, as Mel understood it, she had no special skills. She was to hang back with Remy and somehow assist him as he worked the weather.

Weird.

"Even at a distance," Remy drawled.

Stryker snorted. "Easy there, Gumbo. Save some action for me."

"There will be enough work to go around, boys," Dev said grimly, and the light mood in the kitchen went dark.

After Remy, the steady stream of agents continued with psychics, excedosapiens, snipers, and even transportation and medical people. Finally, at four in the morning, an hour before attack, Mel finished with the last agent, a man named Logan, whose company had, in the past, supplied Itor with weapons. He'd spent the last few months developing countermeasures, and he'd go in to deploy a concussion wave device that would jam the enhanced pistols his company had sold to Alek.

Dev stood. "Thank you, Mel. We couldn't have done this

without you." Before she could reply, he gestured to Stryker. "Gitre wants to see you to go over his geology report."

Stryker gave her a squeeze and a reassuring smile. "Andrew is our head geologist. He's going to help me find the best and worst places to rip into the earth during the assault, and then once we find out where the machine is."

That was one of the many things Mel couldn't help with. She'd never been shown the facility that housed the machine, and it was very possible there were a lot of other hidden buildings on the ranch that she didn't know about.

Stryker left, and suddenly Mel was stuck in the kitchen alone with Dev. There was a long, awkward silence, and then Dev moved to the sliding glass door. "Join me on the patio?"

It wasn't a suggestion.

Swallowing drily, she followed him out. A bench ran the length of the railing, and he sat, invited her to do the same.

"Alek killed my parents," Dev said, without preamble. "He also broke into my mind and used me against my own agency. Because of him, a lot of good people died, and ACRO could have fallen."

Mel's stomach churned. This was the part where he would explain that Alek was so evil, right down to his DNA, that his offspring couldn't possibly be any different, and thanks for the help, but when this was all over, her usefulness was done.

"I'm sorry," she said, for lack of anything else to say. "He's ruined a lot of lives."

His intense gaze caught hers. "Including yours." She must have looked as confused and stunned as she felt, because he cocked an eyebrow. "You expected me to say something else?"

She nodded. "You have every right to hate him and everything associated with him. Including me."

"You can't help who your parents are. And you had no say in how you were raised."

Blowing out a long breath, Mel looked off the deck at the

scrubby trees that shrouded the property in privacy. "I could have fought harder when Phoebe decided to take over the majority of control."

"And what would that have gotten you? More beatings?" He shrugged. "You did what you had to do to survive." He brought one foot up on the bench and threw his forearm over his knee to brace himself. "What else will you do?"

For a moment, she stared, not understanding what he was getting at. And then she inhaled sharply. "You're afraid I'll betray you at the ranch."

"Back in Rome, you told Stryker you'd take whatever side could keep you alive."

Damn. Her and her fool mouth. "I did say that. And at the time I meant it. But that was before I knew all about ACRO. And Stryker." Before she'd fallen for Stryker. But she wasn't going to tell Dev that.

"I want to trust you, Mel. Hell, I need to trust you, for a lot of reasons, some you don't know about. But between the agents I have here and the ones who are staging in Kiev, Madrid, and Tokyo right now, most of ACRO is involved in the biggest battle we've ever faced. I'm playing my best card, throwing all I have at Alek, and if I'm wrong about you, if you betray us, I'll have lost everything, and killed a lot of people who are probably even now questioning this move."

She couldn't begin to comprehend the pressure he was under, and something made her want to give him a hug. Which made her laugh, because he would probably rather hug a porcupine. The best she could do was offer a lame "You don't have to worry."

"I hope not."

The door opened, and Stryker stepped out. As usual, her heart went a little crazy at the sight of him, especially now, dressed in desert camo BDUs. "We leave in half an hour. Dev, can I have a minute with Mel?"

The way Dev looked between them had Mel thinking he was

going to refuse, but he finally nodded and strode through the door. The second it was closed, Stryker grabbed her, hauled her against him, and held her like he would never let her go.

Mel, as always, fit in his arms like she was born to be there.

According to Oz, she was. Maybe one day Stryker would let her know that they were pretty much fated. Although it kind of freaked him out, at least he knew he was with the person he was supposed to be with.

Even if he hadn't known, it still felt fucking completely right.

"I'm proud of you," he murmured against her cheek.

"And you want me too."

"Well, yes." He licked the side of her neck. "Could only help your powers."

"We can't do anything right now. Everyone's watching us," she mumbled.

"They're jealous. And I've never been more sure of anything in my life."

Mel went up on her toes and pressed her lips to his. It was a soft, hot kiss and it turned molten quickly, and yeah, they would either have to do it right here or he'd have to back off.

He did so reluctantly. "It looks like you and Devlin are getting along."

"He seems to understand . . . he hates Alek as much as I do."

Stryker's gut twisted, and he wondered when—if—Devlin would ever reveal his connection with Mel. "Yeah, he does."

She brought a hand up to stroke his face, her palm cool against his cheek. "I've been worried about you. We didn't get much of a chance to talk on the flight over here. But I heard what happened—between you and the agent who had a baby."

Shit. "Who told you that?"

"Everyone's talking about it. The conversation stops when I get close, but I have ears."

"Annika has . . . trust issues."

"With good reason, I guess." She inhaled deeply. "I don't remember seeing her, but she must have been in the jungle, right?"

"Let's not do this right now, Mel. We've come pretty damned far in a short period of time. We'll need to let everyone else catch up."

"We've definitely come far."

His hand stroked her hair. "You're going to have to promise me you'll stay safe during this."

There was so much riding on her. Almost too much, for any agent—but for Mel, who was just learning to control her powers and was often at the mercy of her alter ego, the burden was crushing.

"You really do trust me," she said softly.

"I do." He tugged away from her. "Come on—I've got a surprise for you."

"What?" she asked as she followed around the side of the house, to the far end of the balcony that wrapped around the building. She stopped short when she saw the table—he'd managed to bribe the handful of ACRO support staff they'd brought with them into creating a breakfast that went beyond the instant powdered eggs and dehydrated hash browns they'd made for the assault teams—and while it wasn't much, he hoped it would do the trick.

"It's not what you deserve—it's a little late to pull together what I wanted—but I figured you might need some fuel to calm your nerves," he told her.

She was so entranced by the sight of pancakes on the table she didn't even thank him, just walked over and began to eat, a peacefulness in her eyes, illuminated by the soft candlelight. That was all he needed to see. And even though they'd be in a dangerous situation sooner than later, Stryker pulled up a chair and joined her at the table.

Mel was serving him now—sharing her eggs and toast with such concern for his appetite that he ate every bite.

The smile she gave him afterward was worth it.

"You know, you're awfully calm," she told him when she finally put down her fork. He doubted she was sated, but she was no doubt thinking ahead to the work she needed to do.

For that, it was better to have a little of that hunger burning inside.

"Yeah, well, I've got as much fear as the next person. It's healthy. It's just that I'm pretty good at this helping-to-save-the-world stuff. This frees the world—and you—of Itor. A damned good thing, which makes me more than ready to kick some ass."

"Stryker? I'm, ah . . . scared." Her admission was shaky, but there wasn't a doubt in his body that she would never think of backing down.

"Fear keeps you smart, Mel. You've been practicing. You're getting good at controlling your powers. And you're not on your own anymore. If something happens, and your power's depleted, an ACRO agent will cover you, okay?"

"But—"

"No buts. You're with me, dammit. And that's going to be good enough for all of them."

It was a go. His agents were armed and at the ready. But this time, Devlin felt more of a tug of worry than he usually did. Tried to clear his mind so he wasn't sending out negative messages to his psychic agents—or subliminally to the others.

A team was only as good as its weakest link and he refused to be that link again.

He watched Gabriel, suited up and ready to head out on a semi-solo mission of his own—a mission inside the mission, an important task that could get him killed.

Devlin argued with himself that the boy wasn't ready. But he knew that was a half-truth—no agent was truly ever prepared and Gabriel had faced a battle already and come back wiser, if not stronger.

"Let's roll," Ender said, leading the excedos out of the house.

Gabriel was about to head out last when Devlin called him back into the room.

Words spilled from the younger man before Dev had a chance to speak. "You're not going to pull me out of this, are you? Because I can finally fucking do something for you, and you can't stop me."

"What makes you think you don't do anything for me?" Devlin demanded.

"Yeah, I know—I get you off."

"Dammit, Gabriel." He hauled the man into his arms and kissed him, hard. When he pulled away, Gabe was staring at him. Because he knew something had changed. "I love you, you asshole. I didn't want to say it until . . ."

"Until you knew I survived. Because it would hurt less that way." There was no rancor or judgment in Gabriel's voice. Only understanding.

"How the hell you got so smart is beyond me." Devlin hung his head. "I know it was foolish. It would hurt just as much whether I said it or not."

"I'm just glad you finally copped to it."

"You be safe out there, Gabriel. You hear me?"

"Yeah, I hear you. I think I finally fucking hear you," Gabe whispered in his ear. "When I finish, I'm going to fuck you into the mattress."

Devlin jerked his head up at Gabe's warning—his cock twitched in response, and Gabe smiled as if he knew.

CHAPTER
Eighteen

Thanks to all the activity and preparations for the attack, Melanie had been forced to stay in control of the body she shared with her sister, and though Melanie kept up on the injections, she got less time now between them. Phoebe had mentioned that issue before, saying that using more than three injections in a row would begin a rapid breakdown of their effectiveness. Worse, by about the sixth shot, chest pains began. Mel had come awake a couple of times after Phoebe's run of several injections, only to spend the day in pain—once in an Itor medical unit. Mel kept all of this to herself, not wanting to worry Stryker or make Dev see her as a liability.

But hopefully, today would be the last time she ever had to inject herself more than once in a row anyway. More important, today would be the last time she saw the Itor compound. And her father.

Half the agents closed in on the ranch in vehicles under the cover of darkness and the severe storm Remy fired up. Others went in on foot, while still others dropped in from aircraft.

Mel, Dev, Gabe, Stryker, and Ender hung back while the first wave of the assault went down, which happened immediately after Itor's initial shock from the storm wore off. Zach handled the dogs, but soon gunfire, explosions, and screams coming from all over the property turned the compound into a nightmare.

Mel wasn't sure what Dev was waiting for, but he finally nodded, and then they were all off like a shot from the ridge where they'd been waiting. Stryker kept Itor men at bay by opening up rifts in the earth beneath them, and if the situation hadn't been so dire, she'd have gotten seriously turned on. His confidence, the gleam in his eyes, the dangerous expression on his face as he wielded a power so mighty . . . she couldn't contain a shiver of appreciation.

The ground shook all around them, and enemies tumbled into fissures that closed up as quickly as they'd opened. Any who managed to escape were taken out by Ender so fast Melanie missed it if she blinked.

It was all so horrible, and she had to keep repeating to herself that these people had hurt her. Had hurt a lot of innocents.

As Mel and Stryker mounted the steps to the main ranch house, a whistling sound brought Mel around. Her adrenaline was already a hot flame in her veins, but she screamed, dove for Stryker, and took him down on the deck as a pitchfork impaled itself in the wood slats right where his head would have been. That made her feel a little less sorry for all the dead Itor agents.

"Nice call, babe," he breathed, as he helped her up.

"You said not to use my power." Not that freezing the thing would have helped. But yeah, she was saving it all up for an emergency.

Or for Alek.

Ender zipped away, and for a few agonizing moments fought with the telekinetic who had launched the pitchfork. The sound of a spine snapping cut through the other sounds of battle, and then Ender was back, looking pleased as could be.

Melanie would never understand warrior types. And where

was Gabe? She looked around, but the man was gone. No one seemed concerned, so apparently that was part of a plan she didn't know about, but . . . *damn.*

Pistols drawn, the men entered the house, took down two Itor agents immediately, and then Melanie darted for the door to the right, the one that looked like a closet. The men guarded her while she stood for a retina scan, and then the hidden rear panel slid open, leading to a well-lit staircase that would take them into the underground facility.

As planned, Ender and Stryker remained behind to signal a false retreat. Dev handed Melanie his weapon, put up his hands, and moved ahead of her. Before she kicked into fake-Phoebe mode, she turned to Stryker.

"Be careful."

Though they scarcely had the time for it, he framed her face in his hands, bent his head, and kissed her. "You too."

Ender pushed a button on his watch. "We'll bring a team in ten minutes, unless the doors don't open or Sam tells us different. You in contact?"

Dev gave a sharp nod. "She's with me for now."

The facility was shielded against psychic interference, so there was a good chance that once Dev was belowground, his connection with Samantha would fail—which was why they'd had to set a time for the underground assault to begin. If all went well, Mel would deliver Dev to Alek and then sneak away to shut down the psychic shield and open all the doors around the ranch that led to the various underground buildings.

"Mel," Dev said, "Alek's been in my mind before, and he can probably do it again. Which means that once we meet up with him, you'll need to get away quickly and carry out your part of the plan before he gets inside my mind and finds out you aren't Phoebe."

She nodded. "Got it." She paused. "If he gets in your head and then somehow gets away, could he use the information to—"

"It would take weeks to get everything from me," Dev assured her. "And there are some things I trust other agents with, so no one person, including me, has *all* of ACRO's secrets."

Made sense, and Mel wondered if Alek did the same.

They moved down the staircase, with Mel pretending to be holding Dev captive. They made it past the first three people they encountered—all it took was for Melanie to bark out, "I have ACRO's boss. The assholes are falling back—go help! Now!"

The three tore up the stairs, where Ender and Stryker would take them down.

The fourth, fifth, and sixth people were where the trouble started.

Ian, a wall of muscle who was one of the few people who knew about Phoebe's relationship to Alek, rounded a corner. A man Mel didn't know came up behind Ian, and both drew down on Dev with their pistols.

"I'm taking him to Alek," she snapped. "Move aside."

"Alek gave orders that no one passes this point," Ian said.

Mel snorted. God, she hoped Phoebe snorted. "That order never includes me, and you know it."

"We've never been under attack by an enemy agency."

"ACRO is in retreat, and I hope you enjoy sunburns." She kept her gun hand steady between Dev's shoulder blades and threw out her other hand, praying these idiots would back down in the face of Phoebe's power.

"Phoebe." The voice from her flank filled her with dread. "Stand down."

She turned slowly to see Alek in the doorway to his personal chambers. This was what they'd come here for, but suddenly, she was wishing they'd gone with another plan.

"Dev." Alek smiled, the wolfish one that sent shivers down her spine. "So good to finally meet you. Nice work, Phoebe. Where the hell have you been?"

Phoebe would probably have rolled her eyes at the combination praise and spank. Mel just hoped her voice would work. "I was captured by Maurice," she said, remembering what Stryker had told her about the man who had captured them in Rome. "I escaped, but he got away before I could kill him. He's a traitor. I think he's the one who brought in ACRO."

Alek snarled. "If you have proof of his treachery, I'll make sure he drowns in his own blood." He gestured to Ian. "Bind Devlin's wrists and take him to my office."

So far, so good. Everything was going according to plan. Alek would take Dev, and she would find the control room, where she would open up the entire facility to psychics, satellites, and every ACRO agent. At that point, the second wave would arrive, and Itor would go down.

Dev put his hands behind his back, and Ian cuffed him with wrist ties that he'd plucked from his pocket.

"Got anything to say, Dev?" Alek asked.

"I have a lot to say. In private."

Alek cocked an eyebrow. "We do have a lot of catching up to do. We can go through my old photos. I believe I have a picture of your mother somewhere."

Why would Alek have a picture of Dev's mother? Mel made a mental note to ask Stryker later.

Dev's brown eyes narrowed. "Are we going, or are you planning to bore me to death here in the hallway?"

"I'm planning something involving your death, but you definitely won't be bored." Alek smiled at Mel. "Phoebe, handle the destruction of ACRO's forces, and then join me."

"Of course." She smiled confidently, relieved that this was all going so freaking well.

Alek grabbed Dev by the arm. "Come. We're long overdue for our father-son talk."

Mel gasped. *Son?* Staring in shock at Dev, she felt the ground shift beneath her. Her pistol fell from her numb fingers and clattered on the floor. Shit! Phoebe would never react like that, but before Mel could recover, Alek cursed. He knew.

"Stop her!"

She lurched to the side, summoning her power. But even as the tingle spread through her arm, a fist slammed into the side of her head, and it was game over.

Gabriel had been using his invisibility with greater ease over the past months. All the practice and training had paid off in spades and, thanks to the adrenaline rush, he was moving like a bat out of hell, taking out snipers and generally anyone else from Itor who got in any ACRO agent's way.

It meant dodging some bullets—literally. Because when Gabe was invisible, he wasn't bulletproof. He wore the vest so he didn't have to watch his back as carefully, but even so . . .

He still had to split his energy between concentrating on not dematerializing at an inopportune time and using his strength to kick some ass, but he finally felt part of ACRO. He had a purpose.

He'd been built for this.

A single beep from his watch told him that Mel's ten minutes were up. Her job should be done by now. Dodging debris flying through the air from Remy's storms, he headed back to the meeting point to be apprised of his next moves.

As he approached the main ranch house, his gut twisted at the sight of Ender and Stryker behind the shelter of a brick wall, barking out orders to bleeding and beaten ACRO agents. Something had gone terribly wrong—the agents should be gathering to enter the facility by now.

Ender looked grim as he told Gabe, "The psychic shield hasn't been shut off and none of the entrances except the one inside the house have been opened—Mel didn't hold up her end of the bargain and we don't know where she and Devlin are. It's your job to find them—we'll go in through the only entrance and take out as many I-Agents as we can."

Emotions rocketed through Gabe—no doubt, they showed on his face but, for the first time, Ender didn't call him on it.

No, all the men were close to Devlin—if he was killed, it would be too great a loss for ACRO to bear.

It can't end like this.

He choked everything back and said, "Let's roll."

"Stryker and I will go in first and make a path. You need to open up the facility and shut down the psychic shield. Fast." Ender took off for the house, with Stryker right behind him, both ducking low and firing shots as they ran.

Gabe concentrated, felt the cloak of invisibility cover him like a stinging rain.

This time, he welcomed the slight pain that came with the changing.

Heart racing, he followed the two ACRO agents into the house and into the closet where the hidden entrance to the underground facility was located. They moved silently down the stairs, the passageway growing wider every ten steps, where narrow landings with blind corners made for potentially dangerous ambushes by Itor assholes. Three-quarters of the way down, Gabe's impatience got the better of him, and he slipped between Ender and Stryker.

At the bottom, an I-Agent waited in ambush. Snarling, Gabe slammed the man's head against the wall, and he went down. Fucker. These guys had Dev, and Gabe wasn't going to show any mercy. Crouching, he snapped the enemy's neck, looking behind him as Ender nodded his approval in Gabe's general direction.

Gabe went down farther into the compound, descending into the depths with relative ease, since most of the security was on the first floor. Alek probably assumed no one could get past them.

Alek didn't count on him.

This place had an underground underground, it seemed. He stopped, listened. Tried to hear Dev, but he possessed no damned psychic ability at all.

Yet he could feel the man vibrating all around him. They

were bonding on some level—and that was enough for Gabe to keep pushing forward. Yeah, he needed to open the facility and shut down the psychic shield, but if he found Dev first . . .

He stopped at a door and put his hand through. Then slid halfway in and saw Devlin and Mel . . . and Alek.

The room was solid stone and metal-encased. Fire- and bombproof. Maybe it could even withstand the entire compound falling on it when Stryker did his earthquake thing.

But it couldn't withstand him.

Dev wasn't so much at a disadvantage because his hands were bound but rather because his psychic connection with Sam didn't work in this underground fortress, leaving him vulnerable to Alek's mind-reading ability.

"This is nice—we'll have a chance to bond, like a normal, happy family." Alek pyramided his fingers together as he glanced between Devlin and Mel, who had been seated on the floor next to him in Alek's luxurious office.

Dev snorted. "There's nothing nice about you, asshole." For that, he was cracked across the side of the face. He spat blood out of his mouth and met Alek's eyes. "Ah, Dad, I didn't think you cared."

"I care very much. You're about to find out just how much, when your precious ACRO—and a portion of the free world— dies."

A small gasp from Mel switched Alek's attention to her.

Mel, who'd just discovered that she had a brother. Devlin had been careful not to look at her, even though he felt her trying to catch his eye.

She was stunned. No doubt scared . . . and hopefully worthy of having his trust.

"Where is Phoebe?" Alek demanded from her. "This is your betrayal."

"How do you know it's mine?" Mel asked, her voice sweet as

apple pie, making Dev proud as hell. "Maybe your precious Phoebe felt she could run the place better than you ever could. Maybe she and I kissed and made up and we're trying to take over the world . . . or Itor, at the very least."

"Don't fuck with me, daughter dear. You're going to wish you were dead when I'm done with you." The sinister smile on Alek's lips as he glared at Mel made Dev sick. "Remember that time in the lab? The four days you spent with my favorite psychic torturer and his lecherous assistant?"

Mel swallowed hard enough for Dev to hear. "I have information on ACRO," she blurted, and so much for being on ACRO's side. She crumbled faster than a goddamned cookie. "Stuff you can't get from Dev because he assigns others to keep some things safe in the event that you get into his head again. I know what some of those things are, because I got real close to one of his agents."

Dammit. It was as he'd thought—Mel could not be trusted, should not have been. She might have information that could hurt his agents . . . Stryker had been too unguarded.

Both men had let their guard down too easily. Devlin should've known that no man or woman spawned from Alek could be totally trusted.

He guessed that had to include him as well, even though it twisted his gut to think that way. Because this man in front of him . . . he'd killed Dev's biological mother after she gave Dev up to his adoptive parents. Alek had caught her, and no doubt her death hadn't been pleasant. Years later, he'd used a brutal mind-rape on Devlin, which allowed all of ACRO and her agents to be exposed to the great evil Itor was.

One of the most evil men Dev knew was his biological father.

Getting past that would never be easy. Getting out of Alek's grasp could prove to be impossible.

Alek closed his eyes in concentration and then opened them. "You're worried that Melanie sold you out. That I can get ACRO secrets easily now. That you've betrayed your entire organization by putting your faith in the wrong woman. That you know no good can come from your biological family."

"Always trust your gut, Dev," Mel said softly. "That's what Alek taught me." She shifted, easing away from Dev, which was wise, because he really wanted to strangle her. "Father, I'll tell you what I know about ACRO—and it's a lot—in exchange for my life. I know you don't want Phoebe dead."

"Phoebe doesn't have to die for what I have planned for you." Alek strolled over to the wet bar, opened a drawer, and removed a leather box. "I've given you so many chances, Melanie. Because you're my daughter, I've allowed you freedom and luxuries. But when this is over, you'll have none of that. Your time in that body will be spent in chains, and I'll make sure whoever I assign to watch over you knows that he can enjoy you as much as he likes."

"I told you," Melanie said, her voice trembling with desperation, "I'll tell you everything I know. Please. Just . . . promise not to punish me. Promise, and I'll tell you what I know about ACRO's plans for the attack today. If I don't, Itor will fall, and if ACRO gets hold of me, they won't just torture me, they'll kill me. Which means your precious Phoebe will die too. Ask Devlin."

Alek didn't have to ask. He could read Dev's mind on the matter and Mel was right. Dev would kill her on the spot himself if given the opportunity.

Fuck. Devlin needed to stop thinking about all this shit. Distract Alek so he couldn't read his mind so easily—Dev had practiced his own form of a mind shield, but it wouldn't be nearly as effective as the one the ACRO psychics used when they linked their thoughts with him, and it required a hell of a lot of concentration.

Taking a deep, calming breath, he put it into place, building it slowly while Alek was busy. *Keep him busy.* "Tell me more about my mother."

There was a long, tense silence as Alek opened the box, palmed an object inside, and walked over to Mel. "What would you like to know?" He gripped her arm and injected her with a syringe filled with green liquid.

"Why did she leave you?"

Straightening, Alek smiled. "Because I'm a bastard. Like father, like son."

"And daughter," Devlin muttered, and Mel laughed—*laughed*—next to him.

"Devlin, I thought you knew better than to trust anyone from Itor. Especially me." And just like that, Dev knew Mel was gone, Phoebe in her place. "Alek, maybe we should let him watch the fireworks? It's time, isn't it?"

"See, Devlin," Alek said, as he hit a button on some sort of touchpad mounted to the wall, "that's the kind of forward thinking I appreciate in my offspring."

A wall panel slid back, revealing a large flat-screen TV, on which was a feed from London's bustling Trafalgar Square.

"I hate England," Phoebe said. "So this is going to be very amusing."

"Agreed." Alek glanced at his watch. "In exactly nineteen minutes, my 2012 machine is going to perform a test run and send a killing concentration of gamma rays into London. And you have a front-row seat. We'll make it a family night."

"You sick fuck," Dev growled, and then a familiar tingle of awareness washed over him, and he felt the soft brush of Gabe's fingers on his wrists.

Excellent. In a moment he'd be free. The catch was that if Alek decided to go on an exploratory mission inside Dev's head between now and then, both he and Gabe were dead men.

CHAPTER
Nineteen

There were times when Phoebe hated her father. And then he'd go and do something that made her all warm and squishy with the nearest thing she could feel to love.

Maybe it was love. She wasn't sure. The closest she'd been to the emotion was a few years ago, when she'd slept with an Itor agent named Jacques, and during the month they'd been together, she'd lost interest in all other bed partners. But then he'd gone and screwed some waitress.

Phoebe had killed the waitress instantly, but had let Jacques linger in agony in a hospital burn unit for three weeks before he died.

Hell hath no fury like a woman who can scorch.

And thanks to Alek injecting her with the antidote they'd developed to counteract the suppressant, Phoebe was now out and ready to do some of that scorching on Dev.

Strangely, though, she could feel Mel in the background, almost as if her sister was knocking on a door. Phoebe couldn't hear the knocks, but she could feel their vibration. Annoying, but Phoebe had another sibling to deal with, so Mel would have to wait.

"Oh, brother," she said sweetly, as Alek released her from her bonds, "you are going to die very, very painfully." She stood, rubbing her wrists. "After we watch every living thing in London reduced to a smoking pile of radiated ash, of course."

"You sick bastards," Dev growled. Such a broken record.

Alek shook his head. "You don't get it, do you? I don't *want* to kill those people. I have to." He poured himself a glass of whiskey, neat. "Now, your sister . . . she enjoys killing. A little too much. I think a few of her recreational activities have caused some damage." He tapped his temple. "Here."

Phoebe schooled her expression to hide the twinge of hurt. "Everything I've learned has been from you—" Her words were cut off as his backhanded strike slammed into her mouth.

"I never taught you to kill indiscriminately."

She almost laughed. Almost. Instead, she dabbed blood from her lips and glared at Dev. Surely it was his presence that was making their father so testy. It was definitely making Phoebe testy. That, and the fact that Melanie had stepped up her protest at being locked out, and was now a constant thud against the inside of Phoebe's skull. Figured that she'd choose this moment to grow some balls.

Alek sipped his drink. "Like I said, it's not that I *want* to kill the Londoners. I'm not a monster, despite what you may think, Devlin. But I have to perform a test run on my machine, and when I took aim at the world map, London got the dart in its stiff upper lip." He assessed Dev with eyes that matched his son's, and Phoebe had to bite back a snarl of jealousy that her asshole brother had gotten more of their father's features than she had. "Look at it this way: Scientists perform horribly cruel tests on animals, but they create medicines and medical procedures that help mankind. This is the same thing. Ultimately, I'll be saving lives with this test. I'll work out any glitches we find, so that when 2012 comes, I can be sure that my machine will absorb the gamma rays that would otherwise destroy *all* life on earth. I'll then be able to concentrate the power, end wars, genocide—"

"For a price," Dev snapped. "You'll sell death to the highest bidder. This has nothing to do with wanting to save mankind."

"Of course it does." Alek swirled the amber liquor in his glass, and why the hell didn't he hit Dev for mouthing off, the way he had Phoebe? "If mankind dies, where does that leave me?"

Snarling silently, Phoebe wheeled around to flip on the outside monitors, wanting to know how the battle was going. As she reached for the switches, a blow came out of nowhere, striking her in the kidney, and suddenly, Dev was up and crashing into Alek, and she was fighting with someone she couldn't see.

Gritting her teeth against the pain from the sucker punch, she struck out, heard a grunt, and felt her fist slam against a wall of muscle. Quickly, she released a stream of fire. Didn't hit Mr. Invisible, but she set Alek's couch on fire. A fist sank into her gut, a fucking low blow, sending her stumbling backward. As she caught herself on the edge of the bar, she let loose another blast of flame, and this time was rewarded by a yelp of pain and the hiss of fire burning clothing and skin.

And still, Melanie was fighting for control, a distraction Phoebe didn't need. Especially because it seemed that the bitch had grown stronger.

People were pounding on the door outside—ACRO, had to be. Another blow, this time to the temple, knocked her off her feet. In the space between the coffee table and the leather recliner, she could make out her father and brother battling. Both were bleeding, battered, and though she knew Alek was in top form and a damned good fighter, Dev was younger, in great shape, and no doubt as expertly combat-trained as Alek.

She reached out, prepared to send a fireball into Dev, but Alek wheeled into the path of her weapon, and she cursed, rolled to her feet just as an invisible foot connected with her chin. Again, she tumbled backward, but this time, she swept her legs out as she went down, catching the invisible motherfucker hard enough to knock him into the wall. A picture crashed down and splintered, and suddenly, there was an unconscious, bleeding man on the carpet.

"Asshole," she spat.

Dev had Alek pinned to the floor and was pounding on him, his fists dripping with blood that sprayed in an arc with every blow to her father's face. Rage lit her up so hotly that her veins might as well run with lava.

"Die!" She threw out her hand to blast him with a stream of fire that would make a flamethrower seem like a child's toy.

Nothing happened.

No! She couldn't be empty. Panicked, she reached deep, feeling for her power. Relief washed over her when she felt the nearly full well . . . but she couldn't access it. It was as if there was a shield over the opening.

Melanie! That bitch! Somehow, she was blocking Phoebe, and damn her, she would pay dearly for this. If it was the last thing she did, Phoebe would hurt Mel so badly that she would never recover.

Cursing, she darted to the two men and leaped, landing a spin-kick right in Dev's mouth. He fell backward, and she took instant advantage, slamming her boot into his ribs. She went for a second kick, but he rolled, and then was knocked flat by Alek, who had recovered enough to put a serious hurting on Dev.

A sudden scratching on the inside of Phoebe's skull was like nails on a chalkboard, except searing, agonizing pain came with it. Melanie wanted out . . . fuck . . . no . . .

Something niggled at her, and she cranked her head around to see Stryker looking through the window in the door as his ACRO buddies worked to get the sucker open. And then it started. The low rumble of an earthquake that put a knot of dread in her belly. Terror was a monster inside her, and as she felt herself being sucked into unconsciousness, her one consolation was that Alek had a knife, and he was about to plunge it into Dev's heart.

Melanie came to in a screaming rush. Before she even fully understood what was happening, she saw Alek straddling Dev on the floor, a knife poised in the air and murder in her father's eyes.

He brought the knife down.

With a scream of terror and fury, Melanie sent a blast of concentrated cold at Alek. It struck him like a blow, knocking him off Dev and shredding the skin on the right side of his upper body. Dev rolled, captured the knife, but he was injured badly and—

"Mel! Let us in!"

"Stryker!" She darted to the door and spun the lock, releasing the mechanism and swinging the door open.

Men rushed in, and she heard yelps, thumps, and Stryker tugged her into his arms and held her as the sounds died down.

She didn't need to look to know her father was dead.

Stryker tightened his arms around Mel. "You did it, Mel . . . you controlled your powers. You helped Dev, probably saved his life."

"I owed him that much." The tears welled in her eyes and he stroked her hair. "Alek got what he deserved."

"It's over, baby—he's gone. That bastard can never hurt you again."

That bastard was currently being hauled away by Ender and Trance—his body would be taken back to the ACRO compound for safekeeping. And, probably, experimentation.

Stryker didn't give a damn, as long as the man was gone from their lives. Itor was nearly destroyed—its agents would no doubt scatter and try to regroup, but to gain the same strength Itor once had would be impossible.

"One down, two to go," Mel said as she watched Alek being carried away, referencing both Phoebe and the machine, although the latter was the far more pressing problem at the moment. "We don't know the location of the weapon."

"I do." Dev groaned from where he'd rolled over on the ground. Gabriel was at his side, dazed, and with blood running down his face. "I read the bastard while we fought. That's why I got my ribs kicked in. I was distracted." He spit blood onto what was probably a damned expensive carpet. "Machine's set to go off within minutes. We gotta go. Vehicle. Now."

Stryker fished his phone from his pocket as Gabe helped Devlin to his feet. "Ryan will have a Jeep waiting outside." He sent Ryan a text, knew the guy would be ready by the time they all got topside.

Gabe practically carried Devlin out of the underground compound himself as Stryker scooped Mel up. She was still shaky and there was no time to waste.

"I've got you," he told her. "This is almost over." Almost, but not close enough. Outside in the sun made hazy by remnants of Remy's storm, the all-too-familiar stench of battle struck him in the face—blood, bowels, smoke, dirt. The fight was still going on, the sounds of bodies colliding, gunfire, and electric blasts thick in the air, but it was clear that ACRO now had the upper hand, and it was only a matter of time before Itor fell completely.

"Hurry, Stryker—just hurry," Mel whispered, and he did, easing her into the Jeep's backseat and scrambling in next to her. Gabriel came in on her other side, having put Devlin into the front seat next to Ryan.

"Hang on," Ryan advised them all, as the Jeep had only a bikini top and the doors were long gone. Mel bounced around with men on either side of her, holding on to the roll bar as best she could.

The wind roared in their ears as Ryan drove the Jeep like a madman, Devlin directing him along the crude ranch roads that jarred them back and forth.

"Dev." Mel tapped him on the shoulder. "I'm sorry about

earlier. At the office. I wasn't switching sides. I was hoping Alek would release me so I could help you—"

"I know." Though Dev was obviously in pain, he reached up, took her hand, and gave it a squeeze. "I know now. I should have trusted you. And I should have told you I was your brother."

Ryan did a whiplash thing to stare at Dev for a second, and then he shook his head and went back to watching where he was going.

"It's okay," Mel said, but Stryker knew she and Dev were going to have a lot of talking to do when this was over.

The Jeep slowed as they entered a patch of brush-covered ground. "This isn't it, Ryan," Devlin said, spacing his words between pained breaths. "Keep going."

"There's nothing here," Ryan said, but he did as Dev asked and stepped on the gas. Stryker squinted against the sand and wind, his body practically quaking with anticipation.

Mel was leaning into the front seat, staring out the front window for better visibility. "We're close. I've seen this before." Stryker wondered how she and Dev recognized anything—it was all dirt, rock, and nothingness.

But then, in the middle of nowhere, sharp, unnatural angles caught Stryker's eye. Reaching between the seats, he grabbed Ryan's shoulder and pointed as a sand-colored set of giant doors rose out of the side of a hill. A hangar. The damned facility blended so well with the surroundings they could've easily crashed into the thing.

If there had been a sandstorm, they would have.

"This is the main entrance," Dev said. "I saw some sort of feeding shack that Alek used, but this is for moving large equipment. Unfortunately, I didn't get the code out of Alek's head." He glanced at his watch and cranked his neck to face Ryan. "I hope to hell you can deal with this. We have five minutes until eight million Londoners die."

Stryker slapped Ryan on the shoulder. "No pressure or anything."

"Fuuuuck," Ryan breathed. "Let's go."

They piled out of the vehicle, and Stryker, Gabe, and Dev provided cover as Ryan, with Melanie beside him, did his weird electronic magic on the mechanism that worked the doors.

"This thing is built like a fortress," Gabe muttered, as he kept a sharp eye on the horizon.

"So how do we stop the machine?" Stryker asked, swinging his pistol toward a puff of dust in the distance, but he relaxed at the sight of some sort of rodent skittering out of the brush.

"A drop of blood." Dev's voice was mushy through his swollen lips, but there was the typical Dev determination there. "It's set for Alek's and Phoebe's blood."

There was a funny feeling in Stryker's gut, though, that all of this was a little too easy.

A massive clanking noise rang out, followed by a whir as the huge hangar doors slid open. Stryker slipped through the crack first. Inside, a single male in a white jumpsuit raised his hands into the air. Clearly, the people here were scientists, not soldiers.

He gestured to the others, and everyone followed, Mel in the middle, kept safe sandwiched between Ryan and Dev. Ryan used flex-cuffs to restrain the guy, and then they moved quickly to the rear of the hangar, ran into another white suit, and Ryan repeated the procedure. Stryker hoped to hell the guy had a pocketful of the plastic cuffs.

Fortunately, they encountered no resistance as they moved through the halls, and when they reached the door at the end, they found out why. A man in a white coat ran into them as he hoofed it toward the exit.

"Go! The machine is about to engage."

Dev grabbed the man by the arm. "Why are you leaving?"

"The radiation." The white-haired dude blinked. "Didn't Alek tell you? We've got to be outside the facility when it fires."

"Shit." Dev nodded to Ryan, who did the flex-cuff thing. "You're coming with us."

The guy's eyes bugged out of his head. "But—"

"Get us into that room." Dev nodded at the control panel to the right of the door. "Now, or we all get cooked."

The dude's finger shook as he punched in a code and then stood still for a retina scan. The door whooshed open, and Stryker drew a sharp breath at the sight before him.

Holy shit, the machinery that filled the cavern on the other side of the door could have come straight out of a Terminator movie. Stuff was beeping, shiny metal parts were shifting, and at the front, under a glass cap, was a clock.

2:46 and counting down.

"Now, Mel," Dev breathed.

Mel rushed forward, lifted the glass, and stared at the white pad just beneath the countdown clock. "I need something sharp."

2:38

Stryker unsnapped the sheath on his belt and palmed his Ka-Bar. Mel's gaze met his as she held out her hand to him. "I'd do this if I could," he said, and she offered him a shaky smile.

"I know."

As gently as he could, he pricked Mel's finger with the tip of the knife, held her hand steady, and squeezed the drop of blood onto the pad.

2:22

They all held their breath. Waited for the clock to stop.

2:15

"It's not working," Devlin stated the obvious. "Try another drop."

Mel did. Several more—and it became obvious, with T minus two minutes until mass fucking destruction, that this wasn't going to work.

1:59

"Once the timer hit three minutes, only Alek's blood could have stopped it," the scientist said, and Stryker wanted to fucking kill him.

"You couldn't have said that before we fucking wasted time and Mel's blood?"

The guy shrugged, and Ryan cursed. "We don't have time to go back and get Alek's body."

"I'll take care of it," Stryker said. He studied the reinforced structure, the heavy beams and lead-lined walls and ceiling. It was a capsule built to withstand natural and man-made disasters. Polar shifts, meteor strikes, earthquakes.

But Stryker's earthquakes weren't your average dirt-shakers.

He stared at the ceiling and the floor and he closed his eyes. Fisted his hands. Felt the familiar energy race through him with a hard tingle that went from pleasant to burning in seconds.

This would be a big one—and it was going to hurt. Would drain him badly.

There was no choice.

He vaguely heard Devlin tell the others to get the hell out. It would be a race against time, because Stryker needed to stay inside the building until the cracks began to show.

And no one was moving.

"All for one." Mel remained there, her body trembling as the earth did under their feet.

Stryker opened his eyes. "Run," he growled, and when everyone, including Mel, hesitated, he shouted, "Run! Now!"

This time, they took off, though Mel lagged behind, matching his slower pace, unwilling to leave him. He took up the rear, still utilizing his powers to bring down the building hard enough to smash that fucking machine.

"Go . . . go!" Stryker yelled as they zigzagged between the steel girders that began to crumple, and ducked to avoid falling machinery.

Once they reached the hangar, things got critical as the structure aboveground began to collapse, the light fixtures becoming bombs. One of the giant mountings slammed into Ryan's shoulder, knocking him flat, and only Dev and Gabe's help got him to his feet before a steel beam punched down hard enough to sink a couple of feet into the concrete where Ryan's head had been.

The hangar doors ahead were open, but a crack split the earth in front of them and was racing toward Stryker and the others as they sprinted for the exit.

"Stryker . . ." Mel squeezed his hand, trying to dodge the fissure, but he realized doing so would get them crushed. He tugged her toward the gaping crack, and at the last minute, he swung her over his shoulder and leaped.

The bright sun greeted them as they came down outside the hangar doors and ran like hell for the Jeep. As Dev, Ryan, and Gabe scrambled inside, Stryker spun around with Mel at his side and drilled every last ounce of his power into the earth beneath the facility. Pain streaked through him—at this level, the sexual side effects were negated by the agony of wielding so much energy. It was as if shards of glass were flowing through his veins.

At some point, he hit his knees, and Mel was right beside him, holding him as the ground shook and his body heaved.

When it was over, there was nothing but a giant crater in the land. His watch beeped, and though he scarcely had the energy to look at it, he did, and smiled. Because time was up. The machine, which should have just sent out a death ray, was scrap metal.

"We did it." Dev was standing on Stryker's other side, looking out over the acres of sunken ground. "The machine is dead and Itor is all but destroyed. We couldn't have done it without you." He smiled at Mel. "Without either of you."

"We're all a bunch of goddamned heroes," Stryker muttered, and then he actually felt like a hero when Mel cupped his chin, brought his face around, and kissed him like he was her world.

"Let's go," she said. "Let's put the past where it belongs and go home."

Yeah, ACRO had always been home to him, and now he couldn't wait to share it.

CHAPTER
Twenty

Dev had been nice enough to let Mel and Stryker take a brief detour to Rome so Mel could gather what few possessions she had—mainly, her course books and her mother's topaz ring.

TAG agents had taken down the Rome Itor office and were now scouring the apartment building that had housed agents and served as their command central, so Stryker and Mel had as long as they needed to go through her apartment, but they'd make it quick. Mel had given herself a shot a mere hour before they landed in Rome, and already Phoebe was fighting to get out, even though her time in control at ACRO should have reset the length of effectiveness for each injection. They needed to grab Mel's belongings and get her back on the plane, restrained and knocked out, and they had no time to waste.

Now she and Stryker stood in the hallway of the apartment she'd considered home for five years, and when he asked what he should grab, she just shrugged. "Everything is Phoebe's. The clothes, the decorations, the furniture . . ." She shook her head.

"You've given me more in a matter of days than I've ever had. I just want the books and the ring."

She started down the hall, but detoured into the bathroom to raid the meds box for anything that might be useful to ACRO. Stryker's cellphone rang, and he ducked into the bedroom to talk.

As she tugged open the cupboard, a sharp stab of pain shot through her brain. Phoebe. Son of a—

Clutching her head, Mel staggered toward the door. "Stryker," she gasped. Or tried to gasp. Nothing came out of her mouth.

And then there was nothing at all.

Phoebe blinked. Blinked again. She was in her bathroom in Rome. How the hell had they gotten here? She heard a voice . . . Stryker. Cocking her head, she listened. He seemed to be talking to someone on the phone. Someone named Wyatt. They were laughing, talking about . . .

Holy shit. Phoebe stumbled backward, slapping her hand over her mouth to cover the sound of her cry. Itor . . . fragmented. Headquarters and three satellite offices were destroyed. Itor agents were either fleeing the other offices or surrendering to ACRO. And her father, *oh, God,* her father . . .

The pain went through Phoebe like a bullet. It ricocheted off her bones and tore through organs and turned her heart into an aching, bleeding laceration. Her father was dead. The only person who had ever connected with her personally and emotionally had been killed.

By her own brother. And with Melanie's help.

Icy hot hatred burned her soul to ash. She was going to crush Dev. He would die for what he'd done. But before she could do that, she had to make Stryker and Melanie pay for their roles in Alek's death and Itor's ruin.

Wheeling around, she took the drug box from the open cupboard and grabbed two vials . . . Nullox to kill Stryker's earth-quake ability and a sedative that worked instantly but lasted only a couple of minutes. She didn't care whether or not the two should be mixed; if Stryker died, it would be almost as fun as what she planned as an alternative.

It took her all of thirty seconds to fill a syringe, and then she crossed the hall to the bedroom, where Stryker was still chatting with his buddy about how Itor had been wiped off the face of the planet. Asshole.

He turned just as she raised the syringe. The smile on his face fell as the needle jammed into his throat, and though he struck out, his blow fizzled, the medicine taking instant effect. He made a satisfying thump on the floor when he hit.

Working quickly, she stripped him of his shirt, dragged his heavy ass onto the bed, dug out her toys from the nightstand drawer, and bound his ankles and wrists with metal hoops that locked into place on rails she'd had installed in the headboard and footboard. A button above the headboard railing popped out, and all she'd have to do would be to push it to release him at the right time.

Now she had him. If the Nullox worked the way it did on most people, she would have an hour to get what she wanted from Stryker. Not that she'd need an hour. She had to hurry, be-cause even now, Mel was scratching at the seams of their skull, desperately wanting out. And though it galled to no end, Phoebe had to admit that Mel's strength had increased tremendously, and Phoebe didn't know how long she could hold her off.

He began to wake, so she hurried to the kitchen, made a phone call, and arranged a few things for dear Mel. Stryker's angry shout spurred her, and she hurried back to the bathroom and once again pawed through her drug box, annoyed at how Mel had cleaned it out of the suppressant injections, but she let it go. For the last part of her plan, she wanted Melanie front and center.

Beneath the recreational drugs, she found a baggie of blue rapid-dissolve pills Itor had developed to help its male agents achieve almost instant hard-on. So really, they could also be classified as recreational drugs . . .

She spilled two out of the baggie, snorted two lines of coke to make sure Mel was good and edgy when she took over, and stripped naked. Her bare feet didn't make a sound as she sauntered into the bedroom, where Stryker was lying on the bed spread-eagled, wrists and ankles bound by the device she'd used so many times on so many men and women. His body was motionless, but his eyes seethed with hatred. Excellent.

"What's the matter, Pookie?" she asked sweetly. "Still upset that you got bested by a girl?"

"You are no girl." The deep, lethal rasp of his voice made her go instantly wet. "You're a monster as evil as your dead father."

Dead. She inhaled deeply, summoning as much calm as she could muster. "You play that evil-doesn't-fall-far-from-the-tree tune over and over, don't you?" Before he could hurl some tiresome insult at her, she leaped onto the bed and straddled his broad chest.

Surprise flickered in his eyes as her nudity finally registered. "What are you doing?" he growled.

"What do you think I'm doing? I told you I'd have you, and I always keep my word." She cupped one breast, flicking her thumb over the sensitive nipple. "You've sucked on these, haven't you?" Slowly, she slid her hand down her stomach, was slightly disappointed when Stryker's gaze didn't follow. As she parted herself with her fingers, she moaned. Fucking him was going to be so good. "Have you had your mouth here? Have you eaten this cunt with your talented tongue? Did Melanie scream your name when she came?"

"I hate you."

She laughed and circled her clit with her middle finger. "I'd make you lick me, but I don't trust you not to bite."

"You're smarter than I thought."

"Oh, you have no idea." Lunging forward, she pinched his nose.

"What the——" He didn't have a chance to complete his sentence. She jammed the two pills down his throat, palmed his chin, and forced his mouth shut.

His struggles nearly threw her, but she gripped him tight with her thighs and refused to let go of his head as he bucked and hacked, trying to get the pills up. "No use trying to keep from swallowing. They dissolve within seconds."

He continued to fight for much longer than she expected. Impressive, really. By the time he started to settle down, he was panting through clenched teeth, and her thighs ached.

"Good boy," she murmured, as she released his jaw and nose.

The tendons in Stryker's neck strained, and his jaw was tight as he snarled at her. "What did you give me?"

Smiling, Phoebe slid down his muscular body to unzip his jeans and palm his soft cock. "Just a little insta-Viagra. I had a feeling you'd be less than thrilled to fuck me, so I'm helping you along." It was already working, and she reveled in the sensation of his shaft swelling in her hand.

His eyes shot wide as the implication of what she'd just said sank in. "You *bitch*," he hissed. "You might be able to make me hard, but you will never make me come."

Oh, that would be the ultimate humiliation, wouldn't it? He'd hate himself for the rest of his life if his body betrayed him, reached that ultimate pleasure with a woman he hated. She definitely wanted him to come, but even so . . . "I don't need you to." Gripping him in her fist, she guided him to her entrance. "*My* orgasm is all I need to get what I want."

A slow, wicked smile split his face. "Know what I want?"

"What's that, lover?"

He arched his back, pushing his cock so deep inside her she gasped. "I want to stop playing the awesome images of your father's last living moments in my head. The way he screamed . . . cursed your name for abandoning him as he died . . . oh, yeah, that'll make me come. Total turn-on."

"Bastard!" Phoebe slapped him, raking her nails across his

face and leaving bloody scratches. "I'm going to make you and Mel suffer. And I'm going to kill Dev if it's the last thing I do."

"You kill Dev and it *will* be the last thing you do."

She leaned over, tongued the blood streaming down his face. "I'm fine with that." She rode him hard, letting his hatred fuel her lust. His thick shaft scraped sensitive tissue, and fuck yeah, she'd bet Melanie was enjoying his cock on a regular basis, the bitch. How was it fair that Mel, the useless, weak twin, the one who had done nothing to make her mark on the world, could land a sculpted, hot piece of meat like Stryker? Sure, Phoebe got hot men—and women—all the time. But they were just fucks. Whether they were one-offs or regular lays, they were nothing but booty calls.

Somehow, idiot Melanie had gotten herself a powerful ACRO agent who looked like a god and had a dick to match. And he cared about her.

Man, Phoebe hated that bitch.

The hatred burned in her veins, heating her all the way to her core. Planting her palms on Stryker's chest for leverage, she lifted her hips until the head of him nearly came free of her sex, and then she impaled herself deep, rocking her clit against his pubic bone. His entire body went taut, his lips peeled back from his teeth, and she knew he wanted to kill her.

So. Fucking. Hot.

She repeated the lift-plunge-rock routine until her orgasm hovered within reach. She wanted to take it, wanted to enjoy what promised to be an awesome climax made better by the fact that Stryker would have to watch how his own dick had given pleasure to a woman he hated.

"Remember this," she moaned. "Remember how it was my juices that were dripping down your cock. Not Mel's. Mine. And when she's panting through her climax, remember that the orgasm is *mine*."

"You crazy bitch. What the fuck are you talking about?"

She flattened herself on top of him, still rocking to keep the climax right there. Pleasure rippled through her, pre-orgasm contractions that made her gasp. Quickly, as she went over the edge, she pushed the button that released him from the cuffs, and then she retreated inside the brain she shared with Mel, finally letting her sister come to consciousness.

She smiled as she went, loving the orgasm, loving Stryker's enraged roar, loving the fact that she'd just ruined her sister's life.

"Oh, yes . . ." Mel gasped as an intense orgasm racked her body, even as her body was flipped, her wrists pinned roughly, and the air squashed out of her lungs. Stryker came down hard on top of her, and she felt his cock sliding from her wet core.

Confusion muddled her thoughts, the climax still rocking her, some sort of amazing high making her body tingle.

"S-Stryker?"

His head snapped back as if he'd been slapped, his eyes going wide with shock. "Mel?"

"Mmm . . ." She couldn't catch her breath. Oh, she loved making love to him. He always knew exactly . . . wait. She shook her head in a desperate attempt to dislodge the cobwebs.

"Mel. Shit!" He rolled off her, tucking his glistening—and still hard—cock in his pants.

What . . . *oh, God*. He hadn't been making love to her. He'd been fucking Phoebe. A massive fissure split her heart wide open, and pain spilled through the opening, twisting her insides and turning her stomach inside out. She scrambled off the bed . . . she was naked. Stryker was staring at her in horror, and yeah, she just bet he was.

"You asshole!" She didn't hesitate. Her fist flew out and caught him in the same cheek that bore scratches, because yeah, Phoebe liked it rough. And so did Stryker.

His head snapped back because he'd been struck, but otherwise, he remained still. "Mel, it's not what you think."

"No? Was your dick inside Phoebe? Then I think it's what I think. You son of a bitch!" Unable to stay for one more second in the room, she fled. She didn't know where she was going, didn't care. She just needed to be away from him.

Too bad she couldn't outrun herself.

How could he? How could he have—

She skidded to a halt in the kitchen, her lungs seizing, her mind jittery with what she now recognized as a cocaine high. There was a note on the counter, written in Phoebe's elegant script, sitting on top of her college texts.

I contacted your college's dean and told them I was you. Said that my guilt over cheating on several of my exams was overwhelming. Guess what, you little whore? You've been kicked out.

Mel's knees buckled, and she barely caught herself on the counter before she went down. And then . . . oh, no. *No, no, no!*

Her mother's ring, the only thing she had left of their mother, the only possession Mel owned for herself, was a melted, twisted lump of gold next to the books.

Phoebe had taken everything from her. The man she loved, her fantasy degree, and her only link to their mother.

The pain in her chest turned to a hollow, cold, empty space as she reached numbly for one of the knives in the wood block on the counter. She wasn't even sure what she intended to do with it, but her drugged and emotionally overloaded brain was no longer rational.

"Mel!" Stryker's voice came from behind her. She loved the way he talked, the deep, resonating rumble. When he was making love, it went even deeper, breathless. Had he used that seductive voice on Phoebe?

Slowly, she turned around. "She's taken everything from me," she whispered. "There's nothing left."

Stryker, bare-chested and pants still partially unzipped, held up his hands in a placating gesture. His voice was low, soothing, like a police negotiator trying to talk someone off a ledge. "You have me. Just put down the knife."

"You were fucking my sister!" she screamed. "For what? More information about Itor? For kicks? I know you hate her, but maybe you were punishing her? Maybe she used her powers and got you all worked up?" God, she wanted to throw up. She wanted Phoebe to die, and she put the knife to her throat.

"That's not what happened. Please, Mel, put the knife down. You don't need to do this."

She gave a bitter laugh. "You don't get it, do you? This isn't about killing myself. It's about killing her. Finally, for once, I'm going to take something from her, the way she's taken everything from me."

"She didn't take me away from you." He tilted his wrists to show her the bleeding, raw circles around them. "Go look at the bed. She cuffed me. She shoved some sort of drug down my throat to make me hard. She forced herself on me, Mel. I swear to you, I didn't want it. I swear, I wouldn't have come. She couldn't have made me do that."

Horror replaced the anger inside her, and the nausea that threatened a moment ago became a reality. Dropping the blade, she dove for the sink and fought to keep her lunch down. Phoebe had raped him. Dear, sweet God, could this get any worse? Could her sister possibly be more vile?

Stryker's hand came down on her hair and gathered it back, and with his other hand, he stroked her back gently. How could he possibly be so nice to her after what had been done to him? And after she'd thought the worst of him.

"I'm sorry," she rasped. "I'm so sorry."

He started the water, wet a paper towel, and eased her away from the sink to wipe her mouth. "It's not your fault."

"If I'd been stronger, if I'd just fought to come out sooner—"

"Shh." He pressed his finger to her lips. "We're not going to play that. We won, okay? She didn't get what she wanted."

Mel blinked, but that didn't stop the tears from spilling.

Stryker gathered her against him and held her tight. "I can't do this anymore." She clung to him, but this would be the last time. "I—I thought we could work around her. I thought we could be together, and I could have some semblance of normalcy."

"You can. Once we're back at ACRO—"

"No." Inhaling deeply, she prepared herself for what had to be said. And done. "When we get back, you're going to lock me up and throw away the key."

Stryker went taut. "I can't do that."

"You can, and you will. Phoebe will never stop trying to hurt you and everyone around you. I can't be responsible for that. You forgave me for what happened to Akbar, but our relationship can't survive another death." She pulled away, and her heart pounded against her rib cage in protest. "For what it's worth, you've given me the happiest days of my life. You probably don't want to hear this, but . . . I love you."

"Mel . . ." Stryker's throat worked on a hard swallow. "I won't let you do this. We can work it out. I know we can."

He didn't say he loved her back. Not that she'd expected him to. How could he love someone who was basically the same person who murdered his friend and violated him? And even if he could, she wasn't going to put him or anyone else at risk from Phoebe.

"My mind is made up." Closing her eyes, she turned away. "But promise me that if, somehow, Phoebe ever tries to hurt you or anyone else, you won't hold back because of me."

"Mel—"

"Promise me! Kill her, Stryker. If she hurts anyone, kill her, or I swear to you, I will."

Silence stretched, and for a long time, she didn't think he'd answer. When he did, his voice was broken. "Damn you," he said gruffly. "Damn you for making me do this."

"Is that a promise?"

"Yeah."

Relief made her entire body sag. Stryker caught her, and as he hauled her to him, he put his mouth to her ear. "I'm going to wait for you to change your mind."

She didn't say it, but he had to know.

She would never change her mind.

The marks around Stryker's wrists and ankles would heal quickly. The memories of Phoebe taking him against his will, not so much, but the fact that Mel was pulling back from him because of it made him furious.

The Mel who made him promise to kill her was uncompromising. Unafraid.

God, he loved her. Knew it with all his heart . . . and still couldn't tell her so.

The most frustrating part was, he didn't know why.

"You don't need to atone for her sins," he told her fiercely, the promise he'd just made to her burning a hole in his gut.

She pulled out of his embrace, grabbed a blanket off the back of the sofa, and wrapped it around her naked body, hiding it from his view. "Unfortunately, I do."

"So you're just going to give up on having a life of your own? You're giving up on us? Don't you realize that you're doing to yourself what your father did to you?"

"What are you talking about?"

"With the food—how your father and Phoebe starved you for years. You're going to stop yourself from being with me—you're going to let them win, dammit. They want you to be unhappy and you're letting them."

"I can't let Phoebe hurt you again. I'm keeping you safe," she said stubbornly.

"You're not keeping me safe at all, Mel. This, what's happening between us, it was supposed to happen this way. It's not some goddamned coincidence."

"You were hunting me," she pointed out.

"I was hunting Phoebe," he corrected her. "I didn't believe you existed. And try as you might, you can't fight fate. Trust me. I tried."

She frowned. "What do you mean?"

He sighed, wondered if he should've told her this before. Wondered if it would've made any goddamned difference—if it would now. "Oz made a prediction to me a long time ago."

"Wait, Oz? Have I met him?"

"No. He was Dev's partner for a long time. And Creed's brother—the guy with all the tats you saw in the cafeteria the other day?" She nodded and he continued. "Oz was killed a little while ago. He sacrificed himself to save Dev's life. Before that, he was an integral part of ACRO. And he was kind of . . . freaky. He had this thing he called the spirit posse—he could communicate with the dead; he was psychic and he made a lot of predictions."

She looked slightly skeptical, but she was also part of the world of secret agents, so she wouldn't be in total disbelief. "Did his predictions always come true?"

"Oz was always right." The man had passed his predictions on matter-of-factly, but they were never given in haste or lightly. Stryker was pretty sure there was a lot more Oz knew but never let on.

But the virgin thing . . . well, Stryker guessed that was Oz's way of letting him know that control would be important in more ways than one.

And he'd blown it the first time he'd been with Mel. He looked at her now, thought about the first time he'd had sex with her, her words to him.

Funny . . . but I always thought my first time might be more . . . well, not hateful.

The thing was, even if he'd known, he wasn't sure it would've been different that time. Couldn't have been. He still wouldn't have been able to look her in the eye then. But things were different now. And Mel was threatening to take it away.

"What was the prediction, exactly—about us?" She asked hesitantly, as if she didn't want to hear anything that might change her mind about keeping them apart.

That was his goal and he prayed it would work. "He said I'd marry a virgin. I told him he was off his rocker. And then, when we had sex . . . Christ, you told me it was your first time."

Her eyes widened at the memory.

"I was so goddamned rough with you." He stared at the floor. "I was an asshole."

Mel walked over to him then, touched his cheek, made him look her in the eye. "You weren't gentle, no, but it was good, Stryker. Really."

"You're just trying to make me feel better." Stryker shook his head.

"What's the big deal about virgins?"

"They're a lot of work . . . need a lot of handling. I always went for the more experienced women because I don't have that kind of patience. I didn't anyway. You changed all of that."

"Why did you wait to tell me this?" she asked, after a moment of hesitation.

"I don't know. It's a little freaky. And I didn't want you to think that it was only happening because of what Oz said."

Just because it's fated doesn't mean it's not real, Oz would say. *It's actually just the opposite.*

"I think I would've liked Oz," she said, stroking Stryker's reddened wrist with her thumb. "So, my brother lost the love of his life."

"A great love, for sure." Stryker paused. "He and Gabe seem to be doing okay."

"Love comes at a cost—and seemingly against all odds—for an operative," Mel mused.

"I guess that's why it feels so damned good." He unzipped his pants, let them fall to the ground. The next casualty was her blanket and then he wrapped his arms around her instead. Carried her to the bathroom and started the shower.

"Stryker, please—"

"I'm not letting you go without a fight, dammit. We're going to wash that bitch off us, and then we're going to make it right."

She struggled, but she was no match for him. And he knew she wouldn't use her powers against him, so he held her fast until he got them under the warm spray, pushed her back against the tile wall and released her after he shut the glass door behind him. He grabbed the body wash and squirted it on the puff he found. Gently, he washed her, lathering her breasts, her belly . . . then reached down between her legs.

She stood silently, letting him have his way. And when he was done, she took the puff from him and did the same to him, focusing on his chest, his neck . . . and finally, she brought her hands to his cock and washed him with tender care. And then they stood under the water together, letting the suds run off their bodies and disappear down the drain.

A fresh start. Symbolic.

He'd been hard in her hands, and now he was throbbing against her. "I want you, Mel."

She smiled wanly. "The drug . . ."

"This has nothing to do with the drug Phoebe gave me and everything to do with you," he told her. "You need to believe that, Mel. I've never fucking lied to you, and I'm not about to start now."

As if to prove it, he picked her up, forcing her to wrap her legs around him as his cock probed her sex. With her back once again against the tile, he penetrated her in a long, slow stroke that made them both groan.

"So right," he murmured into her ear. "You can't stop me from doing this to you—from wanting you. You can't deny us, Mel, no matter how hard you try."

"Stryker . . . please." She buried her head against his shoulder as he drove into her, her wet heat like a tight fist, milking him to orgasm. And he needed one—needed to have it inside of her.

"With me, Mel. Come with me." He fingered her clit and she gasped. She was so close . . . and when she began to contract around him, he went over the edge as well, spurting in a hot rush inside her.

CHAPTER
twenty-one

Devlin and his agents returned to ACRO in the early morning hours. First, they were attended to by medical—most of their injuries had been taken care of on the long jet ride home, but there was medication to be prescribed, X rays to be taken. Healing to be done.

Luckily, TAG had sent their biokinetic healer to help out, and though she wasn't even a tenth as powerful as Faith or Wyatt, the Finnish woman had been able to almost completely heal Devlin's ribs. It made for much easier breathing and it stopped Gabriel from fussing over him like crazy. But there were still cuts and bruises, because the fight had not been an easy one for any of them.

After that, there was miles of paperwork to catch up on, various other fires that Marlena and the others left behind had dealt with as best they could—and had done a damned fine job, for the most part.

Still, it was nice to know Dev was needed.

Old man, my ass. He scoffed at Ender's words, because he'd taken this op on and he'd won. They'd all won. ACRO had come out on top . . . and the miserable bastard who'd fathered him was dead and in ACRO's morgue, where he belonged.

As for Mel and Phoebe . . . well, he'd deal with Phoebe. Find a way for Mel to take over the body permanently. And then spend time showing her that she was safe.

So yes, things on the ACRO front were good. Now, faced with more decisions of a different sort, he paced the first floor of his house and wondered if he could really deliver on the promise he'd made before the battle with Alek and Itor had begun.

It had worked out this time. But there would be other battles . . .

"Cut this shit, Devlin—it's called life. You told Gabe you loved him and it was all right, you can't go back on your promise." Oz's voice drifted up from behind him.

He turned and started with, "Oz, what the hell . . ." Trailed off when he saw the man—*really* saw him.

Oz shrugged. "I called in a favor."

Oz was there, truly there, although he was still semi-corporeal. And when he put his lips onto Dev's, Dev felt the familiar thrill.

His mind also went directly to Gabriel.

"Good, that's good, Devlin," Oz told him. "He's the right one for you—always has been. I was simply a stand-in for him."

"You were never just a stand-in to me." Dev heard the tears in his voice . . . saw them in Oz's eyes. They'd been to hell and back a number of times. Some days, Dev still couldn't believe he was gone.

"Thanks, Dev." Oz paused. "I couldn't be there to help you in the final battle . . . and this is the last time I can visit. I've been granted peace. I'd like to give you the same thing."

Devlin sat and listened while Oz laid out his plan, wondering how he could ever truly say good-bye to this man, all the while knowing he would have to.

* * *

The message had simply said *My house, ten P.M.*

So like Devlin it had made Gabe's heart tug.

Gabe had been debriefed for the entire day following his return from Australia. Now he noted that the other excedos looked at him with a newfound respect that he liked. He finally felt as though he'd earned it.

He'd never take his training lightly again. His job—ACRO—was too important to let that slide. He'd been granted a chance he'd never thought he'd have, and he wasn't going to throw it away. Any of it.

When he went to Devlin's house, he found the door open. Called out and heard Devlin telling him to come inside and lock up behind him.

Gabe did, walked upstairs and into the bedroom to see white candles everywhere. It looked like a church and Dev was cursing about wax being everywhere and *all of this is bullshit and don't expect it every time I want to fuck.*

Gabe shut him up with a kiss. Hard and fast, tongues dueling until Gabe could barely breathe. Even then, he didn't want to stop, threaded his fingers through Dev's spiky hair and held the man there as their cocks ground together.

The friction was killing him. Fuck. "I'm going to come in my damned pants," he breathed when he pulled away from Devlin.

The man simply licked his lips, and Gabe almost came right then and there. With a deep breath, he kept it together, because he wanted all of this to last.

"Why now?"

"Why not now?" was Dev's answer. Gabe looked at the candles and finally caught sight of the bags piled in the corner. His bags.

His bags in Devlin's house.

"I'd have put them away for you, but I wouldn't want to be accused of being controlling." Dev's eyes twinkled.

"I think this kind of counts as controlling."

"It's what you wanted. It's what I wanted. Life's too damned short, okay?"

Gabe felt emotion clog his throat, couldn't form the words, and so he simply nodded and let Devlin hug him and they remained there together.

But they weren't alone.

No, the ghost of the past was with them—except this time, it was in the form of the dark-haired man sitting at the edge of the bed.

"Oz," he said, and Dev stared at Gabe, asked, "You can see him?"

Gabe nodded. "He watches us sometimes." He bit his lower lip as Oz reached out and caressed Dev's neck. Smiling, Dev closed his eyes. "Shit, you can feel that?"

Dev nodded. "Yeah, I can."

"I can leave," Gabe said, not sure he wanted to intrude on this and wondering why the hell he didn't feel jealous.

Because he's yours, Oz whispered in his ear, even though he remained where Gabe could see him across the room. *Always was—I just kept him safe for you.*

And then Oz motioned for Gabe to come closer, and what the hell was going to happen here?

But he knew. He only wondered what it would mean when it was all over.

It means that everything's going to be the way you wanted it to be, Oz told him. *Now, stop thinking so much.*

And that's when Gabe felt the touch of a hand running down his back. Oz had moved behind him, was pulling his shirt off, dropping it to the floor, and began to do the same with his cargos. Dev was watching Oz strip Gabe naked, and holy shit, Gabe was so turned on his balls were boiling with come and impending release.

He must've spoken that sentiment out loud because Dev told Gabe, "Don't—not yet."

A shiver down his spine expanded over his body when Dev dropped to his knees and took Gabe's cock in his warm mouth as Oz caressed Gabe's back.

Gabriel shuddered under both men's touches. He was alternately hot and cold, his skin felt too tight and he ached with a need so great he was nearly vibrating. And when Devlin finally let him come, he did so harder than he ever had, barely stayed on his feet as Dev milked every last drop from him.

And then he let Oz lead him to the bed. Lay him down, stroke his brow, and Dev moved to top him.

"Wait," Gabe said, and Dev raised a brow. "I have a request."

"What is it, Gabriel?" Devlin's cock was hard and heavy, brushed his belly, and Gabe wondered if he asked, whether Devlin would laugh . . . say no . . .

Ask him, Gabriel, Oz commanded him, and his dick hardened again at the sound of the . . . man's . . . voice.

"I want . . . I want to watch," Gabe said. "You and Oz . . . I want to see him with you. I've imagined it, but I want to see it."

Devlin smiled then, didn't say no, but told him, "You need to be involved in this, Gabriel."

Before Gabe could respond, Dev kissed him, then blazed a path down his chest as he fingered Gabe's ass, preparing him with a knuckle that brushed his prostate. Two fingers opened him up wide, so he'd feel more pleasure than pain when he was penetrated.

Gabe couldn't see Oz's face, but whatever he was doing made Devlin's normally calm demeanor become frenzied. Dev's full mouth opened and he panted as Gabe rocked against his hand, his cock dripping pre-cum.

Oz rose up behind Devlin, continuing to make Devlin crazy with pleasure. And then Dev's fingers were gone and he moved forward, his cock breaching the tight ring of muscle, and Gabe groaned, grabbed for Devlin.

He was so fucking full and stretched. Devlin didn't move yet,

was watching to make sure he was ready. And when Gabe nodded, he saw Oz's expression go slack with ecstasy at the same
time Dev hissed with pleasure and pain mixed—it all showed on
his face—as Oz penetrated him. Gabe was mesmerized watching
Oz and Devlin having their intimate moment . . . and they were
including him.

Because when Oz began to rock against Devlin, Devlin did
the same to Gabe, and then the three of them were moving as a
single, sensual unit, faster and faster, and even though Gabe
wanted the moment to last, he knew it wouldn't.

When he came, he refused to close his eyes, watched the men
in front of him orgasm at the same time, the groans mixing with
one another, names cried out . . . sweat and tears mingling until
Gabe felt grounded enough again to actually breathe.

And then, Dev bent down and kissed him. Tenderly. Passion-
ately.

"You don't need me anymore. You can handle anything. Just
turn to him," Oz said, for both men to hear. When Dev pulled
back from the kiss, his eyes filled with tears but he smiled at Gabe
through them. And Gabe watched over Dev's shoulder as Oz
floated upward, disappearing before he reached the ceiling.

CHAPTER Twenty-two

Annika had waited for years to go on the mission that would dismantle Itor. There had been no doubt in her mind that she would have spearheaded the operation. She'd fantasized about it, dreamed about it, had pictured frying Alek to a crisp.

So to not have been there when it all went down should have made her as pissed off as a wet cat and grumpier than a bear awakened early from hibernation. But as she sat in her living room listening to Dev recount the events, one hand rocking the bassinet where Renee was sleeping, Annika couldn't be sorry she'd stayed here with her baby and Creed.

Especially because the loss of life in the Australian and satellite attacks had been staggering.

"I can't believe Jason is dead," she murmured. "And Samantha. Henry. Neema. Zach." Jason, Samantha, and Henry had been at ACRO since the beginning, were incredibly powerful in their fields, as well as experienced. They would be sorely missed. Annika hadn't known Neema well, but she and Rik had grown close, and Rik couldn't be taking it well.

"I'm promoting Kira to Animal Division director," Dev said. "Zach's death is hitting her hard, but I know she'll do a great job."

No doubt. And Ender had to be fucking relieved as shit that he'd put his foot down on Kira's request to go to Australia.

Of course, in all the tragedy, the one person Annika would have liked to see killed hadn't been. Phoebe . . . Mel . . . whatever . . . was imprisoned in the fireproof cave—by choice, apparently—but that wasn't enough for Annika. Phoebe had lost her father, Itor, and her freedom, and she wasn't going to go peacefully into the night.

Still, Dev was all defensive and crap, had, in fact, just come from seeing Mel.

"I think that if you talk to Mel, you'll feel differently about her," he was saying, had somehow moved from the subject of Kira to Mel without her noticing; Annika just rolled her eyes.

"She's your sister. I get that." Actually, Annika didn't. Because she'd never had a sister or a brother. The people she let into her life were people she loved because of who they were, not because they were related. "But Dev, she's trouble."

"Annika—"

"This isn't a jealousy thing," she interrupted. "I mean, yeah, okay, maybe a little. But mostly I'm just worried. I have a bad feeling. She's insane. If she could kill Akbar the way she did . . ."

"You know it wasn't Melanie who did that."

Annika shoved off the couch, partly out of frustration and partly so she could get away from the bassinet, which was rocking a little too hard. Nice. She was going to make her daughter seasick. "I'm tired of hearing that! You weren't there, Dev. You didn't see . . ." She trailed off, her throat closing up too tight to speak anymore.

Dev stood from the recliner and folded her into his arms. "I know you don't understand this, but I have to give her a chance. I told you how she helped take down Itor. And I haven't had a family in a long time, Annika."

"We're your family," she whispered, and he hugged her tighter.

"You are. And you, and Creed, Ender, Wyatt, Haley—everyone at ACRO—you can't be replaced. But all the bad shit my father did, it's like my blood was tainted. I have to believe that something good came from him."

"*You* did."

"I know, but he was poison to everything else he touched. If I have a sister who isn't completely evil, then maybe all of the pain he's caused will have been worth it."

Annika didn't completely understand, but Dev had always been a lot softer than he liked people to believe. He'd definitely put up with her shit, when he could have spanked her really, really hard. And probably should have.

"Dev?"

"Yeah?"

She pulled back to look up at him. "I'm not one for the religious ceremony bullshit, but it's important to Creed's parents, so we're having Renee christened. Next Wednesday. And we want you to be her godfather. I mean, I'm not sure it'll be official or anything, because you're not Catholic and I'm not and . . . well, I just don't understand any of it, but . . . will you?"

Dev's brown eyes grew liquid. "Yeah," he rasped. "I'd be honored."

The flight back to ACRO had been interesting. Since Melanie and Stryker had been alone, she'd shot up with the suppressant, and he'd spent the entire time trying to persuade her to change her mind.

He'd seduced her with gourmet food, champagne, and the most fabulous sex ever. He'd even combined the three, and she'd never look at chocolate-covered strawberries or vanilla sauce in the same light again. The way the man could use food and his tongue was sinful.

His plying had almost worked. By the time they landed, she'd been exhausted in that well-used, tingly way that made her want to go home with him and stay there for the rest of her life.

But then they'd gotten off the plane, and Dev had been there, all warm smiles and wanting to take them to the park, where all of ACRO was celebrating its victory over Itor. As much as Mel had wanted to go, she couldn't. Phoebe was fighting the drug— and the damage she could cause if she came out in a crowd of people . . .

The reality only emphasized why Mel had to lock herself away. She longed to be part of the big ACRO family and to get to know her brother, so much it hurt . . . but it would hurt far more if Phoebe killed any of them.

So she'd asked to be taken to the cave. Stryker refused at first, but when she began to wince at Phoebe's clawing inside her skull, he'd been forced to comply.

Now, three days later, he was sitting just outside the fireproof glass, still trying to wear her down. He'd been here every day, bringing her food, talking to her, keeping her company. Dev had come too, and even though she'd been nervous at first, she'd eventually found him to be genuine, friendly, and warm. He'd told her about growing up with loving parents, his time in the Air Force, and his life at ACRO.

She'd been curious about Oz, especially because if his prediction really did have something to do with her . . . well, she couldn't allow herself to hope, but what she really didn't want was for his prediction to be about another virgin.

It was selfish of her, she knew that. She should want Stryker to be happy—and be with someone else, because there wasn't any way she was letting herself out of the cave. Ever. But she also couldn't bear the inevitable; that in time, Stryker was going to come see her less often. Daily visits would turn into weekly visits, and then monthly visits . . . and eventually, he'd stop altogether.

Don't think about it. Stryker was here now, even though he was looking at his watch and getting up from one of the comfy-looking leather chairs Dev had delivered for her visitors.

"I have to go to a christening, but I'll come back when it's over. Will you be here?"

She gave a casual shrug. "I was thinking of going shopping and then maybe to hang out at a bar."

His sensual smile made her belly flutter. "You know what I mean."

Yeah, she did. The frequent use of the suppressants during her time in Australia had thrown off her ability to regulate Phoebe's appearances, and she sometimes popped out without warning and stayed for several hours. The same thing had happened on many occasions when Phoebe had needed the drug on missions. Mel had sometimes been thrown into consciousness, and other times, she'd found it easy to emerge just by thinking about it.

"I'll try to be here. I'd like to hear about the ceremony." She eyed his dark slacks and blue shirt that set off his gorgeous eyes, and imagined herself stripping him. "You look nice, by the way."

One blond eyebrow cocked up. "Yeah? How nice?"

"So nice that I'm drooling a little."

He drifted closer, and even through the thick glass she could feel the raw sexuality coming off him in waves. "Tell me to come in."

Oh, God. Her heart went a little crazy in her chest, her breasts tightened, and damn if her thighs didn't quiver. "You have a christening to go to," she rasped.

He slapped his palm on the glass and leaned in. "I'd miss my own crowning to be the king of England to be with you." His gaze heated, the colors in his eyes swirling, and his voice became a deep, hungry growl. "Let me in."

She swallowed. Hard. Nothing had ever been so tempting. Her hand trembled as she brought it up so their palms were together, separated by an inch of glass that might as well have been a mile thick.

"I can't," she whispered.

Inhaling deeply, he closed his eyes and hung his head. A minute passed. Two. Mel's heart broke open wider with every passing second. Finally, he stepped back, and she gasped when she saw that nothing had changed in his eyes. The heat was still there, hotter than before, and fueled by a fierce determination that actually frightened her.

"I won't give up, Mel." Pivoting, he turned and stalked out of the cave, leaving her shaking with unquenched desire and the certain fear that he wouldn't give up . . . and she would give in.

There was no way any good could come of that.

Sighing, she looked over at the stone table and the burger that had been delivered a few minutes earlier. For the first time ever, she didn't feel the need to eat just because there was food in front of her.

With startling clarity, she realized that she wasn't afraid. Oh, she was terrified that Phoebe would do something awful, but she wasn't afraid of the people who were holding her, who had complete control over her. At some point, she'd grown to trust Stryker, Dev, and even her guards enough to know that they would never keep food from her—or anything else she needed, for that matter.

They were even working on making the chamber larger and more comfortable, turning it from a one-room hole into a sizable living area with a private bedroom and bathroom. No doors, but there would be walls in place to shield her from anyone outside the glass pane.

For fun, Dev was having a TV built into the stone, and then covering it with the fire-and-impact-resistant glass. He was also putting in a small heated pool that would allow her to not only bathe, but to discharge her power. She could freeze the water, and the heating elements in the rock would melt it quickly. Right now she was having to make do with discharging in the air and turning the chamber into a deep freeze.

While she was immune to the cold, it still frosted up the glass pane and made it hard to see through to talk to anyone.

The improvements in the cell would definitely be nice.

So as Phoebe began to knock at the walls of her skull to get out, Melanie smiled. Because for the first time since they'd been whisked to Itor, the tables were turned. Melanie might be a prisoner, but it was *her* choice. Phoebe was trapped, and Mel had no doubt that the bitch was miserable as hell.

"Come on out, Phoebe," Mel whispered. "Embrace the suck that is your life."

Someone had brought Phoebe a fucking hamburger. Or, more accurately, they'd brought Melanie a fucking hamburger. The chickenshit, dumb cow ate like a pig. She was a barnyard unto herself. It was a wonder they didn't weigh three hundred pounds.

But there was nothing better to do in this fucking hole than eat, so she snatched up the greasy burger and took a huge bite. Gross. Who the hell put mayonnaise on burgers? Grimacing, she swallowed.

And choked. She coughed, wheezed, dropped the burger on the floor. She heard the pounding of footsteps, and then the guard, a wiry towhead named Jerry, was at the glass, his hand hovering over the control panel.

"Melanie? You okay?"

She started to nod as the piece of meat finally went down . . . and then realized that she had an opportunity she couldn't waste. Coughing harder, she doubled over and went down on her knees.

"Melanie! Shit!" Still, he didn't enter, but there was panic and uncertainty in his expression. "Dan!"

Phoebe grabbed her throat with both hands and did her best bug-eyed I'm-dying act, and as she fell over, the pane slid open.

She reached for her power, but as expected, Mel had drained it. Looked like she'd be doing the good old-fashioned brand of fighting.

Jerry rushed in, and the second he kneeled next to her, she sprung the trap. In two quick motions, she slammed her fist in his face and grabbed his sidearm. A flick of her thumb took off the safety, and a pull of the trigger took out his brains.

Before Dan got a chance to even draw his weapon or use whatever power he had, she put two bullets into his chest. Hoping no one heard the gunfire, she stripped Jerry, who was the smaller of the two men, and dressed in his BDUs. She tucked her hair up under the cap and then sprinted to the mouth of the cave, where she eased her head out into the bright sunlight. It appeared that the cave had been built into the side of a hill on the edge of the ACRO compound, so unless someone was fairly close by, the shots wouldn't be heard or even paid heed . . . not when the firing range—or, at least, what she assumed from the constant gunfire was the range—was within earshot.

Quickly, she tucked the pistol into her waistband and covered it with the BDU top. With any luck, no one would take note of her—not every individual on the base could possibly be known to everyone, especially given that trainees were probably common. And if someone recognized her, they might think she was Mel.

Turned out that no one looked at her at all. She stayed on the outskirts of the base, keeping an eye out for anyone she might know—especially Dev. Her goal wasn't escape. It was to find her brother and kill him.

Walking purposefully, as if she owned the place, she headed toward the center of the base, where signs indicated the command facilities would be. As she passed a group of squat brick buildings, a lone female recruit wearing an orange training badge exited the gym. Phoebe smiled like they were old friends.

"Hey . . . I'm new here, and I'm trying to find Devlin O'Malley. Do you know where his office is?"

256 • *Sydney Croft*

"Sure." The girl, whose badge gave her name as Alda Lee, pointed down the road. "It's that way. Take your first right, and the building will be on the left. But right now he's probably at Annika and Creed's new baby's christening."

"Christening?"

"It's the talk of the base. Everyone is invited to the party afterward." She glanced at her watch. "Party should be in about half an hour in the reception hall."

"Where's the christening?"

"Hospital chapel. Down the same street, but take a left instead of a right. The chapel is connected to the south side of the medical facility. You can't miss it."

"Excellent." Phoebe threw her arm around Alda's shoulders, doing the buddy thing as she guided her toward the side of the building. "Thank you. ACRO people are just so freaking friendly."

"No problem—" Alda let out a gasp. Last one ever, given that Phoebe had broken her neck.

She tucked the body into the bushes, brushed off her hands, and grinned as she hoofed it to the chapel. When it came into view, her adrenaline spiked, jacking her up with a rush that no amount of cocaine could match.

Overhead, puffy white clouds meandered across the bright blue sky. Birds chirped and flitted around in the trees that lined the sidewalk. A cool breeze made the manicured lawn ripple and the flowers around the chapel wave. It was all so cheery. So perfect. Justice loved beautiful weather. Truly, it was a sign that Dev deserved what he was going to get.

As Phoebe approached the door, she reached beneath her shirt and palmed the pistol grip. Through a narrow stained-glass window, she saw Dev standing on the stage and wearing a smile that said everything was right with his world.

He was so very, very wrong.

"This," she said softly, as she reached for the door handle, "is for you, Daddy."

CHAPTER
Twenty-three

It was weird to think that Annika actually had friends she could ask to come to her daughter's christening, weirder yet that one of those friends was close enough to ask to be the godmother.

Not long ago, even though Annika had been at ACRO for years, she hadn't had friends. It wasn't until Creed came into her life that Annika had opened up, allowing herself to let others in as well.

And now, Haley Holmes Begnaud stood with Dev and agreed to care for baby Renee as if she were their own.

The little hospital chapel on base was full of people who had come for Creed and Annika, and the thing was, most of them had hated her since the day she arrived, a cold-blooded, vicious, out-of-control teenager. So to see Kira and Ender, Trance and Rik, Marlena and Chance, Sela and Logan, Brenna and Hex, Ryan and Coco, Gabe, Remy, Stryker . . . and so many others who had worked with her over the years, was almost . . . miraculous.

Then there were the conspicuously empty seats, the places

where people should be sitting, but whose losses had taken a toll on so many here.

Still, this was a happy time, when ACRO was celebrating a new life in the midst of so much death, and Annika wasn't going to let herself sink into sadness. She only wished Wyatt and Faith's plane from TAG headquarters in England hadn't been delayed, because she'd have loved for them to be here too. They'd promised to make it for the reception party, though, so they'd be arriving soon.

Creed was holding Renee . . . it was so cute to see the big, tattooed, pierced guy holding a tiny infant so gently, the smile on his face bigger than Annika had ever seen. She'd really thought that things between her and Creed couldn't get any better, but in the days since Renee's birth, Annika had never felt so blissful. Content.

Oh, she couldn't wait to get back to the gym to burn off some of the baby weight, was looking forward to getting back to work . . . eventually. Right now she just wanted to enjoy her family and marvel at how far they'd all come.

The door to the chapel flew open, and everyone jerked around, expecting Faith and Wyatt. Instead, Melanie burst inside . . . with a pistol.

Phoebe.

Insanity and hatred so powerful Annika felt it on her skin burned in Phoebe's eyes as she raised the pistol and aimed directly at Dev's heart.

"No!" Annika dove to shove Dev out of the way, the blast of the shot ringing in her ear.

Chaos broke loose. Pain ripped through her chest. She stumbled, but remained upright as another roar of gunfire shattered the air. Blood bloomed around a bullet hole in Phoebe's forehead, and she fell dead in the aisle. Shocked, Annika cranked her head around and gasped at the sight of Stryker standing in the pews, his pistol still aimed at where Phoebe had been standing, a skinny wisp of smoke curling upward from the barrel.

Holy shit, he'd just killed the woman he loved. The flat, emotionless, *dead* expression on his face said his brain hadn't quite caught up with what he'd done. He'd acted on instinct, and there was no doubt that when . . . what? The rest of the thought wouldn't form.

Why were her legs giving out? And why were people screaming her name?

Everything moved in slow motion even as the room tilted and Annika found herself on the floor. Her hearing cut out, but she could read the lips of those gathering around her. *Annika . . . Annika, can you hear me? . . . Someone get a fucking doctor!*

Creed was on his knees next to her, but where was the baby? "Renee," Annika said . . . or tried to say. Her mouth was moving, but only blood was coming out. Shit. Had she been shot?

A gray haze formed over her vision, growing darker, until her sight joined her hearing in the Land of No More.

And then, the weirdest thing. She was standing over everyone. Well, floating, she supposed. She saw her body lying in a pool of blood, saw the massive bullet wound dead center in her chest. Medical staff was rushing in, some stopping to deal with Phoebe, who even Annika knew was a lost cause, and others shoving people out of the way to get to Annika.

Creed and Dev were yelling at the doctors, and Haley was standing to the side, crying, holding Renee tightly in her arms. Thank God the baby was okay.

"Ooh, CPR."

Startled, Annika turned to the big man standing next to her. "Oz. You're dead."

He gestured to Annika's motionless body, where hospital personnel were pumping her chest and squeezing breaths into her lungs with an Ambu bag and mask. "I'm seeing a pot-kettle moment here. Medical people don't perform CPR on live people."

"So this is death? Being stuck with you is what I get?" She looked around. "Is this hell?"

"Funny."

"Why isn't Phoebe here?"

"Probably because she really did go to hell."

Fuck. He was serious, wasn't he? She watched everything happening below, and though her heart was breaking for Creed, she couldn't cry. Dead people shed no tears, apparently.

"So what now?"

Oz shrugged. "You either stay and hang out like a pathetic ghost, or you go into the light to the Other Side."

"What light?" Even as she said it, a golden beam burst through the stained-glass window behind the organ on the stage. A beautiful tranquillity emanated from it, a strange, lovely buzz that drew her.

But so did the people below. *They* were her light. "I don't know anyone over there," she whispered. "My family is here."

"No, Annika," came a female voice, "your family is here too."

Annika looked over to the golden glow, her jaw dropping and her heart—which she was pretty sure wasn't beating in her physical body anymore—racing. "M-Mom?"

The willowy tall, blond woman Annika remembered only from hazy memories smiled. "You're so beautiful. And you gave me a gorgeous grandchild you named after me."

"You were taken from me—"

"Shh. I've always been with you."

"What about my father?" It was a question that had truly never mattered to Annika—she'd never lived in the past, and spending time in pursuit of an answer seemed like a colossal waste of time. But with her mother here, well, might as well ask.

Renee gestured into the light. "Come with me, and you'll learn the answers to everything you've ever wanted to know."

Or she could hang out with Oz and haunt all the people she loved. She watched as her body was loaded onto a stretcher and rushed out of the chapel. Dev and Creed followed, their expressions haunted, eyes liquid with the stark truth of her situation.

"This was what you meant when you said I'd die if I had Creed's baby, isn't it, Oz?" Annika hadn't died in childbirth, but she wouldn't have been here for the christening if not for the little girl, so in a way, this had happened because she had the baby.

He nodded. "Yeah. I didn't know how it would go down, but I knew something would happen."

As Haley, pale-faced and trembling, walked out of the chapel with Remy's arm around her shoulders and with baby Renee in her arms, sleeping with utter obliviousness, Annika smiled. This sucked, but if Annika could go back in time, have an abortion, or use better birth control . . . she wouldn't. That precious baby was worth a bullet.

Annika flew into her mother's arms, instantly remembering how she'd always smelled of the ocean. "Tell me," she murmured. "Tell me everything."

It won't be much longer now, Stryker . . .

Stryker's arm was still raised. It took Trance a few minutes to wrestle the pistol out of his aching grip, and even then Stryker felt made of stone.

He was freezing, was actually aware that his teeth were chattering, as if he was still under the waterfall with Mel. In her arms. Kissing her.

But there was no waterfall in sight and his arms were empty, just like his heart. The sound of the gun firing echoed inside his head, the gunpowder burned the air. And still, it hadn't been fast enough to stop the killing.

He watched the now chaotic scene in front of him as if it was a bad movie. It was like it was happening to someone else, not him. Because if he wasn't involved, it hadn't happened. It wasn't real.

You should go to her. To Mel. But his feet remained glued to the floor, because he knew it was pointless.

He'd shot to kill, and it had been a long time since he'd missed his mark. Emotions welled inside, threatening to overtake him, and he knew that would be very, very bad.

The walls of the chapel shook as if grieving with him. He knelt on the stone floor, vaguely aware that other agents were nearby.

Oz said you'd marry a virgin . . . he never said you'd kill her too . . . or that she'd die before you got a chance to tell her you loved her—or, hell, have the damned ceremony.

His grief was overwhelming. There were men and women on all sides of him, trying to keep him calm. He looked up and saw a doctor with a syringe, waiting to see if she'd need to use the sedative to save the compound from destruction.

He tried to breathe. Forced air in and out, but it sounded harsh and unnatural, like he was breathing through a straw.

"She's dead," he said, over and over again. For what seemed like forever, no one said a word in response. And then finally, there was a hand under his chin, forcing him to look up.

Devlin.

"She's on life support." Dev's eyes were red-rimmed as he spoke the words. "She's brain-dead, Stryker. There's no hope. I'm so sorry."

"Sorry," he murmured, because he didn't know what else to say—or who to say it to. Mel knew the whole time this would happen. That didn't make it her fault, but maybe Stryker should've protected everyone—himself—better. "Annika?"

"Ani's in surgery." Dev spoke to him so gently, the way he had when Stryker was younger and afraid of getting in trouble for causing earthquakes. "They're doing everything possible to save her."

His eyes flicked to Dev's face. "But it was too late to try with Mel."

"Yes."

"So why is she on life support?"

"I wanted to say good-bye to her. I thought you would want

the same," Devlin explained. "Come on—off the floor. We're going outside. Walk with me."

Stryker hadn't realized how much time had passed. Two hours. The chapel was nearly empty. Bloodstains marked the spot where Mel had lain on the cold floor.

The cold wouldn't have bothered her.

Devlin was practically pulling him along, out of the chapel and into the dusk. They walked for a long while, around the compound, as if Stryker could walk off his grief and anger. "You have to hold it together."

"I know, Devlin."

Dev stopped in front of him. "Listen to me, Stryker. You saved me."

"By shooting your sister," he said hollowly.

"And the woman you loved." Devlin's voice cracked. "I can't imagine what kind of decision that was."

"She made me . . . Mel, she made me promise to do that if Phoebe was going to hurt any of my friends again. She said I'd forgiven her once for what happened to Akbar, but she didn't think we'd get through it a second time." Stryker heard the words coming out of his mouth, his voice sounding raw, like he'd been screaming.

It had been hard to promise her. But far more difficult than anything he'd done in his lifetime to actually carry out her wishes.

She'd been right—they'd never get past Devlin's death if Phoebe had gotten her way. He wasn't even sure if he could get over the fact that Annika was dying . . . that Annika had been right about not trusting Mel.

Phoebe. Not Melanie. Although Mel had to suffer because of her sister, again. And this time, she'd paid the ultimate price.

This time, so had he.

"I need to see her," he told Dev.

"I don't think that's a good idea right now. Maybe tomorrow—"

But Stryker had already begun walking toward medical, leaving Devlin little choice but to follow. And, although the building was no more than five minutes away on foot, it seemed to be the longest damned walk of Stryker's life.

News of the shooting had spread quickly—the other operatives were giving him a wide berth. Some darted sympathetic glances his way, others had fire in their eyes.

It didn't matter. They didn't know Mel the way he did . . . the way he had.

His throat tightened and he willed himself not to break down before he got there. He owed her that much, owed her a goodbye.

But when he got to the door, he turned to Dev. "Did the doctor give you the hypodermic with the sedatives?"

"Yes."

"Good. Don't be afraid to use it." With that, he walked into the room and over to the bed.

She had a bandage wrapped around her head and was hooked up to machines . . . so many damned machines and tubes breathing for her. She was pale, her once supple lips white. With a trembling hand, he held hers, the familiar coolness of her palm somehow calming him for the moment.

"I'm so sorry, baby," he whispered in her ear. "I didn't want it to come to that . . . but I kept my promise. I kept my damned promise."

The tears started to fall and he brushed them away with his free hand impatiently. "Mel, I didn't tell you before—should have . . . I love you. I really, truly love you. Always will."

It was too much then. He dropped her hand and turned to the wall. Punched it. Put his forehead to it and felt the walls begin to shake under the will of his grief.

He was vaguely aware of Devlin calling his name, shaking his shoulder. But he didn't respond. Devlin would save the building, he knew that. He felt the prick of the needle in his arm and he didn't resist, let Devlin drug him into sweet oblivion.

CHAPTER
Twenty-four

The scene from the chapel replayed itself over and over in Creed's mind, no matter how many times he tried to turn it off.

Annika jumping in front of Devlin. At one time, that would've been enough to make him jealous, make him believe that Annika could never fully love him the way she loved Dev.

Now Creed knew that Annika had enough for both men—more than enough.

Kat was chattering in his ear, clinging to him tightly, and he stared down at his hands—one blank, one covered in tattoos—and he wondered what good it was to be protected when the woman he loved was left vulnerable.

Dammit, Oz . . . dammit all to hell.

You're the one who didn't listen to him, he told himself. But looking at Renee, he realized there had been no way around this. If Annika hadn't had their baby, if he'd denied her the opportunity to become a mom, he'd never have forgiven himself.

It had been mere days, but Annika had changed because of Renee. Fundamentally, she'd grown up, once and for all.

And now the love of his life, mother of his child, was in surgery. Dying.

He knew that as surely as he knew his name.

Oz's predictions were never wrong. *Never.*

And right now, he hated his brother for that. For everything. And even though he literally felt Oz, knew he was close by to comfort him, Creed shut him out.

"I do not want to talk to him, Kat," he said finally.

He's trying to talk to you, Kat insisted.

"He can fuck off," Creed growled under his breath, paced the hallway in a futile attempt to literally get Kat off his back.

He realized he was also angry at Ani, for not believing him . . . for not taking Oz's predictions seriously.

For leaving him alone like this.

As he struggled to take back that last thought, the double doors that led to the OR opened and Creed resisted the urge to slam them shut, to send the doctor back to Ani and tell him not to come out until he had the right answer. The only one Creed wanted to hear—and the one he knew he wouldn't.

We did all we could.

The words weren't even out of the surgeon's mouth yet and Creed heard Kat's screeching in his ears. He covered them, even though he knew it wouldn't help—it never did—and he let Kat pull him into his own pool of grief, so deep it threatened to drown him.

Faith Kennedy knew something was wrong the moment she and Wyatt stepped inside the chapel. After getting off the plane, they'd gone straight to where the party should have been, but the hall had been empty. Wyatt figured that the christening had been delayed, so they'd headed to the chapel.

Only to find it empty, and with blood on the floor.

"Shit!" Wyatt grabbed her hand, and they were running out of the chapel and down the medical facility's hall to the emergency department, where everyone who had been invited to the christening was waiting. On who?

Thank God they'd called the ACRO day care as the plane landed and made sure Aimee was fine. Kira and Haley had dropped off all the kids there before the christening, so at least Faith didn't have to freak out about that. But still . . .

Faith scanned the crowd, her heart pounding so hard against her ribs that it hurt. *Please don't let it be Renee . . .*

Relief nearly buckled Faith's knees when she saw Haley holding Annika's baby, but in a heartbeat, sheer, utter terror replaced the relief, because why wasn't *Annika* holding Renee? And Jesus, Creed was . . . coming apart at the seams.

No one could calm him. He was pacing, thrusting his hands through his hair. His eyes were red-rimmed, face pale, and when anyone touched him, he jerked away as though his skin hurt. And Dev . . . he was just as distraught, though he, at least, was allowing Gabe to hold his hand as the younger man sat next to him in total silence.

Faith and Wyatt pushed their way through the crowd to the front, just as the facility's medical director and head surgeon, Matthew Ruch, appeared in the waiting room doorway. His scrubs were rumpled and damp with sweat, and his expression said it all.

The "We did all we could" wasn't even fully out of his mouth when Creed slapped his hands over his ears and hit the floor in a crack of kneecaps.

Crying out, Faith rushed toward Creed, but Wyatt caught her by the arm and dragged her down the hall after the doctor. "What are we doing?"

"I don't know," Wyatt said. "But maybe we can do something. Hey, Dr. Ruch!" The doctor paused, swinging around as though expecting to get beaten to a pulp. "Let us see her."

"I don't think that's—"

"*Now.*"

Wyatt didn't get angry often, didn't assert himself with any kind of aggression except once in a blue moon, but when he did, people paid attention.

Ruch inclined his head in a brief nod and led them to the operating room, where staff was unhooking Annika's body from various machines. Wrappers, gauze, and surgical instruments littered the floor, sitting in pools of blood. Faith wanted to throw up.

"I've never done what you're thinking about, Wyatt," she whispered.

"I know. But when you were bleeding out after Cujo's attack, I saved your life with the powers you taught me to use. We have to try."

Faith didn't remember anything Wyatt had done that day, when Rik's beast had nearly ripped Faith's throat out as she took a walk outside TAG headquarters, but Wyatt's use of his power had saved her life when, by all rights, she should have bled to death.

Faith snapped into action. "Ruch, you'll assist us. Get your team back."

"I don't understand—"

"Do it!" Faith walked around the operating table to Annika's left side as Wyatt went to the right. "And don't tell anyone what we're doing. We don't want to raise any hopes." It was probably cruel to let Creed and everyone else mourn, but it would be even more cruel to let them believe that there was a chance this would work, because if it didn't . . .

God, this was horrible.

Wyatt pulled back the sheet covering Annika's body, and Faith forced herself not to react. Annika's skin was gray, her chest cracked wide open.

Faith charged up her power and felt Wyatt do the same. As biokinetics, they could manipulate bodily functions and heal wounds, but neither she nor Wyatt had tried it on something as major as this.

"I'll get her blood circulating if you do what you can to repair her heart," Faith said, and Wyatt went right to work. Next to her, the doctor barked out orders; within seconds, machines were switched on and fresh blood was being pumped into Annika through two central IV lines in her neck.

Summoning as much power as she could handle, Faith focused on Annika. Usually, people—and animals—were surrounded by an aura she would have to penetrate in order to access the body. But there was nothing around Annika, so Faith punched her gift straight into her organs. She did a quick probe of the damage—damn, the bullet had ripped through Annika's heart, lungs, aorta. Shards of bone had penetrated flesh as well as organs, and holy fuck, no wonder surgery had failed.

Ruch had repaired a lot of the damage, but clearly, he couldn't work fast enough.

Well, this was where Faith and Wyatt had an advantage. They might not have medical degrees, but their powers worked ten times faster than any surgeon could, and as the medical team watched in awe, Faith grabbed Annika's heart with her power and squeezed it into a pumping rhythm. Blood bubbled out of wounds with alarming gushes, and Ruch's quick application of suction, as well as an infusion of blood through the IV, helped keep Faith from a full-blown panic attack.

Carefully, she split the threads of her energy and used the other to ease bone shards out of tissue while healing the flesh behind them.

Wyatt went to work on the shredded cardiac muscle as Dr. Ruch guided both of them to the most critical places and gave them instructions on exactly how to fix the massive ruptures.

Faith didn't know how long they'd been working when her power began to wane. She heard one of the nurses mention something about two hours, which seemed about right. Faith had tested herself a few times, working with her power nonstop to see how long she could last.

She'd never gone over two hours and seven minutes.

Wyatt was hurting too; his skin was pale, glistening with a

fine sheen of perspiration. "Babe," he rasped. "If we don't get this done soon . . ."

"Yeah." They were both running low. "Doc?"

Ruch swallowed audibly. "The repairs are almost finished."

God, the room was hot. Faith's muscles were alternating between cramping and turning to gel. *Hurry . . . hurry . . .*

"Done," Ruch said. "If you guys can keep her heart pumping, I'll close her up, and we'll see where we are."

Between the two of them, they kept Annika's blood moving through her veins. Finally, after what seemed like a century, the doctor was finished.

His gaze lifted to meet Faith's, the dark circles behind his glasses standing out starkly in the glow of the overhead lights. "You can stop now. This either worked or it didn't."

Wyatt's power cut off. Faith began to tremble. "I . . . can't." Right now there was hope. If she stopped . . . Annika could be dead. Truly dead.

She sensed more than saw Wyatt come around the table. He slung his arm around her shoulders. "Let go, baby. We did all we could."

Tears stung her eyes as she cut herself off.

Annika's heart didn't beat.

"Paddles!"

A sob tore from Faith's throat. Wyatt dragged her away from the table as Ruch and the others leaped into action. He put the paddles to Annika's chest, and Faith looked away, unable to bear watching as they tried to shock Annika back to life.

Ironic really, given that Annika had used her powers to shock people *out* of life.

After the third try . . . nothing happened. It was over. Annika was truly gone, and—

"We have a pulse!" Suddenly, machines began to beep crazily, and the heart monitor went from flatline to jumping around to settling into a steady stream of peaks and valleys.

"We did it," Faith rasped. "Oh, my God, we did it!"

Ruch shook his head in disbelief. "I don't give a shit how good of agents you are in the field," he said, "I'm asking Dev to have you assigned to my hospital."

Wyatt wouldn't go for that, and in truth, Dev couldn't assign Faith to do anything. She wasn't an ACRO agent. Technically, she was still in charge of TAG, but she'd been toying with the idea of leaving the England-based agency. The work required too many overseas trips, and now that she had a daughter and Wyatt was wanting to grow the family again soon, it was maybe time to stay closer to home.

So the idea that she could use her powers to save lives . . . intriguing. "We'll talk about it," she promised. "Now, can we celebrate?"

Ruch nodded. "We won't know for sure how much, if any, permanent damage has been done until she wakes up, but her brain wasn't without oxygen for long, so hopefully we won't have to worry about that. For now, though, let's go ahead and give Creed the good news."

"Doctor!"

Faith and Wyatt spun around to the nurse, who was gaping at Annika. Annika, whose eyes were wide open and aware. Faith grabbed her hand, and though the other woman couldn't speak, thanks to the intubation tube, she was able to communicate just fine through the tight squeeze of her fingers.

"I'll get Creed," Faith said. "Hold on." Leaving everyone behind, Faith raced down the hall, and after being directed by a nurse, she sprinted to the chapel, where Haley and Remy were pacing with Renee.

Haley's eyes were swollen, tortured, as she gestured to Creed, who was hunched over on a bench, his face in his hands. Dev was sitting next to him, motionless as a stone. "We can't get him to leave. He won't leave Annika."

"She's alive," Faith said, and ignoring Haley's gasp, she ran to Creed and Dev, and sank to her knees in front of them. "Wyatt and I . . . doesn't matter. Creed, Dev, Annika's alive. She's in the operating room. She's awake."

Slowly, Creed lifted his head, and Faith recoiled. She'd never seen such devastation in her life. "I lost her." His voice was a gravelly rumble, as dead as he thought Annika was.

"No, Creed. Listen to me. Wyatt and I used our powers. The doctor operated while we helped heal her. We got her going again. Creed . . . she's alive."

It took about five seconds to sink in, but once it did, Dev and Creed leaped to their feet and burst out of the chapel. Faith followed them, grinning as they slammed into the operating room.

"Ani?" Creed skidded to a halt at her side, his entire body trembling. "Jesus, Ani, you're okay."

Annika blinked slowly, an assurance that, yes, she was all right. Wyatt folded Faith into his strong arms as the storm of emotions swirling inside of her broke, and she dissolved into tears. Annika was okay. But life was so fragile, and death so devastating.

"Let's go home," she said against his chest. "Let's hug Aimee until she gets sick of us, and then let's get to work on a brother or sister for her."

An approving sound rumbled up from deep in Wyatt's chest. "I'm so lucky I have you."

"I feel the same way about you, love." She looked up to see the room filling with ACRO personnel, despite Ruch's insistence that they'd be able to visit after Annika was moved to the recovery room. "I feel the same way about all of them. How lucky we are."

It took a little time for the death haze to wear off.

Annika stared at all the people in her hospital room as the doctors and nurses fussed over her and removed annoying equipment like intubation tubes. Of course, they had to work around Creed and Dev, who parked themselves at her bedside and refused to move until the medical people finally figured out that if they said "This is important," the two would bound out of the way.

It would have been amusing if Annika's chest didn't hurt so bad, and if she wasn't struggling to hold on to the memories of being . . . dead. With every passing minute, the details faded, and there was so much that was important. Oz, her mother, her father . . .

The docs and nurses were talking, telling her to expect things and do things—little pinch here, pressure there, breathe out hard. Mostly, their voices ran together, but when Creed spoke, his words punched straight through the drone from everyone else.

"Annika?" Creed squeezed her hand as the intubation tube came out of her throat. She coughed, gagged, and shit, her throat was going to be sore for a week.

"R-Renee," she rasped, and Haley stepped forward with the sleeping infant.

"I haven't let her go except to change her," Haley said. "She's fine."

Dr. Ruch cleared his throat. "I need you all to clear out. Once we move Annika to her room, you can see her."

Everyone obeyed except Creed and Dev, who gave Ruch looks that dared him to make them leave. Wisely, he didn't say a word.

"How are you feeling?" Creed asked, and Annika scowled.

"Like I got shot."

"Damn you," Dev breathed, as he took her other hand. "What you did was stupid. Reckless." He inhaled raggedly. "And you saved my life."

"Payback." She smiled weakly. He'd saved her years ago when he'd rescued her from a miserable existence on the run, and then he'd given her a life here at ACRO. "So," she said, "how am I here? I died."

"Faith and Wyatt," Creed said, and then he frowned. "How do you know you were dead?"

She swallowed, winced at the tenderness. "Saw it. I was with Oz. And my mom." Dev and Creed exchanged glances, like maybe she was crazy. "I'm not crazy. Oz . . . he said that what happened was what his prediction was about. And he was on his way out of here permanently." She swallowed again and glanced at Dev. "Said he told you and Gabe good-bye."

Dev nodded. "Yeah. Yeah, he did."

"So you saw your death?" Creed asked. "How did you come back?"

The hazy memories were like a rubber band, being stretched impossibly thin, and at any moment they'd break and she'd have nothing. "I don't know. I was with my mom. She was telling me things. We were in the light, but then I was being pulled back."

Her head throbbed as she struggled to remember how she'd seen her body surrounded by medical people. Faith and Wyatt were there. And then Oz was next to her and telling her to go. She had one last chance and she had to take it. *Now or never, Annika.*

Her mother had pushed her, and Oz had brushed her hand in a last good-bye as they both were swallowed by the light and Annika was sucked into the darkness of her own skull.

Creed's hand came up to brush her cheek, and she realized she'd been crying. "It's okay," he said. "Everything's okay."

"I'm going to leave you two alone." Dev stroked her hair gently. "I'll be back after they move you to your room." He gestured to Ruch, who was messing with her IV. "How long will she be in the hospital?"

"We won't know anything until we run some tests to check the state of her healing, but given her condition now, I'd say no more than a couple of days. We'll know more by morning."

Dev nodded. "I'll be here first thing." Leaning in, he kissed her forehead, and after giving Creed a pat on the shoulder, he was out of there.

"I'm sorry I scared you, Creed," she said, as soon as Dev disappeared.

"Don't." His black eyes, which were bloodshot and rimmed with red, sparked with ferocity. "You are what you are, Annika. You protect those you love, and you do it on instinct." Closing his eyes, he dropped his head so it rested on her hand. "It's why you're going to be such a damned fine mother." He lifted his gaze, and her breath caught at the intensity in his expression. "And wife."

Annika's stomach tightened into a knot of terror . . . and then, just as abruptly, it was gone. She and Creed had never talked about marriage, at least, not about *them* getting married. She'd told him often enough that she didn't believe in it. How could anyone promise to be so committed to one person?

But she had a baby—and Annika was beyond committed to the child. Forever. And if meeting her own mother in the Great Beyond wasn't proof that a person could remain dedicated no matter what, then nothing was. Annika was tied to both Renee and Creed . . . in life and death.

So, as he drew a little velvet box from his pocket and opened it to reveal a beautiful diamond solitaire, she knew what she was going to say.

"*What the fuck?* You've had that in your pocket? For how long?" Okay, not what she thought she was going to say, but her mouth had always been disconnected from her brain.

"Awhile." Creed looked absolutely terrified, had gone pale, making his facial tattoo stand out in stark blackness. "So, Annika? Will you marry me?"

Tears stung her eyes, and Creed went even paler, no doubt thinking she was about to say no. But that word had just been deleted from her vocabulary. "Yes," she whispered. "I'll so marry you."

Falling forward, he gathered her in his arms. "I love you, Ani. God, I love you."

She grinned against his neck. "I love you too." The feel of his heavy body against hers was a comfort she never wanted to be without. "I didn't think I'd ever be so happy or be part of such a wonderful family." Even as the last of her life-after-death experience faded from high-def to mist, she remembered one crucial detail. "Speaking of family, I found out who my dad is."

Creed pulled back slightly, just enough so that she could look into his gorgeous eyes.

"Who?"

"Let's just say," she said as she plucked the ring from the box and wiggled her finger into it, "that you're marrying into royalty."

He groaned. "And I thought you were hard to live with before."

"Baby," she whispered against his lips, "you ain't seen nothin' yet."

CHAPTER
twenty-five

Don't let her go before I can say good-bye.

Stryker's last words to Devlin—and Devlin nodding—before the medication took over completely.

When he woke, he was in his room, in his bed, and it was dark out. Three in the morning. There was a message on his answering machine that Annika had pulled through, thank God.

He showered, trying to wake himself up, because he was still foggy from whatever strong shit Dev had shot him up with—a necessity, for sure—and then he dressed quickly. Knew where he needed to be.

He was in the process of sneaking down a hospital hallway when Creed came out of Annika's room and they practically ran into each other.

"I saw Mel . . . but I didn't get to say good-bye," he explained, running his hands through his still damp hair and realizing he sounded like a rambling idiot. "I heard Annika's all right—I'm glad. I didn't like the way we left things . . . and the baby and labor and shit."

He turned away from Creed and just tried, like, breathing.

"Dude, come on, turn around," Creed said quietly. "You've been through fucking hell, okay? You look wrecked—sound wrecked."

"Yeah, I guess I am." He turned to see Creed had his hand on the door leading to Annika's room.

"Come on in here and sit down—Annika's awake."

"I'm sure I'm the last person she wants to see," Stryker muttered.

"No, definitely not the last," Creed said with more sympathy in his voice than Stryker could stand, but he followed the man inside.

He owed as much to Annika anyway.

She was sitting up in bed, the baby sleeping next to her in a bassinet. These hospital rooms were more like hotel rooms than anything—at least the ones for the recovering patients. There were no machines in here, and Annika looked as healthy as ever.

"You look good, Annika," he said, because he didn't know how else to start. "I'm really glad you're okay."

"Wyatt and Faith had a big hand in healing me. And you . . . you had a big hand in saving Devlin."

"No, that was you," he pointed out.

"Both of us," she said, and he didn't argue.

"Look, you were right about not trusting Phoebe," he said. "I'm not saying I couldn't trust Mel, because I'll never believe that. They're two separate people. But Phoebe never should've been allowed to get that close to you and Dev and the baby. I'll never forgive myself . . ."

He couldn't finish. Needed to get the hell out of here, because he still had more true fucking confessions to get out, and he needed air.

"Stryker, wait." Annika's voice stopped him from leaving. "Don't go—not like this. I get it, okay? You don't need to apologize for believing in someone you love."

He did believe. But he also knew Phoebe had left a trail of

death behind her yesterday, including her two guards and a trainee, according to the email he'd seen on his phone on the way into the hospital.

He'd shut down his phone after that. And now he didn't know what else to say to Annika.

"Go to Mel," Creed told him.

"Thanks," he mumbled, left Creed and Annika and the baby behind, because the need to see Mel was too great to ignore. The halls were pretty silent, just light beeps from monitors coming from some of the rooms.

As he approached Mel's room, he saw a nurse leaving and he slid in before the door closed—it was a locking door, just in case, as if Mel was still somehow a danger to all of them.

Even in death, Mel couldn't shake Phoebe and the distrust of everyone around her.

She was in the same position as before, long hair hanging limp around her shoulders, tubes everywhere, her hands down by her side—and he walked to her and lowered a rail, pulled a chair over so he could rest his head near hers.

He took her hand in his as well.

"Sorry I left before. If I could've stayed . . . I would have." He paused. "It's just that I might have taken down the hospital, with you in it, and you don't deserve my temper like that, Mel. I don't know why I couldn't tell you I loved you before all this. Because I do—but I couldn't bring myself to say it. You paid a heavy price for being attached to Phoebe . . . at first, I didn't want to believe, and forgiving you was even harder. But now I know you did nothing that needs forgiveness."

He watched the blinking lights on the monitors, wished he could pretend the perfect waves for the heartbeat were really hers and not the life-support system. And still, he continued to talk to her.

"I wish you'd had more time here. I would've taken you all around—showed you where I used to sneak and hide when I didn't want to go to school or practice." He reminisced as though she could hear him. "I hated school—all the paperwork and memorizing shit. Although geography was cool ... I needed that. I liked studying the terrain of different countries, and earth science too, discovering where the fault lines in each continent were ... all of that felt like such a part of me."

He remembered other things from that time too ... things that had kept him up, tossing and turning at night. Things he'd never told Mel, and he knew he wouldn't get the chance if he didn't admit them now. "I realized then that I could take my gift and put it to damned good use—I could help people. At least I thought I could." He paused then, wondering if he could say it all out loud and knew that he could've told Mel anything—that she, of all people, would've understood.

"It's hard for a kid who thinks he can master the universe to realize that sometimes he's simply a pawn in Mother Nature's game. Usually, she's well ahead of me and I found myself chasing my tail trying to predict earthquakes and the like. It was a horrible feeling, realizing that I was going to lose at that most of the time. When I can't help people in a natural disaster situation, it kills a part of me. Maybe that's how I understood why you hated losing control to Phoebe so much. Because I hated not being able to control the earth to the point of stopping the disasters. It sucks to have partial control over things ..."

He stopped then, put his head down on her arm, and tried to pull it together. Moved onto other topics that weren't as heavy, memories that made him smile.

When he got tired of talking, he just held her hand. He wasn't sure how much time had passed, knew there was sunshine on his back and that another shift of nurses had come on duty.

The new nurse had been surprised to see him, but when she noted he'd actually handcuffed himself to the bed, she hadn't confronted him. He supposed she'd called Devlin, though, because he heard the man clear his throat and then he finally looked up.

"Sorry. Hope I didn't cause trouble, but I needed to be here,"

Stryker said, his voice hoarse from lack of sleep and grief and, yeah, talking so much.

Devlin sounded much the same when he said, "It's okay, Stryker . . . I knew you'd come back. You don't have to stay chained to her bed. No one's going to make you leave."

"You still have the drugs, though—just in case?"

"No. You don't need them. I'm counting on you to keep in control. She deserved that. So do you."

Stryker nodded and reached into his pocket for his keys and undid the cuff. Rubbed his wrist where the red mark remained and then took Mel's hand again.

"They're going to pull the plug now, aren't they?" he asked, and Devlin nodded.

"Yes. I wanted to be here too."

"Do you need some time with her?"

"I already had my good-bye with her before you came," Devlin said. "I told her I wished we had more time together. That she's family. That she was trusted."

"Thanks, Devlin."

Dr. Pauling came inside then, after a quick knock on the door to alert them of her presence.

Stryker recognized her instantly as having treated him once, years earlier, after a particularly nasty knife wound, courtesy of an Itor agent.

Now she simply nodded at him and Devlin, her eyes sympathetic . . . and focused on the task at hand.

"She's really gone?" Stryker asked before he could stop himself.

"She is. I'm so sorry. We tried everything, but she's simply unresponsive," Dr. Pauling told him. "She made her wishes clear to Devlin before going to Australia: She did not want to live on life support."

They all had to submit their medical wishes before each mission—renew it each time, in case they'd changed their minds.

Devlin had made Mel part of the team by doing so.

"If you're both ready," Dr. Pauling said, and no, Stryker knew he'd never be ready. Devlin nodded because Stryker couldn't.

"Okay, then." Dr. Pauling began to switch off the various machines around the bed, and Stryker looked away.

He had one of Mel's hands, Devlin the other. Stryker watched her face as he heard the beeps of the machine—faster first, and then slower . . . and slower, until there was nothing but silence.

Mel really, really hated hospitals. She'd been in way too many of them . . . mostly Itor facilities when Phoebe got them hurt on a mission. But the hospital she remembered the most was the one in Japan, after the earthquake.

It was the smell that got to her. That funky odor of sickness that no amount of disinfectant could get rid of.

And then there were the noises. The beeping and whoosh-whoosh of machines. The clank of metal instruments.

The sobs of people in mourning.

Mel opened her eyes to that sound. Well, not really sobs, but the distinct ripple of breath shuddering from lungs. Stryker's lungs.

He was kneeling next to her bed, his head on the mattress. On the other side, Dev was sitting with one hand on hers, his head hanging loosely on his shoulders, eyes closed.

God, this must be bad. She wiggled her toes, was instantly relieved to realize she wasn't paralyzed. Was she sick? Closing her eyes, she let herself just . . . feel. But she felt fine. No pain except for a headache. Granted, it was a bad headache, and she got the sense that there was something around her skull. A bandage, maybe. An instant of panic welled up . . . but was cut off by a shock that stopped the massive breath she was about to take.

She was alone in her head. Completely alone. All her life, there'd been a faint buzz on the left side of her brain, almost a tickle. Now there was nothing, and she knew as sure as she knew she loved *boeuf bourguignon* that Phoebe was dead.

Grinning, she opened her eyes. "Hey."

Jesus Christ, you'd have thought she'd sent an electric shock through her body. Stryker bolted to his feet, Dev jumped about three feet into the air, and the doctor—who had been sneaking out the door—shouted and knocked her head into the door frame.

"Holy fucking shit," Stryker breathed. "Mel?"

The doctor's hands shook as she palpated the pulse in Melanie's neck. "This is . . . ah . . . let me run some tests." She flipped on one of the machines and adjusted the monitor.

Okay, this was weird. "What's going on?"

Stryker grabbed her hand and held so tight she winced. "You were dead. Mel, you were dead and we had to take you off life support, and . . ." He shook his head as though trying to clear it.

"Why was I dead?" When Dev and Stryker exchanged glances, her stomach knotted. "Phoebe. Oh, God, what did she do?"

Dev explained it, his voice cracking often enough that he'd have to repeat what he said, and Mel felt sick. Phoebe had gone on a killing spree, had tried to kill Dev and nearly killed Annika.

And then Stryker had shot Phoebe.

"I'm so sorry," she whispered, squeezing Stryker's hand. She couldn't even imagine how hard it had to have been for him to do that, and then to sit here and watch as the machines keeping her alive were turned off. But why, if they had been turned off, was she sitting up and chatting like she just woke up from a good night's sleep?

Stryker said nothing, merely wrapped his arms around her and tugged her hard against him.

"Doc," Dev said quietly, "what's going on?"

"I have no idea. She was brain dead. The EEG is showing activity now, but there are some gaps. Hold on, I'm going to get Faith." The doctor left, but what she'd said sparked a thought, and for a few moments, Mel let what had happened sink in before she pulled back a little from Stryker.

"I was brain dead?" When Dev and Stryker both nodded, she frowned. "What side of my brain did the bullet go into?"

"Left," Stryker croaked, and then his eyes shot wide. "That's Phoebe's side."

The doctor returned with Faith. "Melanie, I'd like Faith to poke around in your head a little, if that's okay."

Melanie agreed, and sat still while Faith put her hand on Mel's head, being careful to not disturb the bandage. A tingling sensation vibrated her scalp, but there was no pain, and after a few minutes, Faith stepped back.

"I repaired some of the damaged tissue, but it's weird—the left side of the brain has an area inside that I couldn't access before when Melanie was in control, and now it's just . . . empty. It's like a tumor was removed."

"I knew it," Mel whispered. "Phoebe's gone. I can't feel her."

The doctor nodded at the EEG screen. "The pattern is very different from the readings we took when you first arrived at ACRO. Before, there was an echo we guessed was Phoebe. It's no longer there."

"So how could there have been no activity at all after the shooting if I am still alive?"

Faith and the doctor exchanged glances, and it was the doctor who answered. "Phoebe was in control when the bullet entered your brain. So the death was hers."

Faith nodded. "I think that when you turned off life support, Mel's half of the brain kicked in and took over. Kind of like it woke up from sleep."

"There have been instances of people having entire hemispheres of their brains removed," the doctor said, "and the remaining side takes over the function of the missing half. So with Phoebe dead, Mel took over the other side."

"She's gone," Stryker murmured. "She's really gone."

Mel wanted to shout with joy. "I can be normal. I can finally be free. No more cave. No more drugs. No more worrying about hurting people." She grinned. "We can be—" She cut herself off before she made a fool of herself. What if Stryker didn't want to be with her?

He seemed to know what had made her stumble, and he glanced at Dev, the doctor, and Faith. "Can we have a few minutes?"

They all headed out, but Dev stopped at the threshold. "I'm glad you're with us, Mel. I'm damned happy to have a sister." He left before she did something humiliating, like start crying, leaving her alone with Stryker.

"Nothing has changed, Mel. I told you I want you, and I meant it. I want you to move in with me, but that's up to you. The guesthouse will always be yours. I know you're going to need time to adjust to having total freedom—"

"And time for everyone here to adjust to me having it." She looked down at her hands, realized she was wringing them. "What if they—and you—still see me as Phoebe?"

"Hey." He hooked a finger under her chin and lifted her face. "I don't. They won't. We couldn't have taken down Itor if it weren't for you, and everyone knows that. And even if that doesn't change their minds, they now know you're Dev's sister, and trust me, no one will mess with you. Ever."

She swallowed a huge lump in her throat. "But you," she whispered. "Can you truly get past everything? Can you forgive me?"

For the longest time, he said nothing, and she had to struggle to breathe. "I love you, Mel. I don't know why I couldn't say it earlier, but I love you. You've given me a sense of peace and wholeness I was missing before. I mean, I have a family—my parents, ACRO—and I thought that was enough." His brows pulled tight, and he locked stares with her, the intensity in his gaze so startling clear. "But then Akbar died, and revenge carved out this black hole that wouldn't have been filled even if I'd killed

Phoebe that first day in your apartment. It was like a cancer, eating me alive. You stopped it from growing, Mel. And then you filled it with something a lot less poisonous. So yeah, I stopped seeing you and Phoebe as one a long time ago. There is nothing to forgive."

Doubt rang through her, but somewhere in her mind, his voice echoed.

I don't know why I couldn't tell you I loved you before all this. Because I do—but I couldn't bring myself to say it. You paid a heavy price for being attached to Phoebe . . . at first, I didn't want to believe, and forgiving you was even harder. But now I know you did nothing that needs forgiveness.

"You"—she swallowed another lump—"you talked to me while I was out. Dead. Whatever. You said you loved me and nothing I did needed forgiveness."

"Yeah." His voice was hoarse with emotion, same as hers. "Did you hear anything else?"

She considered that, and then smiled. "You hated school. Except geography. You want to show me the places you used to hide so you wouldn't have to go to your classes."

He inhaled raggedly. "Did you hear me say I wanted to make love to you so often that you might as well not ever get dressed?"

A slow burn began in her belly. "No," she murmured, "I missed that."

"Huh. Guess I'll have to show you, then." He brought her hand to his lips and pressed a lingering kiss into her palm. "As soon as you're discharged, you're mine. And I'm yours. All yours. For as long as you'll have me."

Mel's eyes stung. All her life she'd longed for something to call hers. And now she had more than she'd ever believed possible. She had a home, a brother, and freedom. Stryker had given her all of that, but best of all, he'd given her his heart.

Mel had gone from having nothing to having it all.

* * *

The annual ACRO picnic wasn't usually held at this time of year, but, as Devlin noted in the invitation to his agents, they all had a hell of a lot of celebrating to do. And they also needed time together to mourn, to talk . . . to simply be.

And *be* they were, on this sunny Sunday where the chill of early autumn wasn't in the air, as if it knew they all needed the comfort of warmth.

Now, from his spot under an old oak tree, a cold beer in his hands, black-booted feet crossed in front of him, Creed looked around and took stock of the agents and their families as Kat chattered away happily in his ear.

Annika—his wife—was close, sitting on the ground under the same shade, next to Haley, their children on the blanket in front of them. Annika's powers had returned, better and stronger than ever, and each day she seemed to get more comfortable in her own skin as a mom.

It was the coolest fucking thing to see, ever.

And Haley and Remy's boy . . . well, it appeared he would have his daddy's powers. Haley was simply praying they could get through the afternoon without a temper tantrum, which could translate into a thunderstorm. Nowhere as strong as Remy's—not yet—but the toddler would need to be trained, quickly.

Just then, a little person streaked by—faster than the wind—followed by a much larger streak, which, when the game of tag came to a stop, turned out to be Ender and his third girl, the youngest and smallest at birth.

Two of Ender and Kira's three daughters had Kira's power of animal whispering. But this little one . . .

First female excedo, Ender had said proudly last month when it became obvious she was following in her father's footsteps. Now the tall man strode with his daughter balanced on his shoulders, a wide, satisfied smile on his face.

Faith and Wyatt were hanging out in the sun with their daughter—Faith had just found out she was pregnant again.

And she'd started to work at the hospital, since her gift of healing was growing stronger. Annika was certainly living proof of that, and Creed owed Faith a debt he wasn't sure could ever be repaid.

Nearby, Rik and Trance were whispering to each other, sitting in the same chair, cuddling. They were thinking of having kids—*little Cujos*, Trance called them. Creed could only imagine what the howls of the little wolf pack would sound like.

All these kids were the next generation of ACRO. They'd have bigger and badder enemies than their parents fought, no doubt . . . but they'd also be stronger. Wiser.

And there would be more kids, sooner than later, from the way things were looking. Marlena and Chance were waiting for the former SEAL to have more testing, to make sure passing along the chupacabra gene wouldn't hurt a child. If so, Marlena told him she was open to adopting. Sela and Logan felt the same way—the couples had gotten close on their mission in the Amazon, and remained so. All four of them were playing a lazy, beer-filled, spirited game of cards.

Mel and Stryker were walking around the lake. They'd married as soon as Mel was allowed to leave the hospital, in a no-nonsense ceremony that suited both their personalities—and then there'd been a huge party afterward, one that Mel personally catered. She'd started taking classes again, but only as a hobby. Her heart had gone into opening a gourmet café on ACRO's grounds.

Creed had already taken advantage of her need for someone to sample the food she was thinking of serving. Which reminded him, he needed to spend more time at the gym.

Now he watched Devlin moving through the crowd, talking to the agents, Gabriel by his side. Gabe had moved into Devlin's house, and yes, Oz had foretold that, but Dev and Gabe were much more than an arranged coupling.

Oz.

Creed missed his friend—his brother—more than ever these

days. Could feel Oz's spirit starting to slip away with each passing moment and knew there was no way to hold on to him.

He'd been trying to ignore it, not listening when Oz tried to get his attention, even today, as the spirit tugged at him and Kat tried to get him to pay attention. Blocking it out until now had been the only way not to let Oz's death be real.

But he knew that he wouldn't have that option any longer. Not when a chill ran through him, and when he looked up at the sky, he saw them all, ghosts of the past looking down on everyone. Oz, leading the most recent of ACRO's deceased away peacefully, to the Other Side.

Oz, smiling at him. Letting him know that everything would be all right. As all right as it could be on this side of the light anyway.

Yes, it was most definitely the end of an era.

And so he raised his beer in a toast and watched the men and women smiling as they passed, felt their peace as surely as he felt his own.

But something was stopping him from total contentment. At first, he'd thought it was because Oz was still waiting to pass, but then he knew exactly what the problem was.

"Are you staying, Kat?" he asked, realizing he was about to get his ultimate freedom from the ghost who watched him, and had alternately driven him crazy, for years.

You don't need me anymore. You have Ani and Renee to protect you, she told him. Renee would be stronger than Ani, but would also have his gift with ghosts, Kat had told him last week. *And you'll have more children,* she'd assured him. *Can I go?*

He shut his eyes to drown it all out, wondering why she was leaving this decision up to him. "Kat, I can't keep you here— that's not fair to you. I know my powers will go with you, but you've watched me for a long time . . . kept me safe. I can't deny you peace."

No, Creed. You can still hunt the ghosts—still see them. That won't leave when I do, she explained. *It will just be different . . . the power will be fully yours. You're coming into your own, just the way Oz said you would.*

Oz, who was still patiently waiting.

"Good-bye, Oz. Good-bye, Kat," he said softly, unwilling and unable to draw it out any longer. He felt Kat pull from him, the feeling of being totally alone both unnerving and somehow completing him.

And then Ani was next to him as he watched Kat travel up to Oz, the two apparitions disappearing into the light, leaving behind calm blue skies and puffy clouds and the most overwhelming sense of right he'd ever felt.

"Kat said good-bye," Ani told him when he finally brought his gaze down to her. "Where is she going?"

"She went—with Oz."

Ani grabbed for his hand. "Are you okay?"

"Yeah. She deserved to cross over. She's been here too long," he explained. "So now I'm alone, Ani. First time in forever, I'm alone."

"Creed, you're never alone," she told him fiercely, the promise of her words comforting his soul, because he knew that was true. Especially now.

Fuck Disneyland. Because all in all, *ACRO* was the happiest damned place on earth.

About the Author

SYDNEY CROFT is the pseudonym for *New York Times* best-selling authors Larissa Ione and Stephanie Tyler, who also write under their own names.

www.sydneycroft.com